Her steady gaze held his.

Luke's heart pounded. This close, he could see the different shades of green mocking his words. Cassie knew, maybe even better than he did.

"Talent like yours doesn't just go away."

"Maybe it should."

The words hung between them. Time stilled as his blood raced. How had she focused on the fact that while he said he wouldn't write again, the ability had never switched off? His brain still formed tempos and lyrics, even though he pushed them away every time they surfaced. For two years he'd lived without admitting the truth to himself. And now, by encouraging Cassie to deal with her fears, he was forced to confront his own.

With so little space between them, he looked down at her lips. What would she do if he crossed the line? Kissed her as a way of changing the subject?

Find out, his inner voice taunted.

Dear Reader,

Welcome back to Cypress Pointe, the sleepy Florida town where love and family go hand in hand with bright sunny days and warm tropical nights. The wedding professionals are busy once again, this time performing music in *The Wedding March*, the fifth installment in The Business of Weddings series.

Let's face it, you can't have a wedding reception without music and dancing. Who wants to miss rocking out to "Y.M.C.A."? Or jumping into that line dance you can't keep time to? I can already see you smiling. It takes talented musicians to keep guests on the dance floor. Cassie Branford and Luke Hastings fit the bill.

Suffering from writer's block, pop star Cassie doesn't know where to turn for inspiration, until she meets legendary songwriter Luke Hastings performing at her father's wedding reception. Could he be the answer to her prayers?

Luke left the music industry and threw his life into teaching and starting a program for at-risk teens. He thought he had his life under control, until Cassie captured his heart. Can she convince him to jump-start her muse when he's vowed never to write music again?

Thanks for visiting Cypress Pointe. You'll meet new family members and friends, as well as catch up with previous characters from The Business of Weddings series.

Tara

HEARTWARMING

The Wedding March

—

USA TODAY Bestselling Author

Tara Randel

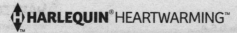

Recycling programs
for this product may
not exist in your area.

ISBN-13: 978-0-373-36828-0

The Wedding March

This edition published by arrangement with Harlequin Books S.A.

For questions and comments about the quality of this book, please contact us at CustomerService@Harlequin.com.

Printed in U.S.A.

Tara Randel is an award-winning, *USA TODAY* bestselling author of eleven novels. Family values, a bit of mystery and, of course, love and romance are her favorite themes, because she believes love is the greatest gift of all. Tara lives on the West Coast of Florida, where gorgeous sunsets and beautiful weather inspire the creation of heartwarming stories. This is her fifth book for Harlequin Heartwarming. Visit Tara at www.tararandel.com. Like her on Facebook at Tara Randel Books.

Books by Tara Randel

Harlequin Heartwarming

Orange Blossom Brides
Magnolia Bride
Honeysuckle Bride
The Bridal Bouquet

To Taylor and Joe Karl. Thanks for sharing your musical expertise and great ideas. You are very talented, wonderful friends!

CHAPTER ONE

THE WEDDING GUESTS standing outside the whitewashed church under a clear, blue Florida sky tossed birdseed on the happy couple as the bride and groom made their way down the sidewalk to the waiting limousine.

"I can't believe I agreed to come to this shindig," Cassie Branford muttered as she brushed the unflattering brown kernels from her new dress.

"It's not a shindig. It's a wedding."

Cassie cast her younger sister, Lauren, a dubious glance. "A wedding I'd rather not attend."

"Dad really wanted you here."

"And therein lies the problem."

Minutes later a dozen white doves were released in honor of the celebration. Cassie barely controlled an eye roll. For her father, the more pretentious the better. This event filled the bill.

"Well, at least the birds get to eat." Cassie chuckled at her own humor as she viewed the ground covered with seed.

Lauren merely shook her head, obviously not amused, and walked ahead of her to the car.

The ceremony had been celebrated at the Methodist church off Main Street. Very elegant, very subdued. You'd think the couple were getting hitched for the first time instead of second marriages for both. Still, Angelica wanted a production and Cassie's father indulged her. It was easy to do when his new wife's family money covered the bill.

"The doves were a nice touch," Lauren said minutes later, as she navigated the charming streets of Cypress Pointe en route to the reception.

"Nice? How about unnecessary?"

"When did you become such a downer?"

"I don't know. When I was commanded, not asked, to come to the wedding?"

"Cassie, we haven't seen you in a while."

"True, but at least I talk to you and Mom regularly. Dad? Never. So his summons kind of turned me off."

Lauren pulled into a space in the country club parking lot. "It's his day. Be nice."

It was always Robert Branford's day, but Cassie got the gist. As they entered the event room, Cassie stopped short. "Really?"

The mood had changed from tasteful to over-the-top. Flanked on either side of the banquet room doors, medieval garbed trumpeters announced each guest in a blast of great fanfare. Crossing the threshold, a trumpet aimed dangerously close to her head, Cassie covered her ear and took in the atmospheric mist courtesy of the dry ice machine. A sultry haze hovered over the dance floor. Hello, could anyone say danger? As she headed to her assigned table, a sudden spate of coughing seized her thanks to the fog irritating her throat. She grabbed a goblet of water from the table for a soothing sip.

Huge white calla lily centerpieces, dripping with crystal beads, took up half the space on the round dinner tables. Spotless linens with the initials *A & R* embroidered in silver and black thread covered the tables. Champagne glasses with silver rims waited to be filled with sparkling wine. A massive champagne waterfall took up one corner of the room, a chocolate fountain positioned in another.

Soon, a six-course dinner would be followed by dancing until dawn.

Held at the Cypress Pointe Country Club, the town elite made an appearance at the flashy reception. Dressed to the nines, everyone tried outdoing each other. Cassie had let her soon-to-be stepmother talk her into a short emerald-colored dress with a sheer lace covering and high silver pumps. She'd have been happier in a casual dress and sandals instead of shoes that pinched, but Angelica would have fainted on the spot. Even Cassie's hair bothered her. She reached up to touch the elaborate style.

"Quit fussing," Lauren hissed, smoothing the skirt of her navy dress.

"I feel like a mannequin in the department store. No one wears their hair like this. And don't get me started on the time spent at the salon. Three hours? On hair?"

"It's better than your usual braid."

"Hey. I like my braid. It keeps the hair out of my face."

"At least the hairdresser hid that dreadful pink streak you insist on. It's not appropriate for a beautiful event like this wedding."

She liked the pink streak. Or any color streak that gave her pizzazz. As a popular music artist, she'd developed her own stand-out look, regardless of family opinion.

"Suck-up," Cassie muttered under her breath.

"What did you say?"

"You look lovely," she answered.

And Lauren did. Both sisters shared a light skin tone, but their hair color differed. Cassie's, a light sandy brown, hung long and straight, while Lauren's, a warm ash, was cut at her shoulders, much more fashionable than Cassie's. Lauren had acquired the conservative gene, which seemed to have skipped Cassie. And while the sisters resembled each other, that was where the similarities ended. Especially with regard to this wedding.

"Thanks. I want Dad to be proud."

That was never going to happen, but Cassie didn't express her opinion. How many times had she tried to earn his approval, only to be shot down? She and Lauren argued time and again over the subject of their father and never made any headway. Today wasn't going to change the impasse.

Angelica came up behind them, her arms circling their waists, catching the tail end of the conversation. "Robert is over the moon. Both of his daughters here for the happiest day of his life."

Cassie bit the inside of her cheek. She liked Angelica, she really did, but sometimes the older woman didn't have a clue. Maybe it was better like that.

"Now, girls, your father would like you all in a picture together. He's waiting by the windows."

Normally, the floor-to-ceiling windows overlooked the lush golf course. For the wedding festivities, however, a huge cutout fairy-tale castle obscured the idyllic view. Light emanating from the early spring evening snuck in beside the garish photo spot. Cassie sneaked a peek. Honestly, the palette of orange, purple and deep blue streaking the sky, hues only an artist could have conjured, would have been a much more appropriate backdrop for a wedding, but Angelica wanted a "fun" background for guests to take commemorative pictures. Hats, feather boas and masks were scattered on the nearby table for the guests to don in their photos, which were digitally printed out seconds later.

As Angelica stepped back, Lauren grabbed Cassie's hand and pulled. "C'mon. We can't keep him waiting."

Cassie allowed herself to be tugged along. If she had her choice, she'd make an excuse not to be photographed, but Robert loved being the center of attention. Tall, his brown hair immaculately cut, his shoulders straight and steady in a custom fitted tuxedo, he was used to commanding the room. A symphony conductor, he moved audiences with his dramatic flair for interpreting musical scores, touching the hearts of listeners. Tonight, his command included the wedding guests and his daughters.

"Here we are," Lauren said as they arrived. She hurried to loop her arm through his. Cassie hovered a few feet away.

Robert held out his other arm for Cassie. "Well?"

She shuffled to his side, begrudgingly taking his arm.

"You could look a little more excited, Cassandra," Robert spoke from the corner of his mouth. "Even when you were a child I never could get you to smile."

Pasting on a fake grin, Cassie returned with, "Better?"

Flashes of light blinded her as the photographer snapped pictures, but she continued to hold her smile. Before long, Angelica joined in. One big happy family.

As soon as the photographer signaled he was finished, Cassie beelined to the ladies' room to compose herself.

Compose. Hah. Like she needed to be reminded that she should be in California writing music for her next album, not a couple thousand miles away in Florida, at a wedding she would have missed if her sister hadn't cajoled her into coming.

"It wouldn't matter where I am," she said under her breath as she stood before the wide restroom mirror hanging on the wall over a bank of gleaming sinks. She was having trouble coming up with new music. To be honest, her lack of inspiration scared her. This next project would make or break her career and so far…nothing.

Keep at it, sweetheart. One day you'll get better.

Her first pop album had been a surprise commercial success. At twenty-three, she'd made a name in the industry with her haunting melodies, her soul-stirring lyrics, her clear voice. Her writing, so pure then, had come from the depths of her soul. Critics had called her work natural and her style heartfelt. The label, thrilled by the interest in their new artist, pushed her back into the studio right away. Caught up in the whirlwind, she went along with the plan to start a second project.

But the label had wanted her to work with new producers, make her music more trendy, they told her. More dance style than ballads and songs with deep conviction, like those on her first record. This time, the music sounded nothing like she'd intended. The process was arduous. There were too many people telling her what to do and how to sound. Because she was so new at this, she went along with the voices of experience. Her manager wanted to please the label. As a result, her second album had tanked.

Could she now be a has-been at twenty-six?

The door opened, drawing Cassie from her morose thoughts. She nodded to a woman dressed in a designer gown, saturated in a cloying floral perfume. Cassie patted her hair again, at a loss as to what else to do. She couldn't play with her braid since her hair was all curled up around her head and she'd left her clutch at the table so she didn't have any gloss to touch up her lips with. With a sigh, she stood, staring at her image.

Was she a two-record wonder?

Would her next project be a disaster, too? She knew she should stop thinking like a failure before she even got started, but after the release and disappointment of album number two, she'd lost her mojo. The critics demanded to know what happened to the genuine songstress they'd admired so much, and to be honest, so did Cassie. She'd disliked the music of her sophomore effort. She wanted, no, needed, to get back to basics. She was tired of second-guessing her talent. Fearful of failing again. She hadn't told a soul, but all the stress had produced a serious case of writer's block.

She couldn't write a thing.

And she had to be back in the studio in less than three months.

Keep at it, sweetheart. One day you'll get better.

The woman came to the sink, eyeing Cassie. "You're Robert's daughter. The musical one."

She nearly laughed out loud. Right now, she could debate that claim. "That's me."

"We're thrilled to have a man of your father's prestige as part of our community."

"I'm so happy for you."

The woman sent a startled glance at Cassie, not sure what to make of her reply.

"See you on the dance floor," Cassie said, returning to her assigned table, more than ready to eat dinner and make her escape.

Across the room, a string quartet and a harpist played soft background music. Before the meal began, Angelica stood, a sparkling tiara nestled in her platinum blond hair pulled back in a tight chignon, her makeup flawless, her white dress covered with glittering seed pearls. She tapped her champagne flute with a spoon and smiled as silence descended upon the room.

"Thank you so much, my dear family and friends, for joining Robert and me on our special day. I am so pleased that Robert's daughters, Cassandra and Lauren, are here to share our happiness."

Cassie ground her back teeth together. *Cassie. My name is Cassie.*

"I've asked Lauren to make a toast." She waved her new stepdaughter to her side. "And Cassandra? Please, join us."

Cassie took her glass and walked over to her new stepmother. Just as Lauren was about to speak, Robert rose and worked his way to her side. He nodded and Lauren began.

"I've been so excited for this day to come. Angelica is such a warm and loving woman, just the right person to make my father happy. My sister and I—" she looked over at Cassie. Cassie held up her glass "—are honored to have been raised by such a wonderful father. We thank him for all he's given us and look forward to what the future brings in his marriage and our lives together." She lifted her glass. "To Robert and Angelica."

"To Robert and Angelica," echoed the guests.

As everyone took their seats, the steady hum of conversation filled the room as dinner was served. Classical music started up again, a quiet backdrop to the festivities.

Cassie leaned into her sister. "Laying it on a bit thick, sis?"

Lauren narrowed her eyes. "I meant every word."

"Really? The part about Dad—"

Lauren cleared her throat.

"—excuse me, Father, raising us? Please, he was never home and then after the split, he couldn't get away from Mom and us fast enough."

"That's not how I remember it." Lauren straightened her shoulders and looked away from Cassie.

"Oh, really? Did he make it to your first soccer game?"

"No."

"Your high school graduation?"

"No."

"College?"

Silence.

"The day you were honored at work as the first woman in your firm to receive the outstanding employee award?"

Lauren pressed her lips together.

"Yeah. Me, neither. Not my musical recitals or band performances."

Her sister glared at her. "Just because he missed a few milestones doesn't make him a bad father. He's here now."

A few? Cassie had a list. "Yes, but for how long?"

"Just because you were stubborn and didn't make contact with him after your first album doesn't mean he doesn't care."

"Oh, he cares. As long as it benefits him."

Cassie hadn't heard from her father for years until her first album became popular. He called, texted, enlisted Lauren to try to make Cassie return his attempts to reach her.

Why, when he didn't have time for her before she gained popularity, would she reconnect with him now? Her loyalty remained with the mother who'd raised Cassie and her sister after he left, working two jobs and keeping a loving, stable home for her daughters.

"Let's not argue," Lauren said, reaching out to take her hand. "Not today."

With a sigh, Cassie took her sister's hand in hers. She loved Lauren dearly. Just because her sister was blinded by their father's charm didn't mean Cassie wanted them to fight. "I agree." She might not want to be here, but was glad for some bonding time with Lauren while she was in Cypress Pointe.

The main dish of roasted chicken, grilled vegetables and risotto was superb, but after a few bites, and the nausea that followed, Cassie picked at her food. Her stomach was twisted in a perpetual knot lately, making it hard to keep anything down. If she didn't get over this writer's block soon, she'd be physically sick as well as out of a career.

The guest sitting next to her left his seat and within seconds her father took his place. She tried not to stiffen, but too many years of bad blood couldn't be denied.

"Nice reception, Dad."

A shadow passed over her father's eyes.

"Thank you. I'm glad you could make it, Cassandra."

"Why can't you call me Cassie like everyone else?"

"It's your given name."

She stretched her neck back and forth, working out the tension.

An awkward moment passed.

"How is work on the new album going?" he asked.

"We're in the early stages so I've mostly been thinking about the project."

She spoke the truth. Coming up with songs was all she thought about.

"You should make significant changes this time. The sound on your last album wasn't exactly you."

She met his gaze, a forest green, as similarly striking as her own. "I'm aware, so yes, I'm going to make changes."

He nodded, pleased his sage words brought some clarity to her decision-making. Even when she was a kid he was always critical, whether it was her piano form or music style.

"Perhaps I can have a small musical part on your next release. I have been known to play the piano quite well."

She blinked. "Come again?"

"It would be fun. Father and daughter making music together. Remember when you were young and I taught you to play the keyboard? It can be that way again."

Fun? Cassie shivered as a memory unfolded in her mind. She was ten, waiting for one of her father's infrequent trips home.

"Daddy. You're home. I did it! I wrote a song."

Robert dropped his suitcase as Cassie grabbed his hand, dragging him to the piano.

"I did it, just like you said."

"Can't this wait, Cassandra?" Impatience tinged his tone. "I just walked in the door."

"Please. Just listen."

He sighed. "Very well."

Cassie jumped on the piano stool, made room for him beside her and began to play, her fingers flying over the keyboard as she sang about flowers and puppies and summertime. When the song came to an end, she waited for his critique, her heart pounding. "Well?"

"Keep at it, sweetheart. One day you'll get better."

Then he rose from the bench and walked away.

Was he serious? She searched his expression but he seemed sincere. Like years of estrangement didn't matter and they could become buddies overnight?

"To be honest, I haven't thought that far ahead."

"Let me know. I'm always willing to share my talent with those who need it."

Those who need it? How about to get his name in the limelight? That sounded more plausible.

She couldn't continue this conversation. Taking her napkin from her lap, she folded it and set it beside her plate. "Please excuse me. I have to go…somewhere."

Robert rose and pulled back her chair. "Of course. Save a dance for me."

With a nod she took hold of her beaded clutch bag and skirted the table, not sure which direction to head. The string quartet moved off the stage to pack up while another band set up for the reception entertainment. Too bad. She'd enjoyed the chamber music.

Work that sound into a song.

She stopped short. Could it be? Her muse finally making an appearance? But just as quickly as the thought flickered through her mind, it vanished.

She stood still near the slightly raised platform set aside for the band, her mind in turmoil. Hot tears burned her eyelids. Not now. Not here.

With clumsy fingers, she opened her clutch,

searching for a tissue. Dabbing her eyes, she slowly steadied her breath. A masculine voice sounded beside her.

"Are you okay?"

Hoping her mascara hadn't run, she turned to find a man with shaggy dark blond hair smiling at her. Dressed in black slacks and a white button-down shirt, his chocolate-brown eyes held a hint of concern. Flustered, she couldn't find her words.

"I didn't mean to disturb you, but you looked upset."

She waved her hand. "It's nothing. You know, weddings."

His brow rose.

"The emotion and all."

"Right."

"It's my dad's special day."

"Congratulations." He paused, then his gaze moved to the platform and back. "I need to get to work."

"Work?"

"Wedding band."

"Oh, right. Sorry."

"No problem. Enjoy the rest of the reception."

"Thanks," she said as he moved away. Was it her imagination or did he look familiar? She hadn't been back to town in years, not since her mother and stepfather settled in Cypress

Pointe her freshman year of high school. Did she know him from school?

With athletic ease, the man leaped onto the platform, then removed his guitar from a case. He set the instrument in a stand by his feet before moving the case behind the curtain backdrop along the wall. When he finally lifted the strap over his head and plugged in his guitar, it hit her.

Luke Hastings. Only one of the best songwriters in the music industry. A four-time Grammy winner. A man who'd churned out hits before retiring to parts unknown at the height of his career. He'd been in Cypress Pointe all this time?

She'd seen pictures of him in tabloids and magazines, but never paid attention to his handsome features. In person, he made her breath hitch. Which surprised her more? That he lived in her old hometown or that she'd never noticed how good-looking he was? Both, actually. She'd worked with plenty of guys in LA, yet not one made her head turn like Luke did.

"Hey, what's up with you?" her sister asked as she came up beside her.

"Do you know who he is?" She covertly pointed at Luke.

"Yeah. Luke. He's a teacher at C.P. High."

Cassie twirled on her sister. "Why didn't you tell me?"

"About a teacher? Why would you care?"

"Because he's *Luke Hastings*."

Her sister still looked confused. "So?"

"So. So? He's only a genius songwriter."

Lauren looked up at the stage, head tilted. "Huh."

"Huh. That's all, just huh?"

"Cassie, I work in finance. I don't know songwriters. That's your area."

Cassie glanced over her shoulder, her heart thumping double time. "He's only a hero of mine. I started writing music after I heard 'Won't You Love Me Always.'"

"I remember that song. You used to drive me crazy singing it nonstop."

She pointed her thumb over her shoulder. "He wrote the lyrics."

Lauren shrugged. "So goody. You get to meet your idol."

Cassie went blank. "Meet him?"

"Well, yeah. He's here. You're here. Go introduce yourself."

Did she dare? He'd left the business for a reason. Besides, he was working. Maybe he didn't want her fawning all over him.

"I… He…"

"You'd better come up with better lyrics

than that," her sister advised as she swooshed off across the room.

Cassie slowly turned. Made her way to the wall where she slumped against it while the wheels turned in her mind. Luke Hastings, a man she'd admired for his song-crafting ability, in the same room as she. Did she dare introduce herself? What did she have to lose?

LUKE HASTINGS LOOKED up from a quick tuning to find the pretty woman he'd spoken to leaning against the wall. She stared at him, as if she'd seen a ghost.

He might as well be, at least in the music industry. He'd walked away from a lucrative career, turned his back on the one thing he loved most in his life, writing music. Sought refuge in this small town after a public divorce cut his heart and soul to shreds. Yeah, he was a ghost and intended on keeping it that way.

"Luke, did you bring the extra music in case we get requests?" his buddy Ryan asked from his position behind the keyboard.

The band had practiced the bride and groom's preselected songs, which Luke could play with his eyes closed, but they always kept backup for the odd song a reception guest requested. Luke set his Mac computer on the stand beside him and booted it up. After a few clicks, the music program opened and the band synced together.

"Got it." Luke glanced over at the drums. "Where's Sonny?"

Ryan scanned the room then smiled. "Hitting on one of the guests."

Luke chuckled. "He does know we're starting in five?"

"Yeah." Ryan waved. "Here he comes."

Sonny jumped onto the stage and held up his cell, a goofy grin stretching his lips. "I got her number."

Brian, the bass player, slapped him on the back. "Great. You can call her when we're finished."

"Dude, you're killing me."

Luke nodded to the empty seat behind the drums. "You have a job to do."

Sonny stepped over the amp chords and picked up his sticks.

Luke loved his buddies like brothers, but sometimes he had to rein them in. Sonny constantly looked for a girlfriend, Ryan constantly worried over money since he'd recently become a new dad, and Brian, well, if he were any more laid-back, he'd be asleep. Luke was the glue that held this small wedding band, Sandy Palms, together.

"Hey, who's the cutie you were talking to?"

Sonny asked Luke. "Maybe I can get her number, too."

"Daughter of the groom."

"She got a name?"

"Yeah. Sit your butt down and play."

Sonny frowned. "That's not a very nice name."

Luke shook his head. "Please, sit. We're about to start."

Sonny took his place and before long, the group started the first song of the set. A few people made their way to the dance floor. Others mingled or finished their meal. After the second song, Luke spoke into the microphone.

"Welcome, everyone, to the wedding reception of the newly married Robert and Angelica Branford. Let's give them a big round of applause as they have their first dance as a married couple."

The smiling couple came forward, dancing to a special song picked out by the bride. Since the couple were the parents, the next dance included the daughters. Luke watched the woman he'd spoken to skirt around her father to dance with the bride, not missing the frown on her father's face at her evasive move. Soon, though, Luke's attention shifted back to the song. Before long others filled the dance floor. They played five more songs, then took a break.

"I'm off," Sonny said, jumping from the stage, in search of Miss Right.

Ryan pulled his cell from his pocket. "I need to call Julie. Check on the baby."

Brian shrugged. "Guess I'll get a drink."

As his band members dispersed, Luke unplugged his guitar. He normally didn't mingle when they played a gig. Most folks in town had heard his history, but for the most part they knew him as a local teacher and left him alone, which suited him fine. He'd put together the band as a musical outlet and as a way for him and his buddies to earn extra cash.

"Excuse me?"

He glanced over to find the daughter of the groom looking up at him, noticing first her striking green eyes, made a deeper shade by the emerald dress she wore, then the indecision written all over her features. "Can I help you?"

"I think so. I hope so, anyway." She bit her lower lip, then said, "You're Luke Hastings."

Great. He knew by her tone she recognized him as the songwriter, not the teacher. "That's right."

Her tentative smile spread, lighting up the deep green hue. "I can't believe it's you."

Here we go. "You've heard of Sandy Palms, have you?"

Her smile faded and she blinked. He'd thrown her off, just as he'd hoped. "Sandy Palms?"

"Our band."

"Um, honestly, no. I'm not from around here. I mean, not any longer."

She didn't move and he guessed more small talk would be coming.

"Listen, I don't mean to be rude, but I need to get ready for the next set."

"Oh, of course."

And of course he'd hurt her feelings. He really wanted to see the sparkle return to those amazing eyes.

"Wait." He stepped from the platform. "Do you play?"

"Yes. I'm—"

"Let me guess. A songwriter?"

"At times."

He chuckled. "Either you are or aren't."

"At this moment in time, no."

"As opposed to other moments?"

She shrugged, the light in her eyes dimming. He tilted his head, intrigued. Then straightened. *Stop*, his inner voice scolded. He didn't need a female distraction.

Still, it had been a long time since he'd been floored by a woman's eyes.

"I didn't mean to bother you," she was saying. "I'm a fan and wanted to say hi."

"You have me at a disadvantage."

"I'm Cassie Branford." After a slight hesitation, she held out her hand.

"Well, Cassie, nice meeting you." He took her hand in his, surprised by the zing accompanying the gesture.

"No, the pleasure is all mine. I remember—"

She stopped when her father approached, losing the airiness from just a second ago. She broke the connection, leaving him bummed that he hadn't heard more.

"Mr. Branford," he greeted the groom. "Congratulations."

The man barely acknowledged him, focused instead on his daughter.

"Cassandra, you aren't thinking of joining the band for a number, are you?"

Number? What was he talking about?

"No. I was just talking to Luke."

Mr. Branford looked Luke over, sizing him up in a less than complimentary manner.

"You do know who my daughter is?" he asked, condescension oozing from the man.

Glancing at the woman again, it struck him. With a name to go with the face, he recognized Cassie. He might not be part of the music scene anymore, but he wasn't dead. Still, with her hair up and wearing a dress that hugged her curves, she didn't portray the confident woman from pop magazine pictures. Her signature braid, a different color always running through it, was missing at the moment, which had thrown him off.

"Dad. Not now."

"Well, if you're going to play he should know. Let you take the lead."

"Know what?" He should have been paying better attention to the vibe around him, because a sinking feeling warned him all was not right.

Cassie shifted and said, "I'm not playing with the band."

"You should."

Luke met her gaze. Read the discomfort there.

"So you're a professional musician?" he asked, even though he knew the answer.

"Cassandra is a successful popular music artist," her father boasted. "You both have many things in common."

Heat flushed through Luke. The protective wall he'd cultivated over the years to keep his old life locked away rose as Cassie's uncertain smile returned. As much as he tried to maintain a low profile, people from the industry found him from time to time. Granted, Cassie was merely a guest at her father's wedding, but old habits were hard to ignore. Better to stop this intrusion before it went any further.

"I doubt it."

Cassie flinched at his tone. "I only wanted to ask about your ca—"

"I'm not part of the industry any longer. I'm sorry, I can't help you."

He turned on his heel and walked away. Yeah, he'd been rude, but he'd sensed where the conversation was headed and would rather tap-dance on hot coals than reminisce about the old days. He was not going to talk shop with this woman. Or any woman, for that matter. His time in the music industry was over and he intended on keeping it that way.

CHAPTER TWO

"Thanks, Dad. You just blew my chance to talk to the greatest songwriter who ever lived."

Her father lifted a haughty brow. "The greatest who ever lived? I believe that's a bit of an overstatement."

"You know what I meant. Luke had a stellar career."

"Which he walked away from. Messy personal life if I remember correctly." His eyes narrowed. "And why is it so important to talk to him?"

Like she'd admit her writer's block to anyone, especially her father. "I'm a fan. That's all."

"Cassandra, he's been reduced to a wedding band singer. Old news. Focus on the future."

Why did she even bother speaking to her father? Fisting her hands together, she turned and navigated through the mingling guests. What had her father been thinking? See, this was why she kept her distance. Her father didn't have a clue about who she was or what she wanted.

She'd just reached the door to leave when it hit her. Luke could help her. She needed his expertise. The question was, how could she get it?

The band started up again. Instead of storming off like she'd intended, she went back to the table she'd been seated at earlier. She angled her chair to face the far side of the room. A bird's eye view of the man in question.

She needed a plan. A way to work up the nerve to ask the legendary Luke Hastings for some tips to help her out of her writing funk. But how? This certainly wasn't the opportune place to approach him. Yet if she didn't talk to him tonight, she might miss her one and only chance.

"I just danced with Father," Lauren said as she flopped into the chair beside her. "He seems distracted. What did you do?"

"Why do you always assume I did something?"

"Because I saw the heated conversation between you two."

Cassie sent her a sideways glance. "Just the usual. Honestly, I'm more interested in Luke. What do you know about him?"

"Like, what subject he teaches? If he's involved with anyone?"

"No. His life here in Cypress Pointe."

Lauren crossed one leg over the other. "Let's see. Moved here a couple years ago. His cousin owns the Grand Cypress Hotel. He teaches English at the high school and started an after-school program that morphed into a community outreach for at-risk teens."

"Wow."

"Kids' Klub has been pretty successful. Redirects kids going in the wrong direction."

Noble and hunky. Perfect combination.

"Why are you so interested?" Her sister's eyes went wide. "Oh, my gosh, you have a crush on him."

"I do not," Cassie insisted, even if she couldn't meet her sister's gaze. "I want to talk to him about something and it would help if I knew more about him."

"So explain why your cheeks are red."

"It's hot in here."

"Right. Don't forget, I'm the one who heard all about your undying love for Chris Johnson."

"Chris Johnson?" Cassie's mouth gaped. "That was like eight years ago."

"And you were crushed when he broke up with you."

True, she was, but moving away from Cypress Pointe and keeping busy had gotten her through that dark period in her life.

"Just so you know, he got fat."

Cassie laughed out loud. "Have I told you lately how much I love you?"

Her sister's quick grin slowly faded. "I miss our times together."

"Me, too."

Cassie's heart squeezed at her sister's soft expression. They hadn't grown apart, exactly, more like distance, time and separate lives put a strain on their relationship. Their differing views on their father, Lauren's insistence on proving herself to him while Cassie didn't want him around, created another, ongoing source of tension between them.

"I'm glad you let me stay with you. Since Mom and Bud are still away, I didn't want to spend all my time in their empty house."

"That what sisters do. Let each other crash on the other's extra bed."

"I was hoping we could—"

Lauren jumped up "Angelica is waving me over. I'll be right back."

"Hold on." Cassie grabbed her arm. "So if Luke is so busy, why the wedding band?"

Lauren shrugged. "You'll have to ask him yourself." Then she was gone.

Cassie blew out a sigh.

She glanced across the room. Luke picked the guitar with one hand, his fingers effortlessly positioning the chords with the other, and sang along with the guys. So in the moment, he moved with the beat, smiled at a band member from time to time. How she missed the total abandonment she experienced when she sang and played her piano, lost in the words and the tempo.

Her heartbeat sped up again, matching the emotions swirling inside. As she studied Luke, she realized she'd first thought his hair was shaggy. The more she looked, the more she realized it had been deliberately styled. It gave him a bit of a free spirit look, yet not out of control. Hmm, some stylist in his past life had taught him well.

His fingers expertly moved up and down the neck of the guitar, bringing an unmistakable sound from the instrument. He certainly had a flair. The band performed mostly wedding standards, she noticed, none of the songs that made Luke famous. From his attitude earlier, he probably avoided those particular songs on purpose.

Twenty minutes later the band took a break. Cassie waited for Luke to be alone, but one of the band members was talking his ear off. She should wander over, start another conversation with him, but she couldn't seem to leave the chair.

Even though he'd made it clear he didn't talk about the industry, Cassie couldn't take no for an answer. Her chest constricted, the noose of her future pulling tighter. She could do this. She'd gathered enough information about Luke to make small talk while she bided her time to get to the root of her dilemma. She just had to wait for a chance to grab his attention. Luckily, she was a patient woman.

She swore he'd looked directly at her during one of the numbers, but the lights were too low to know for sure. Her imagination? Hopeful wishing? She sat through two more sets before the party began to wind down and the band finally performed their final number.

To her surprise, the band members took off quickly, leaving Luke to break down the equipment.

Taking a deep breath, she approached the platform.

"You guys sounded great tonight. Been playing together for a while?"

"Couple years."

"So…I wanted to apologize for my father."

Luke shot her an amused glance. "Overprotective?"

She'd have laughed out loud at the notion if it wasn't so sad. "No, more like too much interference in my life." She moved closer, silently high-fiving the fact that Luke wanted to engage in conversation. "We aren't exactly close."

He nodded. "No offense taken. I stopped worrying about what people think a long time ago."

If only she could adopt the same mantra.

"My sister tells me you teach high school English."

"I do." He unzipped his case and gently laid the guitar inside. She admired people who took special care of their instruments. "Never thought I'd impact any kids, but it's turned out to be one of the best experiences of my life."

"Did you take over for Mrs. Trumbull?"

"No. She was gone before I arrived. She did leave a legacy behind."

Cassie shuddered. "Of fear. I remember sweating out the Shakespeare semester. Her assignments were killer."

Luke chuckled. "I sure hope my legacy isn't that negative."

"As long as you don't pull your hair back in a severe bun, narrow your eyes at your students and make everyone uncomfortable, you should be fine."

He patted the back of his head. "I never considered a new hairstyle. Maybe a man bun would up my cool factor and keep the kids in line."

She laughed, delighted by his sense of humor. He didn't need a bun to be any more good-looking in her eyes.

He snapped the latches on the case and faced her. "Did you do well on the Shakespeare assignment?"

She squinted, thinking back. "B, maybe? I have to say, she laid down a really good foundation. The subsequent years of Shakespeare weren't so horrible."

"Not a fan of the bard?"

"I can appreciate the work that went into writing his tales, but translating old English is like math. I'd rather not work that hard if I don't have to."

"You sound like the majority of my students."

"Then let's hope you make learning fun, not a session in terror."

"I go over Shakespeare, but throw in other more contemporary works for my students to read."

"Writing isn't as easy as everyone thinks."

"I'm sure my students would agree." Taking hold of the handle, he lifted the case and stepped down from the platform. "It's been nice talking to you."

Cassie's stomach dipped. She had to keep

him interested. "Same here." She glanced at his case. "You really know how to play."

"Years of practice."

"I didn't get serious until I was in high school."

He took a step back. "Well, I need to take off."

By the shuddered look in his eyes, she could tell he'd checked out of the conversation. Drat. She'd lost him.

"Well, I'll be in town awhile longer. Maybe we'll run into each other."

"Anything is possible."

"I'd love to talk to you about your songwriting days. You've been—"

He held his hand up "Let me stop you right there."

She blinked. His sudden displeasure indicated she'd gone too far.

"I'm not going to talk about music careers, songwriting or whatever you have your mind set on."

"I didn't mean to upset you."

"You didn't. I just need you to know I'm not available for whatever it is you want."

Her heart sank as he turned and crossed the room. *Good night to you, too, Luke Hastings.*

LUKE STEPPED INTO the mild spring night, his face hot, his chest tight. Upset? Him? Right, not much. Slowly, he eased the pressure of the fist holding the guitar case handle, letting his breath out in slow degrees.

He stopped. Shook out his arms. Tilted his head back.

The dark sky was clear, stars twinkled above him. Cicadas buzzed, hidden beyond the empty golf course. A lonely frog belched nearby. The air, still warm even after the sun had set a few hours ago, held a hint of something sweet, like flowers. In the distance, the sprinkler system sputtered and hissed as it turned on.

All in all, a beautiful night to just let go and not think at all.

If only he could oblige.

He'd gone at least six months without the anger and despair building up. All it had taken this time was an attractive woman with expectation in her eyes to reduce him to this state.

It was clear Cassie wanted something from him. She'd floundered getting to the point, but once she admitted it was to talk shop, he couldn't handle it. He didn't have it in him to go back in time, to the place where another woman selfishly bent on fulfilling her dreams had squashed his.

He hated that he wasn't stronger. But the truth was as clear as the night sky. He hadn't forgiven Tracy. Was afraid he never could.

He continued walking to his black two-door BMW, his footsteps steady against the pavement. It had been two years since Tracy's betrayal. Shouldn't he be over it by now?

Get a clue, Hastings. People will always let you down.

As he unlocked the trunk and laid the guitar case inside, he wondered once again for the millionth time, what was wrong with him. Whoever said time heals all wounds hadn't been cheated on by an ex-wife.

"You're leaving kinda late."

At the sound of a voice in the darkness, Luke froze, until a figure materialized, stepping into the circle of light provided by the overhead fixture. He recognized his cousin, Dane Peterson, a local hotel owner, decked out in a button-down shirt and pressed slacks, his hair cut in his usual short fashion.

He let out a long breath as he slammed the trunk closed. "You want me to have a heart attack?"

Dane held a hand up. "Sorry. Thought you might have noticed me."

"No. I was thinking."

"Yeah, I could tell. With you, that's never good. Tracy?"

"No, actually, I'm…" He paused a beat. "Hey, what're you doing here?"

"Picking up Nealy. Her car is in the shop."

"I saw her a few times tonight. She was running all over the place."

"She loves being an event planner, but this reception was not her dream job. Angelica kept after her until she gave in."

Luke glanced around. "Where is she?"

"Forgot something and ran back inside." Dane leaned back against the car, crossing one ankle over the other. "So, what's up?"

"I met a woman and—"

"Wait," Dane interrupted. "Repeat that. You met a woman?"

"Not met, like I want to go out on a date. I talked to the daughter of the groom."

Dane's deep chuckle echoed in the still night.

"You already knew?"

His cousin nodded.

"How?"

A besotted expression came over the other man's face. "Nealy."

As usual, his cousin's girlfriend was one step ahead of everyone.

"First thing she said when she walked out the door tonight was, 'I saw Luke talking to a very lovely young lady.'"

"Why do I even bother to have a personal life?"

"Dude, it's Cypress Pointe. People notice other people and what they're doing."

"I thought I'd left the scrutiny behind when I moved here." Luke shoved his hands in his pants pockets. "So I was talking to a woman, but it's not what you think."

"Let me guess. Brought up bad memories?"

"Big time."

"So tell me you have a good reason not to ask an attractive woman out," Dane said, settling into the conversation.

"No good reason. More of a hunch."

"About?"

Luke shifted uncomfortably. Suddenly his dress shoes pinched way too tight, the collar of his shirt became stifling. "She wanted to talk about music."

"She knows who you are?"

"Yeah. And she's a pop singer. Cassie Branford."

"Nealy plays her music all the time."

"So you see my dilemma?"

Dane cocked his head to one side. "No, I do not."

"She's everything I've been staying away from since I moved here."

"And you're afraid, what, that talking to her about music will somehow make you face up to the last two years?"

The old stubbornness overwhelmed him. "Maybe I don't want to forget."

"Or more like you don't want to forgive."

Luke ran a hand through his hair. "I never thought I'd end up here, like this."

"Yet here you stand, kicking yourself over something you had no control over."

"It still hurts."

"I get that. But maybe you should let go. Cut yourself some slack. You can't be a martyr forever."

Luke met his cousin's sharp gaze. "Is that how you see me?"

"When you first got here. Lately, less so."

"You're not the only one, are you?"

Dane shrugged. "I don't discuss you with other people."

"Nealy?"

"Nealy's not other people. Besides, she has a good sense about folks."

"Yeah? What does she think about me?"

Dane pushed away from the car. "Luke, when you first got here, you were a mess. Rightfully so. But we both think you've grieved long enough. Tracy doesn't deserve a second thought and you can't keep living this way."

"Believe it or not, I agree. I just can't seem to move ahead."

"What about this woman? If she's caught

your interest, maybe this can be the first step to getting on with your life."

He pictured Cassie. Soft brown hair. Incredible eyes. A little bit of a dimple when she smiled at him. She'd caught his attention, even before he recognized her.

"Not every person in your life is going to hurt you, Luke."

Neither he nor his cousin came from very stable homes. Dane's folks fought all the time, leaving him and his brother to do as they pleased, which hadn't always turned out for the best. Luke's own parents had been abusive. His father and brother were in and out of jail. His mother? Who knew? He'd wanted to change his life when he married Tracy. Thought they'd had a chance. It made sense why Luke was reluctant to place his hopes too high, only to be knocked down again.

Which meant he wasn't about to trust his heart to another woman.

Luke broke the silence. "She's pregnant, you know."

"Tracy?"

He nodded.

Dane blew out a low whistle.

"After years of promises, of stringing me along, she's finally expecting with her new husband."

"Sorry, man."

That's what hurt the most, Luke realized. "I get that Tracy was ambitious. We wrote a lot of hits together. I shouldn't have been surprised when she left me for Andrews or how she talked me into giving her royalties in the divorce for that last song of ours."

"I never got why you would just hand that song over to her."

"At that point I just wanted out of the marriage and would do anything to expedite the matter. The paparazzi hounded me, all because Tracy fed them a steady diet of our marital drama." He ran a hand over the back of his neck to release the tension. "The song hadn't been released so I figured it didn't matter much. Major lapse in judgment." He sighed. Who knew in his haste he'd sign over their top moneymaking hit ever? "But a baby? Talk about a double whammy. She promised we'd have a family. Knew how much I wanted to be a father. Even went so far as to make me think she might actually be pregnant more than once."

"I never liked her," Dane said, sounding like something rotten filled his mouth.

Luke appreciated his cousin's loyalty. "It's like she ended up with it all while I got the pain."

"So, change your future. Take some chances. You might—no, you will—get hurt again somewhere along the line. But you gotta get back to living."

Luke stared out over the deserted golf course. His cousin was right. He would never write another song, but he needed to get his priorities together. He was only thirty-five. Time to stop skulking in the shadows and be open to the possibility of meeting people.

Maybe he should do as Dane suggested. Ask a woman out on a date. Not that he was in a hurry for romance, though. But he did need to start enjoying the present instead of dwelling on bad decisions from the past.

He was about to tell his cousin so when his cell rang. He pulled the phone from his pocket and read the screen. "Gotta run. Trouble down at the pier."

"One of your kids?"

"Looks like." Luke slapped his hand on Dane's shoulder. "Thanks for listening. Tonight threw me."

"Figured. Listen, we're family. You may keep your feelings close to the vest, but I always have your back."

"Same."

A sly grin curved Dane's lips. "And so does Nealy."

"Why does that make me want to run?"

"She wants to see you happy."

"So do I, but I'll get there on my own."

They parted ways. Luke drove through the deserted downtown. All the businesses were locked up tight and safe for the night. A plus to living in a small town. He'd had his share of big cities and found Cypress Pointe suited his temperament.

He reached the marina, pulling up to find red and blue lights swirling from a police car parked in the lot. Shoot. Not what he'd wanted to see. Chief Gardener spoke to a blond-haired teenage boy slouched against the squad car.

Parking a few feet away, Luke met the scene with the right amount of sympathy and steel he'd adopted since starting Kids' Klub.

"Chief. What's going on?"

"Seems young Snyder and his buddies intended to sneak onto a boat moored here. Instead, they broke some glass on the dock. Made a ruckus."

Luke stared down at the teen. "Kyle, we talked about this."

The boy hung his head in silence.

"Are you charging him?"

"Lucky for him he cleaned up the mess after his friends took off." The chief put his hand on the boy's shoulder. "He's free to go, as long as he tells me this is the end of this nonsense."

Kyle, his eyes partially hidden under messy bangs, met the chief's gaze. "I'm sorry."

"That's not a promise."

The teen sighed. "Yeah, I promise."

The chief removed his hand and nodded to Luke. "He's all yours."

Kyle stepped away from the car, head down as he approached Luke.

"Let's get you home."

Once in the car, Luke waited before speaking. Kyle huddled against the passenger door, as far away from Luke as possible. In working with at-risk teens, he'd found that helping certain kids meant making them sweat it out a bit. Kyle was no exception. Luke started the car, motored from the lot.

"Thought you stopped running with that group."

Kyle shrugged, with the feigned nonchalance only teens could pull off.

"Was there an answer in that shrug? Because I sure didn't hear anything."

"It's not easy," Kyle mumbled.

"Nothing is. But if you want me to keep your place in the music program at the Klub, I can't be bailing you out when your buddies leave you to take the fall. This is the second time."

Kyle's head jerked up. "You'd kick me out?"

"If you get in trouble again, yeah, I will."

"I'm sorry, Mr. Hastings. I don't want to leave the program. I'm finally getting the hang of those chords you showed me."

"Then you'd better remember that the next time you go to cause trouble."

Kyle straightened in his seat. "I will."

The remainder of the journey passed in silence until Luke pulled into Kyle's driveway and put the car in park.

The house was situated in a nice, older neighborhood. The homes were fairly close together. He'd noticed a few bikes on the ground in a yard across the street. Heard a dog bark down the block. Very middle class, very reassuring.

Since settling in Cypress Pointe, Luke had bought a house on the edge of town, within walking distance from the Gulf Waters. Separated far enough on each side from prying neighbors, it became less of a sanctuary and more of a prison of his own making. The past few months had been better, but if he were honest, he'd been waiting for something to threaten his hard-earned peace. Who would have thought a woman with incredible green eyes would be the one to disrupt his quiet spell?

Shaking off the thought, he cut the ignition and turned in his seat.

"Kyle, you have talent. Don't blow it over some guys who don't care about you."

"I hear you, Mr. Hastings."

"Do you? It seems like we've had this conversation before."

Kyle slumped in his seat.

"Now let's go talk to your parents."

Apprehensive eyes met his. "Do we have to?"

"You know the rules."

"Stupid rules," Kyle muttered as he opened his door to slide out. In the cover of darkness, Luke grinned at the boy's discomfort. Wished someone had cared enough to enforce rules when he was a kid so he and his brother wouldn't have ended up in hot water more than a few times.

As they walked up to the front porch, Luke said, "You know, Kyle, you could call me if you're not sure what to do."

Kyle glanced at him. "You wouldn't mind?"

"No. So long as it's not a habit. I wouldn't mind helping you out. Before the cops do."

A sheepish grin curved Kyle's lips. "Got it."

When they reached the house, the front door flew open. Kyle's parents stood in the doorway, the bright light from inside silhouetting them.

"Kyle," his mother said, hand over her heart. "Come inside." She opened the door to let her son in while her husband stepped out.

"I'll be just a minute," he told his wife.

Kyle nodded at Luke then followed his mom.

"I'm sorry Kyle inconvenienced you, Mr. Hastings."

"Luke, please. And it was no bother. I happened to be out anyway."

The older man crossed his arms over his chest. "Kyle's doing so much better. He really enjoys the program at the Klub."

"But kids still get lured into what they think is an exciting life. I understand."

"Will he still be able to continue with his guitar lessons?"

"Yes. But I told him if he gets in trouble again, his place will be in jeopardy."

Kyle's father nodded. "Thank you."

"I want Kids' Klub to help kids like Kyle, so I hope he'll use better judgment in the future. Good night."

Luke drove home, his thoughts slipping from Kyle to his own brother. Would a program like the one he'd started have helped Mark or had he been destined to be drawn to trouble? He supposed he'd never know, especially with Mark behind bars at the moment.

But there was one thing Luke did know for

sure. Despite the constant worry about funding the Klub, enlisting help as the programs grew, or even doubting his brother's turnaround, Luke didn't regret starting Kids' Klub for one second. If he helped one kid get away from an abusive home or criminal influence, it was worth the hurt of his old life to get the Klub off the ground.

Dane was wrong in the sense that while it might look like Luke wasn't living, helping kids brought great meaning to his life. Luke may need a personal shake-up, but he didn't want to alter this part of his life. The kids were his family.

The other part? Maybe talking to a perky woman who caught his attention while in town for her father's wedding wouldn't be as hard as he imagined. What was the worst that could happen?

CHAPTER THREE

THE NEXT MORNING, Cassie sat at her sister's kitchen table, feet hooked over the lower rung of the chair, her elbows bent while she balanced a pencil on her fingers. A half-empty cup of coffee, her third so far, sat within reaching distance, while she stared at a blank yellow legal pad.

She'd been up since dawn, still dressed in a tank top, sleeping shorts and a threadbare long sleeve denim shirt. Her guitar, which she'd named Ginger for its deep red wood, still inside the case, sat beside her feet. Normally she'd take Ginger out and strum until a melody caught her fancy. Normally. But with her head in a bad place, she didn't dare touch the instrument.

So far, nothing had come to her. Oh, some random notes. A few words here and there drifted through her brain, words she tried to link together, but she couldn't make them stick. The words lingered, then escaped as if wisps in the wind.

She gathered her long hair and twisted, then tossed it over her shoulder, hating this surge of frustration. Her sister walked into the kitchen, dressed in a flirty dress, ready to go out to Sunday brunch.

"Sure you don't want to come?" Lauren asked. "My friends loved meeting meet you last time you were in town."

"Thanks, but I need to work."

"How long have you been sitting there?"

"What time is it?" she asked. If she didn't get it together soon, she was in big trouble.

"You look terrible." Her sister stated the obvious.

"That's the look I was going for." *Okay, stop.* No point in taking her situation out on Lauren when her sister had absolutely no idea what was going on with Cassie in the first place.

Lauren poured herself a cup of coffee and leaned a hip against the counter, her narrowed eyes trained on Cassie. Uh-oh. Trouble. Her sister hadn't become a successful financial advisor without being perceptive.

Cassie wiggled in her seat.

"So when are you going to tell me what's going on?"

"If I have my way, never."

Lauren sipped her coffee. Cassie could almost picture the wheels turning in her sister's mind.

"So there is something going on. The wedding?"

"No, it's not about the wedding."

"Whatever it is, I'll listen. I'm told it's one of my best qualities."

"As much as I'd love to, you can't help with this problem."

"Music?"

"Of course. What else drives me?"

"If you're having trouble, talk to Dad."

"Yeah, that's not going to happen." She held up her hand as Lauren opened her mouth to argue. Her father had shown her the wonderful world of music, and yes, she'd wanted to please him, but after too many years spent trying to earn her father's love and never measuring up, she'd stopped trying. Excluding him from her life had helped her to focus as she tried to succeed in the business, finding passion in her talent, without his criticism. "Not because we don't talk to each other. He can't help me figure this out."

A knowing gleam shone in her sister's eyes. "But Luke Hastings can?"

Her breath caught. "Why would you ask me about him?"

"Because I heard you humming that song of his again." She snapped her fingers. "You know, something about love."

"'Won't You Love Me Always.'"

"Right. I can never keep all the titles straight. It's like that one of yours, 'Pretty Inside.' I love the message of that song."

Cassie smiled, remembering the story behind the lyrics. She'd gone to a fancy sorority party in college and while her friends were all dressed up in the latest fashion, she'd worn a casual outfit. Big no-no. She'd brushed off the sideway glances and snickers by pretending to be amused, hiding her hurt feelings. Later on, she'd used the experience to compose a song about beauty coming from inside, not the trendy clothes or shoes that a person wore. It had been one of her most popular singles.

"That was a great time for me. I was away from home for the first time. Mom and Bud were strong so we didn't have to worry about her like we did when the three of us were making ends meet. It was like the clamoring inside my head finally calmed down and I could take the lyrics I'd been jotting down forever and put them to music."

"Mom wasn't happy when you dropped out your senior year."

"What can I say? When the opportunity to perform full-time arose, I jumped at the chance. Actually made some money."

"Until LA."

"It wasn't easy, but I was living my dream." She laughed. "I was all about ramen noodle meals, sleeping on friends' couches and pinching pennies to get by while I knocked on one record label door after another."

"And now," her sister asked, "you're interested in Luke?"

She'd been humming Luke's love song, a number infused with such deep longing that the singer didn't know how he'd make it through another day without a commitment from the woman he loved. It was so much a part of her subconscious, taking her back to the painful breakup with Chris around the time of the single's release. As long as she could remember, humming, singing and playing were natural responses for her, but that song? After hearing it, she'd taken out her journal and begun writing snippets about her feelings, which eventually became lyrics to her own songs.

"The guy is a legend. Look at his reputation. Multiple hits recorded by famous artists. Four Grammy awards. If I could just convince him I don't want anything tangible from him, just a bit of his time…"

"From what I've heard, he doesn't talk about his old career."

"I remember reading something about a

messy divorce, but I was busy with my career then so I didn't pay attention."

"Some people don't like to dwell in the past. Luke is one of them."

"It's a shame. He really made his mark on the music world."

"And now his mark is Kids' Klub. When Luke came to town and started teaching, he saw a need for at-risk teens to put their energy into something constructive. He started with music, but soon the concept grew into sports teams and other creative stuff. It still focuses on troubled youth, but the teams and clubs and lessons caught on and developed into an awesome outlet for kids from any background. Not only do the teens in Cypress Pointe take advantage of the Klub, but surrounding towns, as well. And now, local businesses have joined in and will help train kids in their areas of interest. It's quite a success."

"I'm impressed."

"They operated out of the basement of a small community center, but recently Luke moved to an empty warehouse just north of town. He's hoping to buy the property but funds are tight. He runs the program from donations, including whatever he makes with his wedding band."

Cassie pictured his face, his dark blond hair

and those deep brown eyes. How he'd smiled during a raucous number his band performed at her dad's reception, or the faraway look that came over him when he sang a love song.

"You certainly have your finger on the pulse of the town, especially this Kids' Klub," she said, shaking off the vision.

"I helped Luke draw up a business plan when he first came up with the concept. Guided him through the nonprofit maze, set up the organization books and so on. He recently called me for advice on buying the property and warehouse."

Cassie tilted her head. "Last night you acted as thought you barely know him."

Lauren shrugged. "I don't know him, other than as a client. He doesn't talk about himself or his life, only the Klub. So essentially he is kind of a stranger, at least about his personal life."

"Hmm."

"I recognize that look," Lauren said. "You're still determined to get him on board to help you with…whatever."

Did she dare confess her darkest fear? Speak aloud the words that kept her awake at night, drenched in a cold sweat, worrying about her future?

Cassie paused, staring out the window. A

cardinal landed on the birdfeeder in the backyard. Sitting atop the structure, tall and proud, the beautiful scarlet creature surveyed its surroundings, its stature speaking of control in the world. So unlike Cassie's state of mind at this very moment.

She finally glanced at her sister, took a bracing breath before saying, "I'm having trouble coming up with new material. That's why I'm so interested in Luke."

"Since when?"

"Since *Living in Paradise* tanked. The label wants a repeat of my first album and I can't put together words or melodies."

"I remember when we were growing up you were always scribbling in your journal. No wonder you're worried."

"I'm hoping this is temporary, so please keep this between us. At least until I can sort this out."

"I will." Lauren finished her coffee and placed her mug on the counter. "I may not be able to help you with this, but from the look on your face, I hope you come up with a solution, and soon." That said, she walked out of the room, leaving behind troubled silence.

Cassie stared at the blank paper again. Was this it? The end? What happened to the ease of jotting down words over the years? All the times growing up when her dad disappointed her or her mother struggled to make ends meet? Yeah, her life made for good lyrics, even though it wasn't always easy. But still, she had experiences to draw on. Why wouldn't the words come now?

The record label had expectations. So did her manager and fans. She didn't want to disappoint any of them.

The yellow legal pad, still as pristine as when she'd bought it, mocked her. She grabbed the pencil and wrote in big, block letters, WRITE.

Not much in terms of inspiration, but right now, it was all she had.

Tapping her pencil against the paper, she closed her eyes. She thought about her conversation with Lauren, which made her think of Luke and his great club for kids. She should really volunteer there to get her mind off her troubles. She'd given music lessons in college to make money, why not do some good while waiting for inspiration to strike?

The more she thought about it, the more she liked the idea. But would Luke accept her assistance? Only one way to find out.

With her mind whirling, Cassie hurried to the guest room. Even though it was Sunday, she'd go to the Klub and see if Luke was available. If he was as dedicated as Lauren said, she suspected he'd be on site. She chose an outfit, showered and dressed in record time, braided her hair and slipped on chunky ankle boots. Enough worrying. She needed action. Time to make a positive impression like her life depended on it.

After calling Lauren for directions, she drove her rented red convertible, complete with all the bells and whistles, to the Klub's address. The sporty two-seater was similar to her car back home, her one splurge after the first album. As she entered the spacious warehouse, walking into a gymnasium setup, butterflies fluttered in her stomach. She noticed teens hanging out, some playing hoops, others working on some type of project, a good indication Luke was indeed here.

She stopped a young man with glasses. "Can you tell me where I can find Luke Hastings?"

"In his office." The boy pointed to an opening on the far side of the gym. "Down the hallway."

"Thanks."

Hand on her stomach, Cassie ventured to the door clearly marked Mr. Hastings. She lifted her hand to knock on the partially open door when she heard the sudden peal of bells.

Bells? She blinked, realizing the disruption

came from her cell phone. Grabbing it from her jacket pocket, she read her manager's name on the screen. She swiped the screen and said hello.

"Hey, stranger," said Travis. "You don't write, you don't call."

Did he suspect her dilemma? He couldn't. She'd only told Lauren about her predicament. See, she was so off balance she was transferring her fears to everything.

"Sorry. Been busy with wedding stuff."

"Not too busy to work on new material, right? I gotta say, I'm a bit concerned I haven't heard from you."

Travis Bailey had taken Cassie under his wing when she'd first made a splash in the club scene around LA. Without his guidance, there's no telling how she would have navigated the murky waters of the recording industry. The man had a heart of gold, for his clients, anyway. Otherwise his instincts resembled an attack dog, brokering deals and keeping those he managed away from bad contracts and shady characters making false promises. A middle-aged hipster with thinning hair, he had plenty of lines on his boyish face, attesting to years of smiles. He'd become something of a substitute dad to her over the years. Letting him down would break her heart.

"Sorry, Travis. I'm trying to get some work done while I'm here." She bit her lower lip. Not a lie, exactly. She was trying.

"Great. We have to hit this thing with everything we've got. I've spoken to Ron and they're looking for a stellar product."

Cassie swallowed hard. Ron Harding, an executive at the label and the idiot, er, mastermind, in proposing the changes in her sound, was a hard man to please. He'd dropped other artists for less of a flop than Cassie's last album.

She'd always wondered why Travis had let the producer tweak her sound. Travis had been gung ho and she'd been so caught up in the whirlwind excitement of cutting another album, she didn't dare ask. Didn't dare voice her opinion after only one album with people who'd had years of experience. Well, she'd learned. The bad album fell squarely on her shoulders for not expressing her true self. She wouldn't make the same mistake again.

"In the meantime, what about a few touring dates before you go into the studio? You know, for momentum. Any thoughts?"

How on earth could she make any appearances when she was most likely going to get kicked out of said studio? All without her manager realizing any of her concerns.

"Um, why don't you hold off. Or better yet,

start looking at the calendar after I finish the album. Don't want too much on my plate. This project is so important."

And she needed to stay in Cypress Pointe where she had access to Luke.

Travis went silent for a few beats. "You okay? You sound weird. Pressure isn't gettin' to you, is it?"

"We both know this is make or break, Travis. I'd be unrealistic not to be concerned."

"Now, calm down," he tsked in the soothing voice that had pulled her from the edge multiple times. "You've got this."

"And if I don't?"

"We'll figure it out. Like we always do."

His words should have made her feel better, but created the opposite effect.

"You'll keep me in the loop?"

"Yes, sir," she answered, adding a little sass to her tone.

He chuckled. "That's more like it, although I still think you should consider touring."

She winced. "I'll get back to you on the concert idea."

"That's my girl. Talk to you soon."

Hitting the end button, she stared at the dark screen. She couldn't tour, not now or in the future. Planning a concert was on the bottom of her to-do list. If, and when, the album was made, she'd consider going on the road. Until then…

Her manager had faith in her, but did she? "What were you thinking, Travis?"

The sound of a throat being cleared made her jump. She looked up into amused brown eyes. "Talk to yourself much?"

Good grief. So much for a positive impression.

LUKE HELD BACK a grin at Cassie's mortified expression.

He'd been in his office, fingers stalled over the calculator as the same numbers kept appearing on the screen. A sharp ache took residence in his temple. No matter how many times he went over the accounting, there was still a big gap in his operating capital. Contributions came in regularly, but since the move to the warehouse, cash was tight.

A shout came from the gymnasium. Every Sunday, a bunch of the boys gathered for a game of basketball. Luke didn't mind opening up, especially when he discovered how many kids wanted to hang out. To him, the sound of voices meant he was doing something right, justifying his decision to move into this larger building.

He'd been about to abandon his depressing

act of going over the finances when a feminine voice floated in from outside his office door. He recognized Cassie's sweet cadence. What was she doing here? Intrigued, he went to investigate.

He certainly hadn't expected to see her any time soon, if at all. Since the wedding events were over, he figured she'd leave town before they had a chance to reconnect. Yet here she stood, her hair in her signature braid, dressed in a stylish outfit. No wonder he hadn't recognized her at the wedding.

"Sorry to bother you." She held up her phone. "My manager."

He hadn't meant to eavesdrop, but heard enough of the conversation to know she was all about her career.

"Can you spare a minute of your time?"

"Sure. C'mon in."

He gathered the paperwork littering his desk and stuffed it into a file. "I'm actually happy for a distraction." He took a chair from the corner and placed it beside his desk. "Have a seat."

She sat, her gaze taking in his office. Pictures of kids he'd worked with adorned one wall. Another displayed framed certificates of appreciation from local businesses. When she met his eyes, he glimpsed the uncertainty there. Guessed he'd be the one to break the ice.

"So, what brings you by today?"

"I'm hoping to talk to you about volunteering here."

His brow rose. "In what capacity?"

"I was talking to my sister this morning and she told me about Kids' Klub and all the great things you do for the community."

"Lauren helped me in the beginning."

"She said. Thankfully, my sister and I never got into too much trouble, but I have to say, starting a program for at-risk kids is really honorable." She spread her arms. "So here I am."

Interesting.

"While it would be easy to simply write a check, I'd like to propose a more personal touch." A nostalgic expression softened her face. "I used to give music lessons as a way of earning money through college. Piano. Guitar. I love seeing kids get excited when they begin to learn to play a new instrument. So, I'd like to volunteer."

"Volunteer? Don't you have a career you're busy with?"

"Yes, but while I'm here in Cypress Pointe I'd like to be part of your program. You know, something bigger than myself."

"Cassie, I'll be honest. I overheard some of your conversation just now. Won't a concert schedule keep you too busy to be involved here?"

"Oh, I didn't realize…" She stopped. Composed herself. "It might have sounded like that, but I'm staying in Cypress Pointe for a while."

"So no running off to concerts just as you start to bond with the kids? They need consistency. People who stick around."

"I realize that. I remember those angsty teenage years, so I would never intentionally hurt anyone."

He ran a hand through his hair. "I'll admit, the Klub has lots of needs, including volunteers in time and money. I need you to be sure about a commitment, not thinking about concerts or PR gimmicks."

"PR? I wasn't even considering that far in advance. I can do some good and—" A slow smile bloomed over her lips. "You're a genius."

"Come again?"

"You just gave me an excellent idea."

"Which is?"

"How about I give a benefit concert with all the proceeds going to Kids' Klub?"

Surprised twice in the time span of five minutes. A new record.

"Your offer comes out of the blue."

"That's because I just thought of it." Her expression turned serious. "It would be a great opportunity to raise funds and the kids would have fun, as well. Plus, I'd get some musical time with you."

"I don't know what to say."

"Say yes. The idea is win-win for Cypress Pointe and the Klub."

He propped his elbows on the desk and steepled his hands under his chin, quickly doing the math. One concert with Cassie could set the Klub up for at least a year if he was wise with his spending. Or it could be enough for a down payment on the property. His mind went over all scenarios, returning to his initial gut reaction.

Cassie had a career and he knew how consumed some artists could be in that business. He remembered that she'd shown promise on her first album, then appeared to change her style to chase the charts with her second. Would a benefit concert for Kids' Klub just be a media event for her? A chance to grab the spotlight in the guise of helping a good cause? He didn't want that type of tabloid exposure if it was only meant to advance her career.

"I see the benefits for the Klub. What do you get out of the deal?"

A puzzled frown marred her forehead. "Who says I need anything from it?"

"Because I've been in that world, Cassie. I know how the PR machine works."

She avoided his gaze for a second too long before scooting forward in her chair. "Luke, I love to perform live. It's how I made my way before the studio work." Her eyes sparkled. "I also love Cypress Pointe. My sister, mom and her husband live and work here. It's the place I return to when I need a break from the craziness of this business. I'm sure you understand."

He did. All too well. "What about your schedule? Can you make the time?"

Pain flashed in her eyes before going flat. Pain? Where had that come from? She'd been downright excited moments before.

"I don't have to be back to LA for a few weeks."

"Planning a concert is a big undertaking."

"I know, but it won't take much to figure out the logistics. Since it'll be a local event, we can pull it together in no time. The only hitch is that the guys I usually play with will probably be busy, but I'm hoping Sandy Palms can fill in."

Had he heard her right? "You want my band to play with you?"

"Sure. You sounded great at the reception. It may take a couple practice sessions for us to mesh, but they're your friends. I can't imagine them turning you down since it's for a good cause."

"You'd really do this for us?"

"Why not?"

Why not indeed? As much as Luke tried, the cynical part of him kept wondering if after all was said and done, she'd let them down. Last night she'd tried to engage him in conversation that was definitely headed to a place he didn't think he'd like. His past career. Eons and miles from the present.

He looked at her now, with that earnest expression and the hopeful curve of her pink lips. Not wanting to believe this was some sort of trap, he tried to push past the reservations hindering his decision. He'd hate to see Cassie, or anyone, for that matter, use Kids' Klub for their personal agenda. That's how much the program meant to him.

Before he could give Cassie an answer, a knock interrupted them. Denny, one of the teen volunteers, bounded in, his dark hair spilling over his forehead, his glasses slightly askew. Tall and lanky, his sneakers skidded on the tile floor as he came to an abrupt stop. "Oh, sorry. I didn't know you were busy."

"What have I said about knocking?"

"We need to respect each other's space," he replied in mock exasperation. "I get it, Mr. H., but I need the key to the art room. Lizzy forgot her paints and needs them for art class tomorrow."

Luke opened the top drawer to his desk, removed a key ring and tossed it to Denny.

Denny caught it midair. "Thanks. And sorry, again." He took a step, stopped and twirled around. "Hey, do I know you?"

Cassie smiled. "I'm a musician."

He noted she didn't call herself star. Props for her.

Denny pushed his glasses more securely on to his nose. "Cassie Branford, right? My friend Erin listens to your music."

"You're correct."

"I heard some of the kids say your family lives in town." He frowned. "I'm not real familiar with your songs. I'm more of an opera fan."

Cassie blinked and glanced at Luke.

"I know, most kids his age don't have a clue."

"It's my grandma's fault," Denny explained. "She raised me on the stuff."

"There's nothing wrong with opera," Cassie rushed to assure him. "It's an acquired taste."

"Which usually skips teenagers," Luke deadpanned.

"Yeah, my friends think it's odd, but before

long I've got them listening. Some of 'em actually like it."

"Good for you," Cassie said.

Denny gripped the keys in his hand. "I'll bring these back when we're finished."

Luke nodded as Denny hustled out the door. "Interesting young man."

"He is. I've known him since he was a freshman. He was one of the first students to try out the program."

"Troubled home life?"

"If you call having a family who loves you trouble." He chuckled. "No, it might have been because he was bullied when he was younger. He's never admitted it, but I can see the signs. Once he heard about the concept for the Klub, he tagged along and has been an integral part ever since."

"He must be an amazing young man."

"He's getting there. Now, back to the subject at hand."

"I can see you're not convinced," Cassie said.

"I got the distinct impression you were trying to ask me something the other night. Does this offer have anything to do with that?"

"Busted." She sighed. "Yes. I might as well be honest. I do want to volunteer here, no matter what your answer to my next question is, so keep that in mind."

"I know I'm going to regret it, but, what do you need to be honest about?"

As she bit her lower lip, Luke couldn't ignore the rush of attraction. Cute and conflicted. Her hair shone under the fluorescent lighting, highlighting the bright pink streak. Her skin, so luminous, had him itching to trace his fingers over it. And those unforgettable eyes. His downfall so far.

"I have a deadline coming up," she went on to say. "I have to be back in the studio in three months. Problem is, I have no new material."

"That's a problem."

"No kidding." She pulled her braid over her shoulder and tugged at it. "I can't come up with any new songs. You might not know this, but my last album was a bomb."

He'd heard.

"I have writer's block. No matter what I do, I can't come up with anything new. No sparks. No inspiration. Nothing."

So here it was. The real reason behind her altruism.

In the music industry, Luke knew how devastating writer's block could be. He'd never experienced it, but had friends who'd agonized because of it, usually after a big blow, like a bad album. He could sympathize, even though he didn't live in that world any longer, but he found his back up at her request. He could agree to most anything but songwriting.

"So you want, what, help? Suggestions?"

"At this point all I know is that my career will definitely suffer if I can't snap out of this—" she wiggled her hand in the air "—whatever it is."

The music business could be fickle at times. One day you were a star, another a has-been.

"I'm hoping being around you and the Klub might kick-start my muse." She lowered her eyes for a moment, then met his gaze, a captivating grin making his chest squeeze. "No pressure or anything."

Cassie's look got to him. He didn't want to be the guy she pinned her hopes on and who let her down. Or have her get involved only to have her muse show up and then she'd leave him in the lurch. His focus was on troubled kids, not a pretty songwriter who'd lost her way. He glanced at her again. Those green eyes always managed to trip him up. She bit her lower lip again, anticipating his answer.

"If I said I can't make any promises will you still do the concert?"

"Yes. Absolutely."

He knew he was digging a hole for himself, but if this wasn't a publicity stunt and truly a chance to aid his kids, then he might be willing to give her pointers. Still, he'd closely watch her actions after the concert. One sign that she was playing him and he'd sever ties between them. "Then what do you say we plan this concert and go from there?"

At her relived burst of breath, he cringed and forcefully told himself he was agreeing in order to keep the Klub going.

CHAPTER FOUR

WHAT HAD SHE been thinking? How had she expected to pull off a full-blown concert in two weeks' time? Therein lay the problem. She hadn't been. Her only thoughts had been to impress Luke.

How's that going?

Cassie paced the stage, clasping her sweaty palms together as the tech team buzzed with activity around her. A late afternoon coastal breeze picked up, swirling the ankle-length sheer skirt around her high-heeled boots, carrying with it the scent of salt water sweetened by the newly blooming orange blossoms. Her entire outfit, a black mesh with gold embellishments around the waist and hem, fit over a black tank minidress. She'd even dyed the pink streak in her hair black to match.

"Watch out for the loose cords," one of the tech guys commanded as he hurried over with tape to secure the cable snaking out from beneath the keyboard she'd be playing tonight. The sustain pedal kept sticking, giving her problems all during sound check. The team investigated and fixed the issue, a relief after a messy preconcert hour onstage coming right on the heels of a strained two-week practice. Just remembering made her want to jump in her rental car and drive away.

As promised, Sandy Palms filled in as her backup band. From the get-go things were tense. At first the guys were thrilled to work with her. Sonny and Brian were friendly, Ryan, not so much.

"Have I done something wrong?" she'd wondered out loud.

"Nope," Sonny had slapped her on the back. "He's always like that."

As they practiced, nerves got the better of all of them, which made Cassie mess up her own melodies, adding to her already strained confidence. And Luke? He'd been a rock.

"Hey, guys, watch the tempo on the first song. It's a beat slower than you're playing. This is a particularly difficult transition. Once you nail it, you'll be fine. Just have fun with it."

His encouragement had bonded the practices together. But now?

Okay, she'd cornered Luke with this concert idea. So far her plan wasn't going as…planned. She could only hope the turnout for the concert was a success so Luke wouldn't see it as a huge bust.

"Miss Branford?" one of the organizers approached her. "Mandy Rose from the *Cypress Pointe Weekly* wants to know if you have a few minutes."

"Please ask her to drop by Kids' Klub tomorrow morning." Cassie had planned a breakfast blowout to thank all the concert volunteers. "I can give her a few minutes then."

"And your father wants to speak to you."

Just what she didn't need. She'd rather have a root canal. "Not now."

The woman nodded. "I'll let him know."

"Thanks."

"Here's your mic." Another member of the team walked to her holding up her personalized, bedazzled microphone. As a dare from her sister, she'd used pink crystals to jazz up the piece of equipment. After positive comments from fans, she kept it as part of her trademark style.

Luke chose that moment to walk by, eyeing the mic. Today, he'd chosen a well-worn pair of jeans, a pale blue button-down shirt with the sleeves rolled up and boots to complete his very casual, very male concert look. His hair, artfully messy, appeared lighter blond in the late afternoon sunshine. His smile, when he chose to share it, hitched her heart rate up a notch.

"A bit much, don't you think?"

Right now, she was inclined to agree. "Part of my look."

He stopped, gave her a nerve-racking once-over. "You look nice."

Wow. A compliment. From the man who mostly kept his opinions to himself, except when it came to Kids' Klub.

"It's not too much?"

"For tonight, I'd say you nailed it." He scooped up the phone he'd placed on top of a nearby monitor. A blast of loud music startled her, blaring for a few seconds as the sound guys tested volume levels.

"I spoke to them about the crackling coming from your monitor," she said, struggling for conversation. "They're working on it."

He nodded.

"Are the guys ready?"

"As ready as they'll ever be."

"Still tense?"

"They aren't used to playing before big crowds."

At least he was hoping for good attendance.

"We've practiced the songs enough. They should be okay with the lineup," she said, mostly to reassure herself.

"They can play, that's not the issue."

"Issue?" Her stomach plummeted.

He slipped his phone into his back pocket. "Ryan is used to playing the main keyboard so putting him on standby has thrown off his timing."

She was afraid switching the usual setup might not be a good move, but what choice did she have? She always started out playing the piano and moved back and forth between it and her guitar.

"I'm sorry to mess things up, Luke. But since I'm the headliner, I have to give the fans what they expect."

His gaze pierced hers and she felt herself cringe. Had she come off as pompous as she sounded?

"I get it. Ryan is set in his ways."

Evidenced by his less than warm and fuzzy welcome to Cassie.

"And the others?"

"Brian is his usual cool self and Sonny is hitting on the makeup artist, so we're good."

A relieved grin curved her lips.

"Once we get playing, the guys will be fine," he told her.

She had no doubt. Brian was seriously talented, but too laid-back to care. Sonny, so sure the right woman was out there waiting for him, was just plain optimistic all the time. Ryan, probably the least talented, although he could play the keyboard with technical precision, wore a perpetual scowl. Cassie wondered how his wife put up with him.

And Luke? Cassie got the impression he held back. Never truly sharing the real man behind the shadows in his eyes. She spent too much time wondering who'd put them there and why.

Blowing out a breath, she asked, "And you?"

His gaze softened a tick. "The set will go fine, Cassie. You've done this before."

Yes, but never with Luke playing nearby.

Even with her nerves stretched so taut she thought she'd snap like a broken guitar string, his calm voice eased her concerns. Every time he said her name in that smooth-as-butter voice, she fought the tendrils of delight curling through her.

Focus. You're here for the kids, not their handsome program director.

"I know things were a bit rough during practice," he went on to say, "but it'll all shake out in the end."

"I'm glad you think so."

"Always does."

Okay, she'd take his word for it.

Glancing out over the park, she watched as streams of people started to fill in the audience area, carrying blankets, folding chairs and coolers. It was a beautiful spring night to enjoy for a good cause. Luke had secured a special permit allowing them to use the public park for the concert, enlisting his cousin Dane to build a temporary stage, which ran parallel to the beach and the green-blue gulf waters beyond. The venue would be casual and inviting.

The last time Cassie had toured, she'd been booked in large venues, so at odds with her love for intimate settings. Tonight's concert would fall somewhere in the middle.

Another tech hustled by. "Thirty minutes and counting."

Right. She needed to be alone to center her thoughts. "I'm going backstage," she told Luke, whose gaze also overlooked the park.

He turned back, lines forming between his brows. "Nerves?"

"I need a few minutes," she replied, warmed by his concern.

"Gotcha."

She'd just turned to walk away, fighting her silly disappointment that Luke hadn't been more chatty, when Denny, the teen she'd met at Kids' Klub, rushed across the stage, followed by a girl his age.

"Hey, Mr. H. We sold all the tickets for tonight."

Luke clapped Denny on the shoulder. "You're sure?"

"Yep. Miss Branford," he said and gestured at Cassie, "er, your sister, not you. Anyway, she's been keeping track of sales and donations. So far we're right on the mark."

Sounded like her sister. Lauren was in her element projecting the outcome of sales.

Luke looked over Denny's shoulder to meet Cassie's gaze. "Seems your idea worked out."

Her tummy quivered. "I'm glad." Which she was, but she wasn't patting anyone on the back until after the concert.

"Even with the short time span to publicize the concert, so far so good." Denny's grin lit up his face. "Thanks, Miss Branford."

"Please, call me Cassie."

"Really?" He pushed his glasses up his nose. "Cool."

"Who's your friend?" Cassie couldn't help notice his besotted smile as he introduced the girl dressed in head-to-toe black.

"This is Erin."

"Nice outfit, Erin," she said as she stuck out her hand in greeting.

"Thanks. I saw you wearing something like this when you were on the MTV awards show." The young girl's teeth tugged at her lower lip. "Sorta stole your style."

"I don't mind at all. You look great."

With her nearly white blond hair and porcelain complexion, Erin was in the early stages of stunning. Contrast the dark clothing and Cassie understood Denny's reaction. The teen was clearly smitten with the goth girl.

"You did a great job rallying the troops." Luke told Denny, rewarding the teen with a lopsided grin. A grin usually reserved for when he was around the kids. How sad was it that she could use one of those assuring smiles from him right now?

"It was easy. All the kids were excited to help out. Especially since they got free admission. And they got to meet Cassie Branford." Denny's smile couldn't get any bigger. "I got 'em on hot dog duty now."

Luke glanced at Cassie. "Denny came up with the idea to sell food for extra income, so I put him in charge. He's nothing if not industrious."

As were most of the kids Cassie had met before today. The young people were respectful of her time, some shy upon meeting her, others full of questions. It had been a while since she'd looked forward to working in an area other than her music. So far her muse was MIA and she still hadn't written a song, but interacting with the kids gave her an excited outlook she hadn't realized she'd been missing since starting in the business.

"Well, if Mr. Hastings agrees, I'll be hanging around the Klub more often."

"Really, Mr. H.?"

"Yes. Cassie wants to volunteer. Give music lessons."

Erin's face lit up. "You promise?"

"I do. But right now, I need to prepare before we go on. Excuse me."

Cassie gingerly stepped over the cords and between the instruments and monitors. She marched down the steps and strode to the tent set up for the band. As she entered the empty space, her stress level lowered.

She grabbed a water bottle from the large ice-filled tub. The cool liquid soothed her throat as drops from the wet container splashed down on her dress. She brushed the moisture away, taking another swallow before placing the bottle on the makeup table.

Pacing now, she cleared her mind. The ritual eased her nerves. Jitters plagued her whenever she performed, right up until she released the first note of the first song and her passion kicked in. *Nerves are good*, her manager always told her. *Keeps you humble*.

Did Luke see her as a humble musician? Or a career-driven poser? She wasn't sure, but in the time she had left in Cypress Pointe, she was determined to leave him with a positive impression. Why his opinion meant so much to her she didn't fully ponder, just let it simmer below the surface. Funny, she tried not to care what most people thought, but Luke had joined the ranks of those she wanted to please.

She shook off the image of Luke. Continuing to pace, she included vocal exercises. She hummed the scale, her tone clear in the process. Long ago she'd learned to start out by humming so not to strain the vocal cords. Then she added the words of a song, again moving up and down the scale before taking another drink of water.

Minutes passed and she started to softly sing a random melody, eyes closed, final prep for the performance. She let go, her mind free, shaking her arms in the process, working out the kinks. Tonight had to be a success. She needed to show Luke that she was more than willing to work in exchange for his agreement to help her unlock the writer's block. That her motives were not one-sided.

She took another pass across the room when the tent flap flipped open.

"Cassandra. I've been looking for you."

She held back a groan as her father walked in. "I'm busy right now, Dad."

He glanced around the empty tent. "There's nothing going on here."

"I'm preparing."

"It can wait," he said, impeding on her space. "I have a request."

She took a deep breath to control her annoyance.

"I want to play with you tonight," he rushed on to say without waiting for her go-ahead. "It will be a good move for your career."

Incredulous, she stopped short, speechless.

Her father took it as a sign to continue. "Cypress Pointe is small so we need all the star power we can get."

Suddenly the tent shrank in proportion to her soaring temper. "We? There is no *we*."

"Of course there is. We're family."

"Even so, why would you wait minutes before I go onstage and ask to play? We've been practicing for two weeks." Unbelievable. "And aren't you supposed to be on your honeymoon? Where's Angelica?"

"We cut our trip short when I heard about the concert."

"If I'd wanted you to participate, I would have asked." She shot him a glare. "How did you find out, anyway?"

"Lauren."

She should have realized.

Her father, still oblivious to her mood, went on. "You have that wedding band accompanying you. Why not me?"

"Because I want to play with them."

"I don't understand."

The sad thing was, he really didn't. He expected Cassie to knuckle under his pressure. A pressure that kept building since she'd allowed him a small opening into her life.

Keep at it, sweetheart. One day you'll get better.

"We go on in ten. Please leave."

"Cassie, reconsider."

"No." Her voice rose and she was afraid she might lose it. "Please leave now."

To her relief, just as she was about to come unglued, another voice joined the fray. "Trouble here?"

Luke watched Cassie's face change from perturbed to thankful in an instant.

He hadn't meant to interfere, but when raised voices inside the tent alerted him, he didn't stop and think. He acted. By her grateful expression, he was glad he did.

"My father was just leaving," she said in a steady tone.

Robert opened his mouth, then thought better of it. He passed Luke as he left, anger radiating from him.

"Another happy family reunion?"

Cassie ran a shaky hand over her hair. "Afraid not."

"I didn't mean to intrude, but the guys are meeting here in a few minutes. I heard loud voices and came in to investigate."

"Which I appreciate. My father has the worst timing."

"Mine probably wasn't any better."

"Oh, no, you actually saved the day."

Just a cliché, but he liked hearing it.

"Where was I?" she said under her breath.

"Pardon?"

She looked up, her grin sheepish. "My father interrupted my preconcert ritual."

Artists. He'd forgotten how they worked. Or how much they were rattled if that ritual was cut short.

"Anything I can do to help?"

"No. Dad's gone and I was mostly ready anyway." She grabbed the open water bottle and took a quick swallow.

Good for her, because he wasn't.

Practicing with Cassie had put him in closer contact than he'd envisioned when he'd agreed to this benefit concert. He kept waiting for her to talk about her songwriting problems, but she'd never mentioned them once. Instead, she'd focused on practicing with the band. Made sure they were at ease with her music. Visited with the kids at the Klub. Initially he'd decided to keep his distance but found he was drawn to her like a moth to a flame. Soon he looked forward to her bright smile when she walked into a room. He had to admit, his reaction caught him off guard, in a good way.

At first, running through Cassie's music with the guys had been fine. Luke analyzed her writing. She was good, he'd give her that. The melodies flowed and the instrument parts complemented the vision of the song. Nothing overly ambitious, just straightforward and catchy. There was a depth to her lyrics he'd previously overlooked.

He saw now why she'd become a popular artist. He wondered what she was thinking to let the record label change her sound, but he'd seen it happen more often than not. Record labels were out to make money. And in the beginning, most artists went along, hoping for a major push in their careers. This must have been the case with Cassie, which was a shame, since her first record rocked. He really wanted to see her get back to her roots.

Once the guys were comfortable playing her songs, Cassie joined them. Meeting in the

Klub music room had made sense since all the instruments they needed were there. Luke expected the practice to be all business, until she sat down behind the piano and began to play and sing.

He hadn't expected to be moved by her.

Nor had he expected his gut to twist with nerves at the idea of performing in front of her fans.

The guys had all exchanged wide-eyed glances, as if to say, *she is so out of our league.* So he'd put on his band leader hat and led a very rough practice. Read the panic on Cassie's face, ignored his own doubts and made sure the group calmed down enough to get through the session.

Soon, the guys' concerns had begun to fade. Cassie, the consummate professional, made sure to interact with each one, even laughing at their goofy jokes. Before long, they were playing as if they toured together regularly. His reservations faded.

Until the sound check earlier. Monitors crackled. Cords came loose. His guitar string broke. All a musician's nightmare. Yet Cassie weathered it all with calm aplomb. Or so he thought until he glimpsed her stricken expression.

"Are you thinking what I'm thinking?" she asked him.

"About the shaky sound check?"

"Yeah."

"Some of the best jam time I've ever experienced was after a rehearsal we cringed over. You'll be fine. Tonight will be no different."

Her face looked less strained after his pep talk. She fished a water bottle from the tub and tossed it to him.

Luke caught it midair. "I'm not thirsty."

She grimaced. "I needed to do something."

"And chucking bottles works?"

"Apparently."

He laughed. Cracked the seal and drank, not realizing how dry his throat was.

Cassie brushed her braid over her shoulder before checking her hair in the mirror. He'd first found the strip of color crazy, but it had slowly grown on him. Just like she had.

Cassie backed away from the makeup table. "Do you guys do anything special before performing?"

"Usually we spend the minutes before we start playing in a frantic search for Sonny."

Cassie smiled, her beautiful eyes lighting up. "I seem to remember that from my father's wedding reception."

"I guess we can call that our preshow ritual. How about you?"

Her gaze dropped, then rose to meet his, a

flash of humor catching him unaware. "I usually say a few words to the band."

Leaning his shoulder against the tent pole, he crossed his arms over his chest. "I'm intrigued."

"Would they mind?"

He shrugged. "It's your show."

A frown wrinkled her forehead. "I don't see it that way. We're all working together for the Klub."

"Fair enough. Still, you take the lead."

"I have something…" Her voice trailed off as she crossed the room to dig through a large leather bag. She pulled out a piece of paper, bit her lip as she returned to his side.

"Don't tell me you've been holding out? New song?"

He wanted to kick himself at her pained reaction. He'd asked her one other time in the past weeks if she'd uncovered any inspiration. She'd told him no then. Must be the same answer now.

"I wish." She unfolded the paper. "When I was a kid my mom always had these positive sayings she'd recite to us. No matter the circumstance, she'd tell us to buck up or don't cry in our milk, which is weird, or tell us what doesn't kill us makes us stronger."

"Your mother put you in situations that might kill you?"

She laughed, just as he'd intended. "After a while I wrote them down from memory. I always quote one before we go onstage."

"Sounds like a great strategy."

"Thanks." She set the paper on the nearby table, then smoothed her skirt.

"You know we'll be fine once we start playing," he assured her again.

"Doesn't help the nerves right now."

"Are you always so antsy before a performance?"

She shyly glanced at him. "It's not every day I play with Luke Hastings."

"It's no big deal."

"To me it is."

He didn't want to be flattered, but he couldn't deny the pleasure her words brought. After his ex had pretty much flattened his ego, Cassie was a breath of fresh air. She didn't try to railroad him, didn't go on and on about her place in the music business. She liked his friends. Had come up with this idea to raise money for the Klub using her own resources.

"Anyway, I appreciate you going along with my idea."

A tiny crack fractured a portion of his emotional wall. He'd fought it. Fought his reluctant admiration of Cassie. Until now.

As he watched her repeatedly ball up her hands and open then, he set down the water bottle. Took her hands in his.

"Cassie, you're good. And generous. Thanks for doing this concert."

She smiled up at him. "It's my pleasure, especially since meeting the kids. Your Klub's pretty special."

As he gazed at her, her floral perfume flitted about them. He got lost once again in the green depths of her eyes. So much for his resolve to stay unaffected by her.

The air grew heated. Luke took a step back but still held on to her hands. She tilted her head, as if to say something, when voices came from outside and the guys barged into the tent. Sonny, in midsentence about a woman—no surprise—stopped short.

Cassie quickly pulled her hands away. His lingered in the air for mere seconds, missing her warmth, before dropping to his sides.

"Hey, you guys okay?" Sonny asked, rubbing a hand over his buzz cut as he watched them move apart.

"Nerves," Cassie answered.

"Really? You get gummed up before you play?" Brian questioned.

"You bet. My manager says jitters are a good thing but my stomach disagrees."

"Take an antacid," Ryan grumbled.

"Okay, then," Cassie said, swiping her paper from the table.

"Guys," Luke said, brushing off his reaction to holding her hands. He needed his wits about him. And besides, Ryan was closely watching him. He didn't want to explain what he hadn't quite figured out for himself. "Cassie has some words of wisdom to share before we go out there."

She cleared her throat, not meeting anyone's gaze and recited her quote. "When life gives you lemons, pucker up, because life's about to squeeze you dry."

The room went silent.

"What happened to making lemonade?" Sonny asked with a straight face.

Luke struggled to contain his laughter at the quip, drawing a reluctant grin from Cassie as she moved away from the guys to drop the paper back in her bag. Mission accomplished on her part.

"I don't get it," Ryan griped as Sonny and Brian chuckled.

"Dude, there's nothing to get," Luke replied. "It was meant to lighten the mood. It worked."

Ryan glanced at Cassie and back, his eyes accusing. "You *like* her."

"What's not to like? She's helping Kids' Klub."

"Are you sure that's it?"

It was all he was ready to admit to at this point.

The tent flap opened and Denny came speeding in.

"You guys ready?"

"We are," Sonny answered.

"There's a big crowd out there. The town really stepped up to help us."

When Luke mentioned the concert idea to the town council, there hadn't been one minute of hesitation. Kids' Klub had become a mainstay in Cypress Pointe and those serving the community were happy to facilitate any fundraiser that benefited the town.

"Hey, Denny, I have an idea," Luke said, the boy's excitement becoming contagious. "As the ambassador of Kids' Klub, why don't you introduce the concert?"

The kid's mouth gaped open. "Are you kidding?"

"No. You put more work in on this project than anyone."

Denny punched his fist in the air. "Awesome."

"Gather a few of the others kids who helped you and have them stand around when you introduce Cassie."

"And the band," Cassie rushed to add. "Please include the band."

"You got it." Denny sprinted outside to assemble his friends together.

"Hey, Cassie," Brian said after Denny left. "We want to thank you for including us."

"You guys are helping me. I'm glad I don't have to be up there by myself."

"Then let's kick this thing off." Sonny held out his hand, palm down. "One for all?"

Brian slapped his hand over Sonny's.

"What are you guys, five years old?" Ryan crabbed but placed his hand on top.

Luke glanced at Cassie. "After you."

A warm smile crossed her lips as she set her hand on Ryan's.

"Okay, boss man, you're next."

Luke moved in at Sonny's command, close to Cassie, his hand resting gently over hers. When her body pressed next to his, it was all he could do not to bolt.

Sonny counted, "One, two, three," and all hands went up in the air, then separated. Cassie's braid flew around her shoulder and landed on his arm, the sweet berry scent of her shampoo stealing his senses. He closed his eyes to savor the moment.

When he opened his eyes, he met her searching gaze. "Um, sorry," she said in a small voice, her breathy uncertainty washing over him.

Minutes later, they climbed the steps leading to the platform. Denny stood center stage, thanking the crowd for coming out and supporting Kids' Klub. Then Cassie was moving with the band, stepping onto the stage to wave at the fans. When she turned to take her place at the piano, their eyes met again, hers with a sparkle Luke wouldn't soon forget. Gone were the nerves. In that one broad smile, the mild-mannered woman from seconds before melted away. This was the Cassie who'd been born to entertain.

He lifted the guitar strap over his head and settled it on his shoulder. Cassie winked at him, the gesture sending a wallop to his gut, just as Sonny counted a three beat with his drum sticks and they launched into the first number.

They played for an hour. Cassie entertained the fans not only with her music, but by engaging and laughing with them, as well. The urgency of her wish to overcome writer's block struck him as she sang. If she didn't come up with new songs, would her career truly be over? Glimpsing the joy on her face right now, he knew he wanted to help her move forward, even if it meant tearing off the bandage still covering his emotional wounds.

As he considered the future, he couldn't keep his eyes from Cassie as she regaled the crowd, and him, with the magic of her music.

CHAPTER FIVE

ERIN ATHERTON PULLED her knees up closer to her chest, resting her forehead on her damp tights. She'd missed her curfew again and her parents refused to let her in the house. Their tough love act was getting old. By the time she'd walked home and found she couldn't get in the house, all her friends were home in bed. She was tired of searching for somewhere to sleep when she couldn't get anyone to let her crash at their place. Tired of trying to get her parents' attention when they should be concerned about their daughter.

Except for sleeping outside, most of last night had been incredible. The concert rocked and Cassie Branford actually talked to her. Watching offstage with the group from Kids' Klub had been a first for her. Afterward, she'd helped load up the stuff they'd brought over from the Klub and unloaded back at the warehouse. Then they set up tables for the appreciation breakfast Cassie had organized for today.

If the experience was so great, what possessed you to pocket the money?

She groaned.

Denny had entrusted her with the zipper bag for the food sales. With shaking hands, she pulled out a wad of cash from her jacket pocket. Counted it. Grew horrified when she realized she'd taken two hundred dollars. She thought she'd only grabbed about fifty bucks.

As she curled up on an uncomfortable bench in the park's gazebo, tears leaked from her eyes. Her plans to make her parents acknowledge her, even for stealing, had worked. Until she'd had second thoughts. She'd taken too much money to explain it away as a mistake. Could she give it back without getting in trouble? Would Mr. H. call the police on her? How could she have been so stupid?

She tried to sleep, but even for April, the nights were still chilly. The damp air and her guilt kept her awake. She'd hoped the tumbling waves rushing onto the adjacent beach would lull her to sleep, but when she closed her eyes, visions of the police dragging her to the station in handcuffs played over and over in her mind like a movie scene.

Eventually she dozed, only to wake as the first streaks of light crept across the horizon. She covered a gusty yawn, trying to decide her next move. Cold and clammy, she hiked to the Klub and settled in to wait for the first person to show up for breakfast duty.

Ten minutes passed. She'd just decided to head home since her parents would be awake now. But the thought of facing their disappointment, of them calling the police when she confessed her sin, stopped her. As she argued with herself, the sound of someone whistling a Cassie Branford tune reached her ears. Her head jerked up. Denny Price. Figured. The one guy she didn't want to run into this morning, but the one most likely to be here early to unlock the doors. Could her luck get any worse?

The whistling stopped short. "Erin?"

Swallowing her pride, Erin slowly rose. "Yeah. It's me."

"What are you doing here so early?"

Finally, a break. Apparently he hadn't noticed she was wearing the same outfit from last night.

"Waiting. I volunteered to serve breakfast."

Keys jangled in Denny's hand as he unlocked the main door. "I think we got it under control, but more hands will help."

She stuffed her hands in her jacket pockets, her fingers brushing the cash. Swallowing hard, she said, "Cool."

"You been here long?" Denny asked as

they stepped inside and he flipped the bank of switches on the wall. The lights high above the gymnasium floor flickered to life.

"Nah."

His task done, Denny looked her over. "I'll be right back," he said then sprinted to the guys' locker room.

Erin stood in the silence of the vast space, her arms crossed at her waist, hugging tight. Alone. She was so alone.

Moments later Denny returned and held out a denim shirt. "Here."

It took a moment for her to register what he'd done. He had noticed her clothing. Slowly, she reached out to take the shirt, her pride taking a hit. "When was the last time you washed this thing?"

"You're welcome." He turned and called over his shoulder as he walked away. "I'll be in the kitchen."

Could this be any more mortifying? Why had she come here? She should have stretched out on a lawn chair on the back patio at home, but honestly, facing her parents was too daunting.

She dragged her feet to the restroom, cleaned her face and tried to fix what was left of her makeup. What a mess. She ran her hands through her hair and shrugged on the shirt before joining Denny. The end of the shirt came to her thighs, covering the short skirt. She noticed a small tear in the black tights and tugged the hem of the shirt lower, not even close to covering it.

"Who cares?" she muttered as she left the room.

"I'm making coffee," Denny said as she entered the midsized kitchen area. Pulling a cabinet door open, he peered inside. "Nick should be here soon with the breakfast food, but until then we've got oatmeal, crackers and some protein bars."

"Wow. Gourmet."

Denny chuckled. Why was he always so happy?

"With all the excitement of the concert, I guess someone forgot to go shopping."

"Wouldn't that be your job?"

"I do a lot around here, but Mr. Hastings usually sends one of the adults to the store."

Erin leaned against the counter, arms crossed over her chest, shoulders slumped. "Maybe there's some money around here we can borrow. Blow this place and go get breakfast alone."

Wait for it... And there it was. Denny's frown. The one he gave her when she suggested doing something dumb. If only he knew.

"You know I can't take any money."

She shrugged. Yeah, she knew that. "Just testing you. I've got a couple bucks."

He closed the cabinet door and tossed her a bar. "Did you go home last night?"

Why couldn't he be clueless like the rest of her guy friends?

"I, um, kinda got locked out."

"Really? Did you lose your keys?"

More like her parents had changed the locks last time she'd been late and hadn't given her a new key. But Denny didn't need the details.

"Something like that."

His brown eyes, always so perceptive and appearing much older than his sixteen years, seemed to figure out the situation.

"Missed your curfew?"

"Only this time I had a good reason." She ran the toe of her scuffed boot over the tile floor, keeping her gaze averted.

"Don't your parents know you were working with us?"

"They don't care."

Especially about her.

"C'mon, they must be worried."

If by worried he meant what the neighbors might think, then yeah, they were worried.

"I'll call 'em later."

Denny crossed the room to lean against the

counter next to her. His shoulder brushed hers and a funny flutter kicked up in her belly. Why did he have to be so close? And why did he confuse her? The strong urge to confide in him overwhelmed her, yet she never did. It was a line she never wanted to cross.

She'd met Denny in middle school, before "the incident." They'd kinda been friends, until she started hanging out with a bunch of cooler kids. She knew he didn't approve, no surprise there, but he never judged her, either.

"I can give you a ride home if you need. Tell your folks you were working here last night."

Would it matter? If Denny told them, probably. But after he left, the lecture would start and once again she'd be the worst daughter on the planet.

"I don't need your help," she said, lifting her chin as she tossed her hair over her shoulder.

Oh, how she wanted him to save her, be the knight in shining armor she read about in the romance novels her mother disapproved of. But then he'd see how things were at home. See her for the thief she'd become. She couldn't face the embarrassment.

Denny pushed away from the counter. "Whatever. I've got stuff to do."

As he left the kitchen, tears welled in Erin's eyes. He was always so nice to her and in return she lashed out at him. She swiped at her cheeks, not willing to let Denny, or anyone, see her weak side. Even though her chest burned with wanting a real friend she could count on.

"So, WHAT DID you think?" Cassie asked Luke. They'd been passing out breakfast for thirty minutes now. The bright morning sun with the temperature hovering in the seventies drew people here this Saturday morning to eat and visit, all at Cassie's invitation.

The idea had come to her about five days before the concert when she'd seen how the community pitched in to support the Kids' Klub fundraiser. She'd wanted to thank everyone involved in making the concert a success, so she'd called an old friend from high school to set up this last-minute breakfast on the grounds of Kids' Klub. Teens, adults and even little ones chatted and laughed, enjoying the food compliments of Pointe Cafe, a mainstay in Cypress Pointe.

The line finally dwindled, giving her time to consider the question that'd kept her awake all night. The scent of rich coffee and freshly blooming flowers vied for her attention until she spoke to Luke.

"So, how do you think it went last night?" she ventured.

"The crowd loved you."

"And?"

"And what? You rocked the place."

The pressure in her chest eased.

She couldn't read his eyes, hidden as they were behind dark sunglasses, but his smile assured her last night had been a big success. At least in making Luke realize she really was doing this to benefit Kids' Klub, not just for the writing sessions that would come later.

Any minute now, Lauren would be joining them to announce the final tally from the concert. She'd been crunching numbers when Cassie left the house, assuring her she'd be there for breakfast.

"The kids from the Klub stayed busy yesterday," she went on to say. "Do they always work together so well?"

Luke laughed. "Not usually. They were a little in awe of you."

She waved away the compliment. "Please. It was a great time for a good cause."

Luke removed his sunglasses and sipped his coffee, peering at her over the rim of his cup. Yes, he made her nervous. His blond hair seemed lighter in the daylight, strands lifting in the gentle breeze. It looked like he hadn't shaved this morning, which only made him more handsome. His long fingers held the cup with ease, the same fingers that played the heck out of his guitar last night. She'd hoped working together would break the ice, since he was always reserved around her, and, as evidenced by his good mood this morning, her strategy must have worked.

He smiled at her and her stomach dipped. How did she explain the sparks whenever they were together? She'd noticed him sneaking glances at her last night, or at least she'd hoped he was. Her heart had danced, just like right now. Probably the attraction was one-sided, but she wanted to explore the heat between them.

But what if he didn't return her feelings? She would be sunk, because if he found out, then working together on her songwriting would be so awkward. For now, she'd have to corral these feelings for Luke.

He rested the cup back on the table. "The guys had a blast playing to the crowd. All in all, a great night."

She relaxed, able to enjoy the breakfast event for the first time. The sun warmed her shoulders as a young mother she'd gone to high school with waved at Cassie as she pushed a baby stroller. Cassie waved back. One of her mother's friends called hello as she passed by, the leash to her golden Lab taut as she reined in the dog exploring the path.

"You didn't have to go all out with breakfast, you know," Luke said, drawing her back to the conversation.

"I wanted to."

"Are you always so generous with your time?" Luke asked, as a young boy ran up for another bagel.

"I try. Most organizations I help quietly, others I lend my name to if it's a big cause. My mother always instilled the importance of being considerate to others and I guess her lessons stuck."

"Where is she, by the way?"

"She and my stepdad will be here soon. They were out of town and got back late last night."

"Will I get to hear any of her sayings?"

She chuckled. "If you're lucky."

"Why did she come up with them?" Luke asked as he moved a few leftover pastries from one platter to another.

"It's a long story."

"And we have time to kill until your sister shows up."

True, but how much of her family story did she want to reveal?

"You've met my dad," she hedged.

Luke arched a brow.

"He traveled a lot when we were little. Became successful and found another woman who recognized his gift. Like my mother didn't." She paused, controlling her temper. "So he left. We didn't understand why at the time, so she tried to cheer us up."

"I see."

Cassie covered the pastries with clear wrap. "My mother worked long hours to provide for us, but we pitched in. Another reason I volunteer when I can."

"I noticed the tension whenever your dad is around."

"He's decided we should bond, which means he wants something."

Luke removed the empty platter. "Pretty cynical thinking. Maybe he just wants to spend time with his daughter."

"By showing up ten minutes before the concert to insist I let him join the band?"

Lines bracketed Luke's mouth as he grimaced. "Point taken."

She really didn't like dredging up old memories, not on a beautiful day like today, working next to a very attractive, very guarded man. She enjoyed the small talk he'd initiated for a change.

"What about your family?"

"I'm not any more thrilled talking about mine than you are about yours."

"Vague, as usual."

"I'm just not comfortable sharing details of my life."

"Or you're stubborn."

Surprisingly, he chuckled at her spot-on character trait.

"I shouldn't have pushed," she quickly said. "You've made it pretty clear you have no intention of talking about yourself."

"I'm beginning to guess pushy is your MO."

Her mouth fell open. Had she been pushy? If anything, she'd tried to be cautious.

She was about to give him an explanation when a dark-haired man approached the table, a large garbage bag in hand.

"Nick, you don't have to clean up," Cassie scolded. "We'll get it."

The cafe owner winked at her. "All part of the service."

"C'mon, you catered this breakfast. I don't want you working so hard. Go sit down."

"You make it sound like I'm eighty. Besides, you know me better than that."

She did. His parents had owned Pointe Cafe and ever since she'd known Nick, he'd worked there. He ran the cafe now and by the big smile on his face, he loved every minute in the community.

"Thanks, Nick. Tell your parents I said hello."

"You can tell them yourself if you're in town for a while."

She snuck a quick glance at Luke, then smiled. "I'll do that."

Nick went back to weaving through the tables, cleaning up and greeting people along the way.

She enjoyed the camaraderie of small-town life. Living in LA had its perks, but other than Travis, she hadn't developed a network of friends. Recording and touring had been her only focus. Her only world. Suddenly, she realized she missed Cypress Pointe. She'd spent so many years away and after last night, she wanted to belong again.

Kids' Klub was a perfect place to start.

"Now that the concert is over, when can I start volunteering?"

"Are you sure? I mean, since you need to concentrate on—" he glanced around and lowered his voice "—writing?"

"Being busy would get my mind off my problem and besides, I really would like to give music lessons."

Was he rethinking her offer? She'd taken a huge chance by asking him to help her with her songs, but he'd seemed on board. Why the reluctance now?

After watching a group of teens laughing

and clowning around, Luke turned back to her. "I get that you want to help, but what happens when you go back to LA? What happens to the kids whose lives you touch?"

When she opened her mouth to argue, he held up his hand. "I'm not going back on my word. I just need you to be sure."

"Luke, I told you I'd never hurt these kids. I remember how it feels to be confused and out of place at that age. Even as I got older, my father's leaving left scars. I may not be here full-time, but I will come back when I'm not working."

"You know as well as I do how time-consuming recording an album can be. And that's only the beginning. You'll be doing promo appearances, probably go on tour again."

"That's all very possible, but I'll need down-time, too. I can come here and continue where I leave off."

He still resisted. "I don't want them to get attached, then be disappointed when you go."

She placed a hand on her hip. "How many full-time people do you have on staff right now?"

"Two."

"And the rest? Volunteers, right?"

"Folks help as needed. Or if we run special classes, I bring in experts."

"So consider me one of your experts. If I'm not here all the time, no one gets bored with me."

A reluctant smile curved his lips. "Boring is hardly your problem."

She didn't know whether or not to be pleased by his comment so she let it fly.

"Look, I'm no parental figure since I've never had children, but I remember the angst of being a teen. I took those uncertain years and made a career out of them. I'd love a chance to advise teens on how to channel their some-times negative energy into something good."

Luke remained silent. Had she finally come up with a solid reason he couldn't argue with?

"I know the Klub means everything to you, Luke."

"Do you?"

His sudden intensity startled her.

"If I don't, then fill me in."

Running a hand along the back of his neck, he let out a long breath. "Don't misunderstand me. I'm not trying to run you off. I've put my heart and soul into this organization so at times I'm a little overprotective."

She got that. Made him an inspiring leader for the kids. "Why don't we revisit this con-versation when you're less defensive?"

"Is that what you call it?" He sent her a

stomach-whopping smile. "Sounds like a wise idea."

Before she could mention an appointment to set up a schedule and finalize duties, a spunky red-haired young woman appeared out of nowhere, a small recorder in her outstretched hand. "Miss Branford? Mandy Rose, *Cypress Pointe Weekly.*"

Right. Cassie had forgotten.

Mandy flashed her thousand-watt smile. "Can I have a few minutes of your time?"

She looked over at Luke. He nodded in the reporter's direction. "Go on. I'll hold down the fort."

"Gee, thanks."

She heard his chuckle as she walked to the shade of a mature oak a few feet away.

"This is so exciting," Mandy said, starting the interview. "Having two famous women in town. You know Jenna Monroe lives here."

"I do." Jenna had been a celebrity chef in LA before moving to Cypress Pointe with her twin daughters. Cassie had met her at a function in LA and they'd become friends.

"Who knew Cypress Pointe had the panache to draw two celebrities?"

"You do know I used to live here, right?"

Mandy blinked furiously. "Why, yes."

Cassie resisted an eye roll. Most of the time

she didn't mind interviews, but she'd hated being interrupted when Luke was opening up to her.

"Let me pull up my notes." Mandy scrolled through her cell phone. "So, tell me, when is your next album due?"

"I haven't gone into the studio yet, so it'll be a while."

"I'm sure your fans will be disappointed."

Not as much as the label if she didn't get some inspiration soon.

"Will the sound be like your first or second album?"

Bending over to pick up a few leaves from the ground as she decided how to answer the question, Cassie tried for nonchalance. "I'm hoping to get back to my original style."

"Because your second album didn't do well?"

She bit her lip. Everyone was a critic. "That would be a good reason, wouldn't it?"

"So can you give us a sneak peek of what you have in store?"

"And ruin the wait? Come on, Mandy, you should know better than to ask."

Mandy leaned closer, a speculative gleam in her eyes. "So, what aren't you telling me?"

As if Cassie would reveal her deep-seated fears. If the label even suspected her dilemma, her dreams would go up in smoke.

"Every woman deserves to be a little mysterious, don't you think?"

Mandy drew back and Cassie could almost envision her mind rebooting.

"So why a benefit concert here and now?"

"Since I spent my formative years in Cypress Pointe, I wanted to help Kids' Klub."

"Were you a troublemaker?"

Cassie laughed, tossing the leaves in her hand to the shady ground. "Far from it, but that doesn't mean I can't appreciate an organization that does good work in the community."

"Did you know Luke Hastings prior to his moving here?"

"No. I was recording when he left the business."

"Will you and Luke be collaborating on a song or two?"

None of your business, Cassie wanted to answer. "Right now Luke and I are focusing on my place at the Klub."

"I can't say I blame him. His divorce was pretty messy before he showed up."

"I wouldn't know."

"He also comes from a troubled childhood. Father and brother in jail. Mother's whereabouts unknown."

Yikes. Cringing, she said, "I'm not sure it's

in anyone's interest to discuss Luke's private life."

"It's not a secret."

Still, Cassie doubted he wanted his family history, or any part of his life, revealed in an article because of her.

"Can we just spotlight the value Kids' Klub brings to the community?"

"Well, you have to know the history before you can understand the value."

Mandy had a point, but Cassie refused to engage in what she feared was verging on TMI. Luke made it very clear that he kept his personal life personal.

"Listen, I have to get back. We still need to clean up."

"One more question. Are you and Luke a couple?"

"What?" The surprise question threw her off guard. "Why on earth would you ask me that?"

"It's common knowledge you two have been spending time together."

"On behalf of Kids' Klub."

"We both know that forced proximity can lead to attraction."

Good grief. The woman had morphed from Mandy the gossip to Mandy the detective.

"I'm sorry to disappoint you, but we're

friends. Really more like acquaintances, coming together for the common good."

Stop babbling. She been around enough reporters to know how to keep her mouth shut. Why not now?

"Just an observation."

"An incorrect one."

A sly smile crossed Mandy's lips.

The cell phone ringing from Cassie's back pocket saved her. She pulled it out to find Lauren's name on the screen. "Would you please excuse me? I need to take this call."

"Certainly. Thanks for your time. I'll be around in case you want to expand on anything."

"I'll keep that in mind."

As Mandy walked away, Cassie tapped her phone screen. "Hey, sis."

"You sound stressed."

"Reporter."

"Ah. You've met dear Mandy."

"She looks so innocent but asks questions like a seasoned cop."

Lauren chuckled.

"Where are you?" Cassie asked. "I've been expecting you."

"The warehouse."

"When did you get here?"

"About ten minutes ago. Can you send Luke to his office?"

"Is there a problem?"

"I need to bring him up to speed."

"Okay. Want some coffee?"

"In a gallon mug if you have one."

She ended the call and returned to Luke. He was in conversation with another man and from what she could hear, they were discussing the man's son.

"Don't worry, Mr. Harrison. I'll talk to Blake myself."

"Thanks, Luke. We appreciate the time you've spent with him."

"He's a good kid."

When the man walked away Luke turned, a small smile curving his lips when he viewed her expression.

"You look shell-shocked."

She lifted a hand to shield her eyes from the sun. "That obvious? I always forget how nosy reporters can be."

"Can't say I miss them."

"Wish I had that luxury. Right now they're a necessary evil."

"Mandy's not so bad."

"Really. Has she interviewed you?"

"Nope. I stopped her in her tracks as soon as I came to town."

Cassie dropped her hand. "You could have warned me."

"What's the fun in that?"

"Mr. Hastings, I believe you have a mean streak."

He chuckled. "Mandy's mostly harmless."

Cassie wasn't so sure. "Yet you keep your distance."

"I have a no-tolerance policy."

Okay, then. "My sister just called. She wants us to meet her at your office."

"That can't be good," Luke said, closing the top of a to-go box.

"Pessimist much?"

He froze.

Oh, crud. Now what had she done? "Are you okay?"

"Yeah. Ah, let's go."

Cassie scooped up the coffee she'd poured for her sister and followed. Somehow she'd managed to get his back up. Her turn-off-Luke skills never ceased to amaze her.

CHAPTER SIX

LUKE STRODE TO the warehouse, deep in thought. A pessimist? Even his cousin alluded to this. In spite of his shades on, he narrowed his eyes against the sun's bright glare, his mind working overtime. Was Dane right? Had he turned into a bitter cliché—the spurned ex-husband?

With Cassie on his heels, now was not the time to review his personal life, especially since her arrival had upturned everything. While he'd been watching her charm the crowd last night despite the writer's block she was dealing with, a brick or two had loosened from his emotional wall. He realized she sang because she loved it. Yes, it was her career, but he imagined she'd find a way to keep singing no matter what, even if she never recorded again.

The fact that she'd planned this breakfast still rocked him. All because she was a caring person, not out for what she could get. Not every woman was like his ex. He'd pegged Cassie all wrong.

From here on out, he'd juggle his responsibilities. Help her get her mojo back while focusing on the kids and expanding the Klub.

He slowed his pace. Centered himself as Cassie drew up beside him. "You know, Lauren probably wants to go over the donations from last night."

"You're probably right."

She tilted her head, those gut-wrenching eyes of hers incredulous. "Really? Cuz more times than not I get the feeling I bug you."

His lips quirked. Yeah, she got to him all right, but not how she assumed.

"How about we start over?" she queried as they continued to stroll over the neatly cut grass leading to the warehouse sidewalk. "I'll try not to annoy you while you pretend you don't mind me volunteering."

"You don't annoy me." Far from it. In fact, he kinda liked being around her, a fact he was learning to admit.

"You're saying I can volunteer here?"

"Yes, but how about we table that discussion until after the meeting with your sister?"

His chest tightened at her full-fledged grin. And not in a heartburn kind of way.

Once inside the cool warehouse, Luke removed his sunglasses and hooked the arm into his shirt neck opening. He waved to a group of boys throwing around a ball, trying

to make baskets. Lauren stood outside his office, dressed like she'd just come from work,
with her briefcase in hand as they approached.

"Finally, you're here," she said.

"You have good news, right?" Luke pulled
out his key to unlock the door. "The concert
was a success?"

"Yes." She looked around them. "Can we go
inside and shut the door?"

All his tangled-up emotions about Cassie
faded at the unease in Lauren's voice.

Upon entering, he flipped the light switch.
The fluorescent bulbs hummed as they warmed
up. He watched Lauren take over his desk, her
face a serious mask as she removed file folders
from her briefcase and placed them in an orderly
fashion on the desktop before taking the coffee
cup from Cassie's extended hand. He pulled out
a seat for Cassie then lowered himself in another
chair beside her.

"Why do I get the impression you have bad
news?"

Lauren glanced at her sister. "Thanks for
the coffee, sis. Would you mind waiting outside until I finish talking to Luke?"

"Oh. Of course not." Cassie started to rise
but Luke stopped her by placing his hand on
her shoulder. For some reason, he didn't want
to be alone for whatever Lauren was about to

drop on him. Besides, after last night, Cassie had earned the right to know how the Klub faired. "Please, stay."

"Are you sure? I don't mind leaving."

"Please."

She sank back down.

Lauren took his usual seat behind the desk, her hands clasped before her, and regarded him with grave concern.

Lauren hesitated. "About the concert."

"Please don't tell me we lost money," Luke groaned.

"No, the concert brought in a significant amount of capital." Lauren opened a file to show them a spreadsheet of the final numbers. Luke read the information, once, then twice to make sure he'd got it right.

"Awesome." Cassie high-fived her sister.

"Not enough yet to buy the property outright, but definitely closer than you were a few days ago."

"So what's the problem?" Luke asked, confused by Lauren's serious demeanor.

"I'm just going to tell you straight out." She placed her palms flat over the open folders. "Someone took cash from the till. The total doesn't reflect the dollar amount I counted against the receipt of sales."

"The cash till involved...?" Cassie looked at him, then her sister, for answers.

"Food sales." He reined in the dread enveloping him. "Remember the kids got together to cook hot dogs to sell, along with bags of chips and sodas."

"Right."

He squared his shoulders. "The difference?"

"Sales came to just over eight hundred. Two hundred is missing."

Luke's stomach felt like someone had just gone fifty rounds with him as the punching bag. "Denny was in charge."

Cassie's eyes went wide. "Denny, your right-hand man?"

"Yes. But I don't believe he had anything to do with the missing funds."

"Have there ever been problems with him, or any of the other teens before?" Lauren probed.

"No. But usually an adult handles the money at our events."

"Last night was different?"

He ran a shaky hand over the back of his neck. "I trust Denny."

"That's not what I asked."

"I gave him control."

"I see." Lauren made a note. "You'll need to question him."

His chest grew tight. "Yeah. I know."

"Luke, since you started this project you've entrusted me to keep your finances organized," Lauren continued, all business in a navy jacket and skirt, hair severely pulled back, even on her off time.

"And you would have advised me differently about last night?"

"You've always been diligent. Made sure there was adult supervision. That's what confuses me."

He leaned forward, resting his elbows on his knees, head hung low. Between his laser focus on how to raise funds to purchase the property and warehouse for the Klub, and trying to ignore the hurt of Tracy's baby news, he'd given Denny more adult jobs lately As a result, someone had helped him or herself to Klub funds. He wanted to kick himself right now.

A soft movement beside him brought his head up as Cassie gently laid her hand on his arm and squeezed. He met her gaze, embarrassed by his mistake, but not questioning the comfort from her solemn look. Lauren gathered up the pages to return them to a nice, neat pile. "I'll leave this file with you. Go over it, then get back to me. But I have to ask, why did you change your protocols?"

"Denny's been with me a long time. He's been asking for, and deserved, more responsibility. I thought last night was a good time to put him in charge."

"I hate to point out the obvious, but this is petty theft. A misdemeanor charge."

Still trying to wrap his mind around his current dilemma, he nodded. Just what he needed, the Klub involved in a criminal investigation.

"If you need any other advice, just call." Lauren stood. Bad news delivered, she started to refill her briefcase.

Words escaped him as he stared at the closed folder.

Lauren came around the desk and spoke to her sister in a low tone. "Can I still get in on the breakfast?"

Cassie pushed her chair back and stood. "Sure. We were cleaning up when you called."

"I know this is a bad time, but care to join me for more coffee?"

Luke felt Cassie's eyes on him. "Yeah. Just give me a few minutes."

"I'll be outside."

As the door closed, Cassie half sat on the edge of his desk, her hands griping the wood on either side of her.

"Well, this is awkward," he said after a few moments of unbearable silence. Needing to do something physical, he moved the two chairs he'd pulled out for them back against the far wall.

"It's a delicate situation, but we can figure it out."

He glanced at her, surprised to find only support reflected in her eyes.

"Cassie, this isn't your problem."

"No, it isn't, but you allowed me in and I'll do whatever I can to help you uncover what's going on."

The tightness in his chest loosened a fraction. Someone to share the burden of this discovery went a long way in making him feel less a fool. Less guilty that he'd put Denny in a situation that backfired on both of them.

"Kids' Klub is important to me on many levels. That's why this is so devastating to me." He paused, considering what to tell her. "When I came back to Cypress Pointe, I was at a low point in my life. My marriage had failed. I'd walked away from the music business.

"I went back to my first career, teaching, and discovered my past wasn't so easy to forget. My brother got arrested the first month I was home. I tried to intervene, but Mark didn't want me involved. In my frustration, I came up with the Klub concept." He met her gaze. "Full disclosure. My dad is doing time, as well."

"I've heard."

"Then you probably know about my mom?"

She nodded.

Super. Was she wondering why she'd hitched her wagon to his? Why he hadn't been more vigilant with the kids last night?

"The Klub has been my vehicle to give others a chance, when I couldn't help my own family. Especially Mark. I tried, but…"

"Luke, I appreciate your motives for the Klub, but as for your family, take it from me, they make their own decisions. You have no control over them and shouldn't feel guilty."

"I'm the only one who made something of himself. The only one to earn a college degree."

"Which you should be proud of."

"I always wished a place like the Klub existed when Mark and I were kids. That we had been exposed to committed adults who shared their time and experience with us, gave us alternatives to acting out because of a dysfunctional family or peer pressure. Maybe Mark would have chosen a different path. That's what I've offered with the Klub. And for this to happen?" He nearly choked on his own good intentions.

"*Maybe*s and *what-if*s will get you nowhere."

He allowed himself a slight grin. "One of your mom's sayings?"

"No. A Cassieism this time."

"Got one for still being angry at an ex?"

Her eyes dimmed. "Nope."

Just as well. "I'm afraid I let my ex-wife distract me lately."

She held up her hand. "You don't have to explain if you don't want to."

He didn't. Not on the tail of Lauren's news.

Shaking off the past he said, "That's why the thought of one of my kids stealing money is killing me. I'm always on top of things. I've been concentrating so much on securing this property that I allowed myself to fall short on my standards."

"Luke, I hate to break it to you, but you're not flawless. We all make mistakes."

"This mistake could cost the kids we're trying to help."

"Not if you figure out who the culprit is. Maybe you can get the money back."

"It's not just the funds. It's the trust." He began to pace. "Some of these kids have already been in trouble with the law. How can I question them and still have them feel like this is a safe place?"

"Maybe. But they need to be responsible, too."

Yeah, he knew that.

"Before you begin the questions, start with the obvious people and branch out from there."

He nodded. A list was already forming in his mind. But that would have to wait for later. He glanced at his watch. "We'd better get outside. Can't have unsupervised kids running around for too long."

Before leaving, Cassie stopped him at the door, placing a hand on his chest. His heart knocked against his ribs. They stood so close, he could see the variegated shades of green in her eyes. Noticed a few freckles scattered across her nose. How easy would it be to kiss her right now? Forget about the betrayal that came from his shortsightedness and lose himself in the pleasure he knew he'd find with her?

Too easy. And not fair to her.

He drew back.

"Don't blame yourself, Luke Hastings. You'll figure this out."

"What makes you so sure?"

"You didn't change your family situation and become a celebrated songwriter and dedicated teacher by giving up. Don't start now. These kids depend on you."

As much as he needed them.

Cassie opened the door. He took a breath at the space between them. His intentions to keep her at arm's length were failing. If he wasn't careful, she'd convince him that writing songs would be cathartic for him. Hadn't he sworn he'd never go there? Watching Cassie walk away, he couldn't recall why.

Quickly locking the door behind him, he sprinted to catch up with her.

"Cassie. Thanks."

"You got it."

He held open the door and they both exited the building into the bright sunshine. He'd taken two steps when ice cold water rained down over his and Cassie's heads.

"What the—"

On pure instinct, he wound his arms around Cassie, protecting her from the icy onslaught. Her back against his chest, he tugged her close and spun, taking the brunt of the freezing shower.

"Surprise," came a chorus of voices.

Cassie sputtered in shock.

He wound his arms tighter, enjoying holding her close. He was treading on dangerous territory here. Moisture dripped from his hair and down his face, landing on the creamy skin of her slim neck. When she shivered, he loosened his hold, using one hand to wipe his eyes. It was then he saw his kids standing on either side of them, laughing their fool heads off.

"We got you good, Mr. H.," Denny crowed, clearly the ringleader.

Shaking water from his hair, Luke noticed

the tables they'd set up earlier against the building on either side of the entrance. Since they'd gotten dumped on from overhead, he assumed the empty ice chests on the grass had been the ones filled with ice.

"What's this all about?" Cassie asked, finally finding her voice.

"You've seen how sports teams dump water on the coaches after a victory?" Denny explained. "We wanted to show you how much we care."

"This is caring?" Luke asked, wringing the hem of his shirt.

Kyle tossed Luke a towel. "We just meant to have fun."

Erin approached Cassie, handing her a towel that she immediately wrapped around herself. Despite the warm day and blazing sun, their body temperatures would need a while to warm up.

Luke eyed Denny. "This was your idea?"

"Well…" Denny glanced away.

"It was mine," Kyle admitted. "We used to get my coach when I played peewee football."

"I need to keep a better eye out in the future."

"C'mon, Mr. H., you liked it," another boy called out.

He wrapped the towel around his neck. "*Liked* is too strong a word."

"Are we in trouble?" Erin asked from her spot a few feet away.

"Nah. But I want to remind you, payback is never fun."

"Ooh, we're shaking," Kyle cooed in a mock frightened voice.

Luke grinned as he viewed the scene before him. Denny and Kyle high-fived, laughing, while a group of kids clapped over their success. Erin stood on the periphery, biting a fingernail. Cassie stood beside him, dripping wet, but smiling. Despite the fact that Luke had just learned someone had stolen money from the Klub, his heart expanded. He'd figure out what was going on and fix this mess, just as Cassie suggested. Maybe even with her at his side.

CASSIE WATCHED LUKE'S FACE, relieved to see a smile. Yes, they were cold and wet, but the prank had taken his mind off money matters. For a while, anyway. Knowing Luke, he'd go back to this office after the party broke up and get to work on who'd pocketed the money from the Klub.

"That's a good look on you, sis," Lauren said

as she strolled over, bagel in one hand, coffee in the other.

"The drenched animal look? Exactly what I was going for."

"Mission accomplished."

Cassie rubbed the fluffy towel over her face. Her makeup was sure to be gone, but at least she hadn't taken the soaking alone. Luke looked a mess, too. A handsome mess, though.

When he'd grabbed her to shield her from the brunt of the dousing, her shock had been more from his actions than the surprise attack. She hadn't needed his protection, but she wasn't going to lie, his arms locked around her felt good. Almost like they fit together. Which was ludicrous, since they'd only known each other a short time.

Maybe it's meant to be.

And maybe the cold water had knocked the good sense right out of her head. She had no expectations that Luke might be interested in her. Now or ever. At this moment they were friends. She'd take it. And if he offered more? Well, time would tell. She wasn't about to tempt fate.

Sidling up beside her, Lauren spoke out of the side of her mouth. "You should make a quick trip to the ladies' room before Mom arrives. She'll be all over you to change and probably even lick her thumbs to smooth down your hair."

Cassie hands flew to her head. "No."

"Yep. It's sticking out all over." She pantomimed drying her head with her hands.

"Why didn't you tell me sooner?" Cassie hissed at her sister.

"And ruin the fun?" She tossed Cassie her gym bag. "Lucky for you I keep clean workout clothes in my car. Go. Change."

Noticing Erin hovering nearby, looking miserable and out of place, Cassie grabbed Erin's arm. "I'm going to the restroom. Come with me."

Erin's dark-lined eyes crinkled. "Me?" she choked.

"Sure. You know girls can't go to the restroom alone."

"Um…okay."

Cassie tugged her to the building, the voices of the boys ribbing Luke fading in the distance. Once out of hearing range, she said, "Thanks for going along with me."

Erin lifted her shoulders in an offhand shrug. "I didn't embarrass you, did I?"

"No, it's… I've never hung out with anyone famous before."

Cassie laughed. "I'm far from famous. Just a woman who needs to fix herself up." She glanced at the teen. "You could give me some serious makeup tips."

"Really? I mean, no one usually notices, well except my parents but they don't count, so I wouldn't know what to tell you." Erin stopped rambling to inhale a breath. "Sorry."

"Hey, I hijacked you. It's okay."

Once inside the building Cassie stopped. Looked around.

"This way." Erin took the lead, walking toward doors to their right.

Inside the ladies' room, Cassie stripped out of her wet clothes. Her sister's tank top and shorts fit, even though she still shivered from the cold water. Her mouth formed an O when she viewed herself in the mirror.

"Just shoot me now."

Erin joined her. "It's not so bad."

"I do look like a drenched animal."

Her hair matted to her head on one side, stuck up on the other. Mascara ringed her eyes. The foundation she used to cover her freckles had melted away. "What a disaster."

"Don't worry. Even wet you're pretty."

"Stylish was more what I was going for." With practiced hands, Cassie unraveled her braid. Once loose, she fluffed out the wet, heavy mass. She took the towel and rubbed, hoping to make herself presentable again.

Erin stood nearby, gnawing on a fingernail.

"Now, you," Cassie said in hopes of setting the girl at ease, "are gorgeous. Do you know what women in the business would give for your hair and complexion? A fortune."

Her hands shooting up to touch the hair falling over her shoulders, Erin looked in the mirror. "I doubt it."

Cassie noted the uncertainty on the young girl's face. She remembered those days, worrying over every little detail of her appearance. She snorted. Guess she hadn't changed that much.

Erin shot her a questioning glance.

"Just thinking that no matter the age, we all care about our appearance." She ran her fingers through her hair, trying for a semblance of control. "So, do you hang out at the Klub?"

"When I can." Erin leaned a hip against the counter. "Mr. H. is always coming up with cool stuff for us to do."

"Like what?"

"Music. Sports. Stuff like that."

"What are you involved with?"

"Nothing."

"What would you like to be involved with?"

Erin pressed her lips together before she spoke, a lost little girl expression on her face. "I like music. But I'm not good at it."

"What kind of music?"

"I'm in chorus at school."

"That's fun. You'll learn technique and theory."

"I guess."

"Listen, I may teach some music classes here. Come by and check it out."

"I don't know. My parents may not like it. They're weird about musicians."

"I can talk to them. Are they here today?" Cassie asked as she tried in vain to braid her straight hair once again. She finally gave up and twisted it into a messy bun and secured it with the band she'd used at the end of her braid.

A shadow crossed Erin's face. "No. They, um… This isn't a good day."

Home issues? Probably. Who didn't clash with their folks at Erin's age? Given the edge in Erin's voice, her need to make excuses, well, the tension prompted Cassie to wonder if it went deeper, but she didn't know the girl well enough to stick her nose in Erin's business.

"Oh. No matter how old you get, you're always their kid."

Erin turned away, but not before Cassie saw the hurt in her eyes.

"This is the best I can do. Thankfully Luke, er, Mr. H., shielded me from most of the water."

"You should have seen your face." Erin giggled.

"I'm glad I didn't." She faced Erin. "Presentable?"

"Are you kidding?"

"No, I'm not. Tell me the truth."

Hesitating a moment, Erin motioned to her ear. "You've got some loose strands hanging there."

Glancing in the mirror, Cassie fixed the problem. "Okay, let's head out."

She held the door open for Erin. They cut through the now empty gymnasium to the exit.

"Thanks, Miss Branford."

"For what?"

"Dragging me to the bathroom. I had fun."

Cassie looped her arm over the girl's shoulder. "If that's your idea of fun, you need to get out more."

Erin laughed, but it sounded stilted to Cassie's ears. "I meant it when I said to come by the Klub. I'd love for you to be in one of my classes."

"For real?"

"As real as it gets."

"I'll try."

They joined the group gathered around Luke, who'd also changed into a dry T-shirt and shorts, when she heard a voice say, "Cassie, what on earth happened to you?" She turned to find her mother, hands on her hips. "Your hair is soaked."

Was it too late to hide behind the towering oak tree or sprint to the back of the warehouse?

"You said something about breakfast, not water games."

"Not games, Mom. Only overzealous teens playing a joke on us."

Dottie Jackson had to be the most gentle woman on the planet, but mess with her kid and the claws came out. "Are you okay? You don't want to catch a cold and hurt your throat."

"It's okay. I'm already warming up."

Bud, her stepfather, joined his wife, a grin on his face. "Heard you took one for the team."

Cassie sent a lethal look at her sister, who shrugged and sauntered away.

Dottie hugged her. "So sorry we missed the concert, honey. Bud mapped out the entire trip in advance, so we couldn't get back here any earlier."

"It was last-minute. I knew it would be tough for you guys to swing it." Cassie disengaged and grinned at her mother. "It's not like you've never seen me perform."

"Yes, but I hate to miss your shows."

In the early years, Cassie had flown her mother to as many shows as possible. As her career took off, her mother only managed to make it to nearby venues.

"Mom. Bud. I want you to meet someone." She took her mother's hand and steered her in Luke's direction. "Luke Hastings."

"We've met." Her mother's eyes narrowed. "Are you responsible for the attack on my daughter?"

"Actually, I'm a mutual victim."

Bud stuck out his hand to shake Luke's. "Dottie's like a mama bear with her young'ns."

Luke took his hand. "Surprise attack. No causalities."

"I should hope so," her mother grumped. "Cassie, you need to get home and put on warmer clothes."

Normally Cassie didn't mind her mother's fussing. She'd gotten used to it growing up. It had been her mother's way of making up for their father's desertion and the subsequent long hours she'd worked because of it. Whenever Cassie came home, she reveled in the attention the woman loved to lavish on her. But right now she'd rather be viewed as an accomplished adult, especially in Luke's eyes.

"I know I can't force you," her mother relented. "But I worry."

"I'm fine. I promise."

"Let's get some of that coffee before it's all

gone." Bud slipped his arm around his wife's waist and winked at Cassie.

She grinned, thankful he stepped in.

Dottie's serious gaze met Luke's. "No monkeying around, young man."

Cassie rolled her eyes.

Luke's lips twitched.

After her mother and Bud walked away, Cassie finally looked at Luke. "Sorry."

He shrugged.

By now most of the kids had dispersed.

"I...ahh, should be headed home."

Luke's gaze held hers. "You didn't mind the shower, did you?"

"No. The kids were just having fun. And who am I to ruin their good time?"

"As long as you aren't upset."

"Far from it." She paused. "Thanks for protecting me."

"Now, what kind of man would I be if I hadn't protected you from the brunt of the attack?"

Luke might not open up easily, but he was a decent man. His work with the kids proved it every day.

"You're a stand-up guy, Luke."

His good humor faded. Was he thinking about the missing money?

She reached over and touched his hand.

"You'll figure out what's going on, Luke. Lauren and I will help you any way we can."

His troubled gaze met hers. "I'm gonna take you up on that offer."

CHAPTER SEVEN

"HEY, LAUREN, I took a towel from the linen closet." Cassie yelled as she padded down the hallway in her bare feet while twisting the towel over her hair.

The aroma of brewed coffee spiced the air, along with the apple-cinnamon candle her sister burned regularly. Homey. Just what Cassie needed after traveling so much. "I'll make sure—" She stopped short as she came into the kitchen, finding her father seated at the table with her sister.

"Look, Daddy's here."

Cassie thought back to the day of the reception when Lauren rebuked her for calling him dad. Daddy? Father? How was she to address the man?

"Dad," she went for, tugging the collar of her robe closer while sending her sister a dirty look.

"He just stopped by. Unannounced."

Her father pushed his coffee mug to the side and rested his elbows on the table. He watched Cassie with a measured gaze. Great. Now what?

"The concert went well," he started. "You put on quite a show. Although less interaction with the crowd would have better served you."

"I always give the fans their money's worth," she responded, pulling out a chair to join the happy family surrounding the table.

"Perhaps next time you'll want advance notice of my availability."

Like that was ever going to happen.

"How is the writing going?" he asked.

It was all Cassie could do not to glare at her sister. Dad would catch the exchange and know something was up. "Slow. You know you can't rush the process."

"I remember when I penned the score for *Speed City.* The ideas flowed so easily. And with the film's success, the music became iconic."

They'd been hearing about his one foray into movie fame for three years. There'd been a spin-off movie, but no offers to work with the team again. He still continued to conduct, but even his touring schedule had slowed significantly. By his actions lately, she got the distinct impression he was trying to reinvent himself.

Lauren smiled at their father. "Everyone remembers your music."

"I have a call in with another director friend of mine. He's considering a project he thinks would benefit from my musical skills. I'm hoping to be asked to compose another score."

"How exciting," Lauren gushed. "Can you give us any details?"

"Not yet. It's hush-hush."

Right. Crossing her arms over her chest, Cassie noticed the slight frown on her father's normally smooth forehead. Perhaps he wasn't as sure of his career path as he'd once been.

"They'll call you, Daddy. I'm sure of it."

He dropped his gaze for a beat, then met Cassie's. She read the great big question mark there before he blinked. Yes, something was up.

"So, Cassie, when will you return to LA? Angelica and I have a home out there. You must come see it."

"Dad, you have three houses scattered around the country and you've never invited me over once."

"Times change. Angelica has reminded me how important family is."

"Ooh," Lauren cut in, "Wouldn't it be fun to have a family reunion? I'd love to visit you."

"Yes, of course." He acknowledged Lauren briefly. "Certainly my doors are always open to both of you."

Cassie wanted to believe he meant it, but Robert Branford had always been out for number one. Was this a true change of heart or did he have an ulterior motive? She didn't plan on engaging him long enough to discover the truth.

"I have no idea what my schedule will be like once I head out west," she said. "I'm sure I'll be busy."

"Not too busy to visit your father."

"Like you visited us when we were kids?"

Her father drew back in the chair. "You know I was focusing on my career. Travel was part of the deal."

"Oh, I get it. Leaving Mom and us behind was all for the greater good, right?"

"We've gone over this numerous times, Cassandra." He struggled to keep the exasperation from his voice, but it leaked through anyway. "I can't help that the means to support you meant I was in and out of your life."

She nearly snorted at the notion of him putting his family first. "Support? Is that what you called it?"

"I worked to take care of you."

She reined in the mounting resentment she always fought against when her father showed up in her life. "No, Mom worked to take care of us. She's the one who stuck it out—looked after us when we were sick, cried with us when we were hurting, was there for the accomplishments in our lives. She made us a family when you couldn't bother."

"And I regret the choices I made."

She might have believed him if the timbre of his voice didn't come off so annoyed. "Do you?"

"Cassie," Lauren cut in. "Stop it."

The stricken expression on Lauren's face was the only reason she didn't lash out more.

Her father straightened his shoulders. "I want to be present in my daughters' lives now."

Cassie rose, griped the back of the chair with undue pressure as she slid it under the table. "Too little, too late."

"You're not being fair, Cassandra. I've changed."

"Tell that to someone who actually believes you."

She stepped away, intending to return to the bathroom. But she stopped. Spun around. "And my name is Cassie. If you really want a relationship with me, try using the name I grew up with."

That said, she marched down the hallway, her face flaming. Softly closed the door behind her and sank against the hard surface. Would there ever be a day when she wouldn't resent her father? Try as she might, she just couldn't forgive the man. She always waited for the other shoe to drop and the man never failed to disappoint. Did he really mean what he said this time? And if so, what was she going to do if he actually kept his word and did change?

She pushed away from the door. Stared at her face in the mirror. "Just give him time," she counseled herself. "He doesn't get a free pass just cuz he says so."

Shaking off the dread, she got dressed. Before long, the steady drone of the blow dryer calmed her frayed nerves. She'd agreed to meet Luke at the warehouse this afternoon, to find out her assignment.

Fifteen minutes later she'd braided her hair, changed into a pair of new jeans, a sparkly shirt, a black leather jacket with rows of zippers, and chunky boots. Her footsteps thudded on the hardwood floor as she entered the kitchen to find only her sister seated at the table.

"Good going. You managed to tick Daddy off."

"Hey, I spoke the truth. I can't help it if he doesn't like hearing it."

"You always do this. Keep him at arm's length when he's trying."

"Trying to do what?" With a sigh, Cassie

rested against the counter. She had to keep her distance. It was the only way to stop him from hurting her. "Honestly. I don't know why you give him the benefit of the doubt."

"There's no question he won't ever win Father of the Year, but I want a relationship with him."

Cassie lifted her shoulders. "Then go right ahead."

"He wants us both in his life."

"I'm sorry, sis. On this particular topic, we disagree."

The stubborn look Cassie remembered from when they were kids took up residence on her sister's face. "You won't even try."

There was no winning this conversation, not for either of them. But Cassie wanted to be close with her sister again, like they'd been when their mother worked and they were left home alone, taking care of each other. Lauren might not choose to remember how exhausted their mother had been after holding down two jobs, but Cassie did. She might not recall the nights their mother had cried in her bedroom after their father so callously broke up their family over his quest for fame, but those tears broke Cassie's heart. Or even the times when he promised the girls a visit and never showed. It was all burned in Cassie's heart, but for Lauren's sake, she'd put her bitterness aside. Because she loved her sister, first and always.

"How about this?" Cassie countered in a quiet voice. "I'll see how much Dad's word is really worth this time. If I'm wrong about him, I'll apologize."

Lauren wiped the tears brimming in her eyes. "You'd really do that?"

"For you. Because I know how important it is."

"I'm not sure what to say."

"Really? This is a first."

Lauren sputtered out a laugh. "Thank you."

Cassie held up her hand. "I'm not making any promises, but I'm willing to see where this goes."

"I understand. And I agree."

"A little bit of compromise goes a long way. On both our parts."

"On both our parts."

"Pinky swear?" Cassie held up a pinky.

"We haven't done that since we were kids," Lauren said, but rose and hooked her finger with Cassie's.

The gesture was one of comfort and hope in tough times. They'd been tight once. A sisterhood bond not even their father could break. Or Cassie hoped, anyway.

Together they recited, "One for all, no matter the fall."

Laughing now, Lauren pulled away. "We really thought those words would protect us."

"In reality, we protected each other."

"We did," came her soft reply.

Deciding to quit while they were ahead in the healing process, Cassie grabbed the keys to the rental car. "I've got some things to do. See you later."

Just before she walked out the door, Lauren called after her. "Daddy won't let us down this time."

Wishful thinking. She donned her crossbody Michael Kors bag and left before her generous mood faded.

Arriving at the Klub fifteen minutes later, she dodged a raucous game of hoops as she crossed the gym to Luke's office. The mingled scent of sweat and pine cleaner brought her back to high school. She hadn't been athletic, but she'd spent enough time in gym class for the indelible odors to remain etched in her memory.

She had to admit, she was curious to find out what he had in store for her. She needed an activity other than focusing on her lack of muse and troubling family dynamics. At this point, teen angst would be pretty refreshing.

Luke's door was ajar. "Cassie Branford reporting for duty," she said.

Luke shuffled together the papers he'd been reading. "C'mon in."

"Sure you're ready for me? I could go throw some hoops with the guys."

"They're pretty hard-core. You might get hurt."

"Or get some much-needed exercise."

He chuckled. "Sit down."

She took the same seat she'd been in only a few hours ago when she'd brought up her volunteering. He'd changed out of his more casual clothes from earlier as well, sporting a polo shirt and chinos. His artfully messy hair and the steady gaze made her blood buzz, but she wasn't as nervous as she'd been the first time she visited his office. Now she was more familiar with Luke. A little less afraid to make the wrong move and lose the opportunity of getting him to help her.

"I've been giving your role here considerable thought," he said.

"Should I be worried?"

He settled back in his chair. "Working with troubled teens is not for the faint of heart. Between hormones and peer pressure, it can be challenging."

"Most of the kids I've met so far are real sweethearts."

"Yes. But the ones that need real help, they aren't all sunshine and roses. Some of these kids face issues that aren't easy to overcome."

"I've thought about this a lot, Luke. I know I can't just waltz in here and expect to solve problems and make their lives better. But I can bring the gift of music."

Luke leaned behind him to reach a bookcase. He snagged a binder from a shelf and slid it across the desk to her. "There have been studies conducted about teens and music. As a teacher, and having had experience in the music world, I read up quite a bit on the subject before opening the Klub."

Cassie leafed through the pages. "And what did you discover?"

"Music can be an outlet for teenagers in multiple ways. Getting the kids to be creative helps them deal with emotions, gets them comfortable with their personalities. I consulted with a professor who's done extensive research in this area."

"Do you have a specific program in place?"

"Yes. We encourage the kids to listen to all kinds of music, learn to play and even create their own sounds. When a person identifies with a certain sound, they can take some of the negative energy and transform it into a positive way to express themselves. The success they find here can then transfer into their daily lives, whether it be dealing with family or self-esteem issues. Even staying away from situations that draw them to trouble. The program also focuses on the kids who have a hard time communicating by giving them an outlet for self-expression. I can't tell you the number of kids who can't articulate why they act out, but once they begin immersing themselves in music, they finally find their voice. It's amazing and affirming to watch."

"Impressive." She glanced at the pictures of the kids on Luke's wall. "What's your success rate?"

"More often than not we've had positive results. Usually it comes with parents who are engaged and will do whatever is needed to get their kids on the right track. Those without parental support are tougher to reach. I'm not saying it can't be done, but these kids have deeper problems and the road to healing can be slower or more difficult.

"Bottom line is, we work hard to make every teen who walks through our doors feel like they are important. We've only been open a few years. We still tweak the program on a per-child basis. And we're open to ways to better assist these kids as they navigate through life."

A chorus of shouts reverberated from the gym. Positive proof that Luke's program worked.

"The more I hear, the more I can't wait to dig in."

He grinned. "I was hoping you'd say that."

While Cassie was happy he was finally on board with her involvement, she hoped he wasn't being nice to her because he could see the benefit of her name drawing attention to the center. Yes, she'd managed to draw a concert crowd, which meant much-needed funds for the Klub, but she wanted to donate her time and talent. Wanted to be needed as Cassie the musician, the core of her being, not Cassie the popular artist.

Please, don't let him be like my father, seeing me as a means to an end.

She brushed away her negative thoughts. "Okay, lay it on me."

He rose, rounded the desk and leaned against it.

"I have talented musicians already giving lessons and teaching the students the art of performing."

She tilted her head. "Then what do you want from me?"

"Someone to lead a songwriting workshop."

Her eyes went wide at the same time her stomach plummeted.

"I can't think of anyone more qualified than you."

After the heat flushing her body subsided, she leaned forward, eyes narrowed.

"Songwriting? Are you being intentionally cruel?"

"Hear me out."

LUKE WASN'T ONE bit surprised by Cassie's less than enthusiastic response. He was taking a chance here. A chance he hoped would benefit not only the teen program, but even more, would unbury the hidden abilities still inside her.

"Well, I must differ," she said, her voice tight. "If anyone is qualified, it's you."

"I don't write music any longer."

"Neither do I."

He held back a frustrated sigh. Just like so many of the kids to come through the doors, Cassie was doubting herself. Unsure of her future. Granted, she was an adult, but age didn't change the fact that she had a problem. As it did for the kids, the music program would help her, too.

He crossed his arms over his chest, shifting to the daunting Mr. H. persona he used when dealing with an unusually hardheaded teen.

"I went back and listened to your music."

Surprise flickered in her gaze. When she remained silent, he continued.

"The first album was real, Cassie. The rich texture of your voice brought out emotion. I believed you. No matter what you were singing, whether a sad ballad or upbeat tempo, it was honest. Was it technically perfect? No. And that's what sold your songs."

The pain etched on her lovely features spoke volumes about her passion for music. How much it hurt her to question her abilities.

"The second album was technically perfect. No rasps in your voice. No cracks when the emotion of the story touched your heart. Your vocal power remained equal in every song, no dynamics or range. Even the lyrics, which were thought out and measured on your first effort, didn't ring true. I'm guessing after making the second record your doubts kicked in."

She looked away and swallowed. Met his gaze again. "I knew before the release date that the album was going to tank." She blew out a breath followed by a nervous laugh. "First time I ever said it out loud."

"And saying it out loud makes you…?"

"Relieved."

"So what happened?"

"A new producer came to the label. He

thought he had the magic formula for a hit record all figured out, so the label paired him with me." She pulled her braid over her shoulder and brushed the ends through her fingers. "He refused to listen to my ideas. Reworked my songs."

"Just like a bad manager can tank a career, so can a bad producer."

Dropping the braid, she sat up taller in the chair. "Part of it was my fault. I didn't want to rock the boat and by the time I brought my concerns to my manager, it was too late. The project was more than halfway finished. Travis suggested I hang in until the end." She grimaced. "Even he didn't realize how different the sound came across until we heard it for ourselves."

"Is that when you first noticed the block?"

"No. I went on tour. Suffered with critics taking potshots at the album. When the dust settled, Travis sat down with the executives and worked out a new deal, one that allows me to go back to my original style of music. Only now..."

"You're stuck."

"Bingo."

"If you would seriously consider it, teaching a songwriting workshop to draw creativity out of the kids will in turn do the same for you. What have you got to lose?"

"Nothing I don't have right now," she grumbled.

He chuckled. "Very true. It's a chance. One I think you should take."

Slumping back in the chair, her expression was one of a recalcitrant teen. "Why do this when I could just as easily work with you? You agreed to sit in with me, get me to focus on writing again."

"You know it's more than just sitting down and coming up with a song. Technically, if we worked long enough, we'd write something. But I can't give you back your confidence. You need to find it on your own."

A sulky pout crossed her lips. One that made him smile inside, because Cassie didn't realize she wore her emotions for everyone to see. How refreshing, to be herself, not yet jaded by an industry that could make or break a career. Not trampled by others to get what they wanted, at the cost of her dreams. The last album was a blip on the radar. Her songs were honest, just like Cassie, which he found more and more fascinating every time they were together.

Her disgruntled expression had him wishing he could lean over and kiss her doubts away.

He'd been there. His chest housed the ragged heart to confirm it. A move like that would be selfish, sure, but Cassie intrigued him. Around her, he forgot to keep his defenses engaged.

Now was not the time, and certainly not the place. He refocused. "Talent like yours doesn't go away, Cassie. Can it be buried? Sure. I personally don't believe we've heard the last of you. Or seen the depths of what you have to offer. A songwriting workshop might just jar loose the lyrics hiding in your psyche."

She seemed to consider his words for a moment. Zeroed in on him in a thoughtful way that made him nervous. "The same could be said of you," she countered.

He pushed away from his desk. Walked back to take a seat in his chair. Ignored the tug in his chest. "We aren't talking about me."

"Maybe we should."

He wanted to scoff at the idea, but instead, spoke words he realized were true. "My time is over. I have other concerns now."

"How can you say that?" She jumped up. "Especially after the lecture you just gave me?"

"There's a difference. You need this for your career to flourish. I don't need, or want, to write music anymore."

Very slowly she placed her palms dead center on his desk and leaned toward him, speaking in a measured voice. "I don't believe you."

For a second, a mere second, anger flashed through him. Not the kind he'd nursed against his ex. Not the kind he'd experienced whenever he heard the last hit song they'd written together playing on the radio. No, this anger went soul deep, to a place he'd closed off for so long he'd pretended it didn't exist.

He rose. Placed his palms on the outside of hers. Leaned in until he was inches from her face. Breathed in her sweet fragrance. "Believe me. I'm not going back there."

"Really?"

"I'm dead serious."

Her steady gaze held his. His heart pounded. This close, he could see the distinctive shade of green mocking his words. She knew, maybe even better than he did.

"Talent like yours doesn't go away," she echoed.

"Maybe it should."

The words hung between them. Time stilled as his blood raced. How had she managed to resurrect this one painful aspect of his life? How had she focused on the fact that while he said he wouldn't write again, the ability had never turned off? His brain still formed tempos and lyrics, even though he ruthlessly pushed them away every time they surfaced. For two years he'd lived without admitting the truth to himself. And now, by encouraging Cassie to deal with her fears, he was forced to confront his own.

This was why he hadn't wanted to make a deal with her. Yet at the same time, was secretly glad he did.

With so little space between them, he looked down at her lips. What would she do if he crossed the line? Kissed her as a way of changing the subject?

Find out, his inner voice taunted.

He moved that last fraction closer, his lips hovering over hers. And still she stayed put, as if waiting to see if he would carry out his intentions. So he did.

His lips covered hers, silencing her gasp. He moved slowly, savoring the unexpected delight. The air around them grew heavy as he coaxed a trembling response from her. Adrenaline buzzed through his system, much like the feeling he experienced when a melody came together. Only this wasn't a song. This was Cassie. Alive and in the flesh. Returning his kiss now with the enthusiasm he'd seen when she performed onstage. A passion he couldn't deny. Or fight.

One of her hands moved over his, satiny

soft as she twined their fingers together. The kiss continued. Slow and unhurried. Until a shout from the gym reminded him that his office door was wide open. Everyone and their brother could get a gander of him kissing the pop artist who'd come to the Klub to volunteer her time to the kids, not him.

He snapped back to his senses, jerking away from her.

Smooth, Hastings.

After opening her eyes, Cassie drew in a shaky breath. Wrapped her arms around her middle. Did he regret his impulsive action? Much to his surprise, he found he didn't.

"I'm, ah… That was totally unprofessional," she stammered.

"I agree. But I can't promise it won't happen again."

They stood in uncomfortable silence. Voices rose from the gym again.

"I should probably go out there and referee."

"And I should get going." She straightened the bag crisscrossing her chest. "When do you want to start the songwriting workshop?"

He walked her into the gym. "How about Tuesday? We have a free flow poetry class at four p.m. I'll spread the word we're turning it into a songwriting workshop for the time being. Should get more participation that way."

"I'll be ready."

Would he?

Before he had a chance to say anything else, Denny sauntered over. "Hey, Mr. H. We need you to settle a disagreement."

Good. A distraction to get his mind off kissing Cassie.

"Sure thing." He smiled at her. "See you Tuesday."

Her eyes narrowed, which concerned him. "Oh, yeah. I'll see you."

Why did that sound like a threat?

He watched her head for the exit. She waved and spoke to a few teens before pushing through the door and disappearing from sight.

"Earth to Mr. H. Come in."

He shook off the trance she'd enchanted him with. "Right. What's up, Denny?"

"Kyle says we should charge kids to use the art room. For the paints and stuff. I don't know if it's a good idea."

Denny went on to explain the dilemma. This was what Luke needed, to focus on the routine of the Klub. Figure out what was going on with the missing money. Anything to get his mind off Cassie and the fact that she made him hear the music again.

CHAPTER EIGHT

ERIN DUCKED INTO the songwriting class ten minutes late. Slipping onto the only available seat, beside Denny, she immediately slumped down and shivered. The cold metal chilled the back of her legs.

Maybe no one would notice her. She peeked around. Right. Everyone had watched her come in.

"You're late," Denny said under his breath.

"Obvious, genius," she retorted. She wasn't in the mood for another lecture, not after playing twenty questions with her parents just so she could leave the house.

"You didn't miss much." Denny pushed his glasses over his nose, not sounding at all like her tone bothered him. "Cassie's just getting started."

Crossing her arms, Erin tried to listen, but the conversation with her parents kept running through her head. When she'd come home from school to dump her books, grab something to eat and change from the short skater dress before hitching out to Kids' Klub, both her mom and dad were home. Unusual for a workday. At first Erin thought something bad had happened, like the day her sister had vanished. Turned out today, her older sister had called her mom. That explained the funk hovering over the house.

Ever since her sister had taken off with her baby daddy, a guy in a bad rock band, Erin had become the focus of her parents' anger. *Where are you going? Who will you be with? Don't make the same mistakes as your sister. And especially don't get pregnant.*

Yeah, like that was gonna happen. She was only sixteen. Like she wanted a baby.

Still, because of Shannon, her parents now treated her like a bad daughter, too. So now there were rules and expectations and burdens. She just wanted to be a kid. Instead, she'd turned herself into a copy of her wild sister. Might as well fulfill her parents' dire predictions, which she'd already done by stashing the stolen money in her bedroom.

Thanks, sis.

"I'm not going to tell you songwriting is easy." Cassie was speaking as she paced the front of the music room. Three rows of chairs stretched across the room usually reserved for poetry class. A big white dry-erase board hung on the wall. When Erin normally showed up here on Tuesday afternoons, there were only three or four kids.

"You saved me this seat?" she whispered to Denny.

"Yeah. You said you were coming."

She looked around. "Full room."

"It's because of Cassie."

She was super glad Cassie had come to the Klub. Never in a million years would she have thought she'd meet someone famous. And nice. She was totally down-to-earth. But Erin liked the small poetry class where she was invisible most of the time. No expectations, except her own. No one's words, but hers, written in the tattered notebook hidden at the bottom of her bag. Her secret words, about her life, disappointments and dreams. She'd never share them. Not with Denny. Not with anyone.

Cassie continued. "There's one important ingredient to being a songwriter. Telling a story. I bet every one of you here today has a story to tell. The more personal, the greater the emotional pull of your song."

She stopped pacing the small area in front of the chairs. Erin noticed she'd changed the colored streak in her hair to bright orange. If she tried that look, she'd come off like a loser and everyone would laugh at her. On Cassie, it worked.

"Everyone pull out a notebook. I have some paper if you didn't bring one. Now think of your favorite song. Jot down the words and let's see what we all come up with."

Denny opened a composition notebook. "Need some paper?"

"No. Who comes to writing class without paper?"

"Girls in a bad mood?"

She rolled her eyes. As the students started to work, Erin considered pulling out her secret notebook. She actually had the words of her favorite song written inside. She'd reread them after a bad day with her parents or if her friends got her down. And weirdly, they were from a Cassie Branford song. The lyrics of "Pretty Inside" were so her, like Cassie had spent a day in Erin's messed-up life and knew exactly how she felt. Nah. Cassie would probably laugh at her if she really got to know her.

"C'mon," Denny urged. "Get started."

She tugged her bag onto her lap and searched through the bits of stuff to find the cherished notebook. Her fingers closed over it, snagging the elastic band she'd wrapped around it when the binding fell apart.

Looking up from his assignment, Denny

nudged her with his elbow. Sent her a smile. When had she started to like him? Well before he gave her his shirt the other day, but it had been building slowly. She couldn't have a boyfriend. Would never bring a nice guy like Denny to her house. Her parents would scare him off anyway and then he'd realize what a loser she was. So no, she wasn't revealing her notebook.

Her cell phone chimed. She pulled up her text message.

Meet at park. 911. Gary

She quickly got rid of the message when she noticed Denny watching her.

"I gotta split."

"Now? We just got started."

"Yeah, now."

Denny would never approve of her friends. Her parents didn't. She didn't even like them all the time. But they let her be her, nothing else. She could breathe with them.

She slung the bag strap over her shoulder. "Later."

No, she'd never be good enough for a guy like Denny. Her parents had harped on it every single day until she'd finally believed them. She'd demonstrated it by taking the money. Why even try?

CASSIE WAITED AS her students scribbled down lyrics personal to them. The butterflies in her stomach slowly began to settle down until a movement in the back of the cramped room caught her attention. Erin. Leaving? Was she that bad that kids were escaping already?

She grabbed the end of her braid. Tugged it to remind herself she was here for a reason. She couldn't wimp out, especially because Luke had given her this shot. Her stomach might be in knots, but she'd facilitate this workshop, even if it killed her. Which it might do if she didn't fire up her runaway muse soon.

And great, now she was thinking all melodramatic. Maybe this class would be to her advantage.

"How are we doing?" she asked the group.

"Is it okay if we don't use your songs?" a girl two rows back asked.

"Please, use whatever songs resonate with you. I don't care if it's one of my songs or not."

"What if it's rap with, you know, certain words?" a boy with a mop of shaggy hair questioned.

"As I would tell any writer, use your words carefully."

"What if it's Italian?" Denny asked. A couple of the kids laughed but it didn't faze him. Proved he was a true opera buff.

"Can you translate?"

"Some."

"Then for today, use English."

She snatched up a red marker and uncapped it. "Now, throw words out to me."

Pushing back the sleeves of the oversized shirt she'd paired with skinny jeans and flats, for the next ten minutes she filled one half of the board. *Boys, chillin', school, money, summer, beach*—just to name a few. The kids yelled faster than she could keep up.

"Vero amore."

"English, Denny."

"True love."

She chuckled. Who knew Denny was a romantic?

"Now, partner up. Take the words that stuck out to you and discover a theme for a song."

"Is this how you do it, Miss Branford?" a boy with glasses, asked her. Jack, she remembered.

"Usually. I like to think of lyrics as poems to music."

"Show us how you'd do it," Denny urged.

She placed the marker on the ledge under the board. "Okay. Let's take the word…*butterfly*."

"Ooh, I love butterflies," a girl named Taylor squealed.

Hopefully not like the ones flapping around in Cassie's stomach.

"Yeah, we've seen your tattoo," Kyle snickered.

"It's only fake."

The boys laughed louder.

"First of all," Cassie said as she walked over to the group, "we aren't laughing at anyone in this class. If you want to goof around, go play basketball."

"Basketball is serious," a tall, skinny boy told her.

"So is my time. And I want your input, so think." She pointed to Kyle. "Especially you."

"Got it." Kyle shot her a thumbs up.

"Back to what I was saying."

"Butterflies," Taylor repeated.

Cassie wrote the word on the blank side of the board. "So I take the idea and write down things that describe it. Give me a few."

"Wings."

"Colorful."

"Monarch."

The marker squeaked as she jotted the words. "A great start. As the words come to you, you keep writing them down because you never know which ones will come to life in your story.

"Next, I get my guitar." She removed Ginger from the stand. "How many here play an instrument?"

About half raised their hands.

"So, you play around with a chord progression." Her fingers moved over the fret as she strummed out a random beat.

"You mix the two?" shaggy head asked, clearly interested in the process.

"That's right. Your name?"

"Alan."

"Do you play?"

"He's in a band," a petite girl sighed.

"Where's your guitar?"

"In the back."

"Go get it and we'll continue."

Alan bolted to the back of the room to remove his guitar from the stand. Cassie continued to lightly strum. "Now, take some of the butterfly descriptions and match them to the tempo."

The room filled with raised voices as the teams worked together. Alan, his guitar strapped on, quickly matched Cassie's beat.

"Taylor, go on up to the board and write the words you hear in the room."

The teen, ponytail flying, darted up front. Before long there were phrases across the board. The chatter level rose as the kids grew more excited. Cassie nodded to Alan as she stopped playing. Quiet resumed.

"So now you have a loose example on how to write a song."

"But isn't it easier if you already have an idea?" a student asked.

"Sure. It's like writing an essay in English class. If you already have the premise, it flows much easier."

"Like 'Pretty Inside'?"

"I wrote that song from a real experience and how I felt because of it."

"So we can use our moods? Like if we're happy or sad?" Taylor asked.

"You sure can."

"What about if you have a melody first?" Alan asked, strumming out a new sound.

"Of course. There are no rules. Sometimes the melody comes first, then the words. Or the other way around. The main idea is to get your thoughts and the notes written down then figure out where they fit and how to use them."

The kids asked more questions and before she knew it, the hour was up.

"Over the next week, if you have any impressions, music or words, write them down. There's no right or wrong. Next week we'll take a look at what you come up with."

As she placed her guitar back on the stand, the kids mingled. She caught Denny's eye and motioned him up front.

"I saw Erin leave earlier. Is she okay?"

"I don't know. She got a text, but she was pretty uptight when she got here."

"Any idea why?"

"She never says, but I bet it's her family."

Cassie could relate. "Would it help if I talked to her?"

"Not sure. She's not real open to advice."

"Maybe girl talk, instead of an adult asking questions and prying into her life?"

He shrugged. "She's a mystery," he said just as Luke walked into the room.

He slapped Denny on the back. "They all are, buddy."

"Hey, I resemble that remark," Cassie protested.

Luke chuckled. "How'd it go?"

"Awesome," Denny said. "Cassie knows what she's doing."

Cassie met Luke's gaze over Denny's shoulder and struggled to maintain a straight face.

"Yeah, she's good."

His praise lifted Cassie's sprits. Even if it wasn't earned just yet. "I enjoyed the class. They weren't afraid to try."

Luke grinned. "Imagine that."

Cassie returned the smile. "Smart aleck."

Denny looked between them both. "Am I missing something?"

"Yes. But right now I need you in the art room."

"Okay." Denny scooped up his notebook and pen. "See you later, Cassie."

"Thanks, Denny."

When Luke followed the teen from the room, Cassie exhaled a long breath. She really didn't want him psychoanalyzing her right now. Exercising her writing muscles with the kids had taken a lot out of her.

She opened the guitar case with the intention of putting the instrument away when she noticed her songbook inside. Reluctantly, she reached for it. Sifted through the pages. Mostly, they were empty. She found the last page she'd scribbled on, because at the time, that's all she seemed to be doing. But a few words and phrases jumped out at her. Taking a seat, she went over them again.

Don't be afraid to try. A voice, sounding suspiciously like Luke's, reverberated in her head.

Swallowing, she reread her previous entry. As she did, her heart rate kicked up.

It isn't as it seems,
it feels like a dream.
I thought I knew myself,
but never faced the past.
The voices in my head
remind me I'm alive,
But every time I look at you,
I ask the reason why.

Rattled by the words catching her heart, she glanced at the date. A few days before her father's wedding. Had she been pouring out her mixed emotions about her father remarrying? Gotten the wedding celebration mixed in with her fears of never writing a decent song again?

Unbidden, a scene from her childhood flooded her mind of her sitting at the piano with her father, while he gave her basic lessons. She'd been a chip off the old block, he'd lovingly said. She'd pushed herself, wanting to make him proud. But the older and more accomplished she became, the less he seemed interested, until he didn't acknowledge her talent at all. He began missing recitals and school musicals. He said it was the job, but right this very moment, she recalled the envious gleam in his eyes. Had he resented her talent?

She sat back, stunned by her revelation. Certainly it explained the distance between them. So why did he want into her life now?

Tentatively, she picked up a pen. Began adding more sentences as they formed in her mind.

What seemed to matter then,
can only come to an end,
There's more to me than fame,
a child with a name.
If you asked me where I am,
you might not like the answer,
I have a life to live,
with only me as the master.

Rough, but the beginning of an idea. One she wouldn't let escape.

She wasn't sure how long she worked on the verses or tweaked the chorus. Once finished, she settled her guitar on her lap. Plunked out a melody line, very similar to the one she'd come up with during class. Pleased, she picked up her phone, scrolling to the recorder app. She hit record and played through the line in its entirety. Once she'd saved the recording, she played again, this time adding in the lyrics.

Tears leaked from her eyes as a sense of relief and gratefulness surged through her. The satisfaction that always came with completing a concept was like welcoming home an old friend. One she'd missed more than she'd ever imagined.

But she couldn't get too excited. Not until she knew she could take more ideas and turn them into songs. Maybe, just maybe, she'd have a positive update for Travis before long.

Rising, she went to put her guitar away and noticed Luke leaning against the doorframe, arms crossed over a beige button-down shirt, legs covered in dark blue jeans. His hair, more tousled than usual, fell over his forehead. A small smile lingered on his face.

Discovering he'd been eavesdropping, the butterflies took up flight in her belly again.

"You heard?"

HE'D HEARD, ALL RIGHT. The raw emotion grabbed him, right down to his toes.

She looked beautiful, her teeth worrying her lower lip as she acknowledged his presence. The way her hair, with the new orange streak, shone in the overhead lights. Even from across the room he got a faint whiff of her berry-scented fragrance. She gripped her guitar for dear life, all because she wanted his opinion.

No pressure there.

"Pretty good for someone fighting a block."

"Was it awful?"

"Not even close."

"It's just the start. I need to make some adjustments." Her green eyes turned bright, but her expression remained timid. "Care to join me and give me your opinion?"

He froze. He'd known she'd eventually ask this question, but still, no matter how many times he'd played this scenario out in his head, he wasn't ready.

"We both know you have experience collaborating with another lyricist."

"Probably not the best reminder if you want me to take this seriously."

She shrugged. "You had to know the past would come up if we ever got to this point."

"I'd hoped it wouldn't."

Patting the seat beside her, she said, "Let's give it a try."

"I need to get my guitar."

He strode back to this office, convincing himself collaborating with Cassie would be easier if he just looked at it like ripping off a bandage. Quickly, painfully, and done with. Maybe then he'd settle in and work. Because he knew a good sound when he heard it, and Cassie's work in progress qualified, with a few edits here and there.

When he returned, Cassie still studied her notebook, biting the end of her pen. She glanced over at him when he sat down beside her. "I'll play the melody through. Stop me if you think of anything."

She played and sang, the textures in her voice taking his breath away. When unencumbered, her gift soared. He knew in his soul she would conquer her fears and once again bless the world with her special brand of music.

"Who are you thinking of when you sing?" he asked after she'd completed the song.

She colored. "My father."

"Why?"

"I have a lot of deep-seated anger."

He nodded, pulled her notebook closer. Held out his hand for the pen she'd slipped over her ear. "May I?"

She handed him the pen. He jotted down a few ideas.

"Oh, that works."

They incorporated the new parts seamlessly and before he knew it, he was harmonizing with her. Adding new chord variations. She caught on quickly and transitioned right along with him.

"Once more." This time she tapped her phone and he knew she was recording them. His fingers froze on the strings.

She didn't notice until she started strumming without him. "What's wrong?"

"I swore I'd never do this again."

Cassie turned off the recorder. "Because of your ex-wife?"

"You know what happened?"

"Not really. Rumors mostly."

He hesitated, but it only lasted a few seconds. "Tracy cheated on me. With the label executive we worked with. Stu Andrews was my friend, or so I thought, anyway. Seems I was only a stepping stone for Tracy. Andrews gave her what she really wanted."

"Which was?"

"A more prominent place in the industry. He was a shark of a lawyer who skillfully got her what she coveted, which turned out to be the royalties to our last collaboration."

She cringed. "I heard about that."

"Not my smartest move."

"I imagine emotions were running high. No one thinks well under those circumstances."

He sent her a questioning glance.

"I still remember my parents' divorce. Not pretty."

"Neither was mine. She used me. Dragged our personal life through the tabloids. I've never forgiven her for that."

Cassie's face fell. "So in the end, you'll always question people's motives, won't you? Just like me offering the benefit concert."

Would he? Life hadn't exactly panned out any other way. "My folks were always out for what they could get," he explained. Or was it an excuse? "At the expense of my brother and me. Mark turned out just like them. I guess it's burned into my DNA to be cautious."

"Not everyone has ulterior motives."

"Tracy did. After all was said and done, I retreated here."

"Which, honestly, was probably a good move. You started the Klub."

True. He'd never thought of it like that. When he'd come to Cypress Pointe all he'd wanted was to be left alone to lick his wounds. But the idea for the Klub had flickered to life once he started teaching and never let go.

"While I'm glad I got this place up and running, I've left the music industry for good."

She scooted a bit closer. Opened her mouth, then thought better of it.

"What?" he urged, honestly curious to hear what she had to say.

Tucking a loose strand of hair from her braid behind her ear, she started. "I think I know what caused my block. Fear. Not wanting to disappoint all the people who depend on me. But you? Finding out what your wife had done, with a friend? Luke, that's a devastating situation to go through. Major. I might be afraid to tank again, but to lose my family and career? All in one swoop? I truly see why you don't want to take a chance."

He frowned. "I don't have writer's block."

"You don't? C'mon, you're more emotionally messed up than me."

He'd have laughed at her simple statement if it weren't so true.

"Are you saying you still get ideas?" Cassie prompted.

"All the time."

Surprise turned her eyes a deeper shade of green. "What do you do with them?"

"Nothing."

A scowl marred her forehead. "That's almost worse than retreating from the world."

He silently disagreed.

"Thank you," she said after a few contemplative moments.

"For what?"

"Sharing your story. Explaining why you don't write any longer. It had to be difficult confiding in me."

Actually, it felt good getting it off his chest. Some of the chronic tightness shifted. He could almost breathe freely. "You're a good listener."

She shrugged. "All in the day of a song workshop leader, teen motivator, Kids' Klub volunteer."

"Busy girl."

She grinned before sobering just as quickly. "You know, something just occurred to me."

"What's that?"

"Your wife. I haven't heard of any songs she's written in the past two years." She picked up her phone and tapped the screen.

Could Cassie's statement be true? He hadn't been paying attention to Tracy's career, too busy putting her out of his mind and getting the Klub off the ground. Trying to figure out how to purchase this property, along with school and band commitments, kept his mind focused on Cypress Pointe, not the music world in LA.

"Nope. I checked. Nothing recent."

Huh. Had her plan backfired? Maybe she couldn't work with anyone else? Then again, she could have been working on a family all this time and left the songwriting behind. Either way, he realized, it didn't matter.

"So, this song," he said, changing the subject. "Got a working title?"

She rejoined the conversation as if her news about Tracy hadn't been a major revelation to him. "'Butterflies.'"

"That's a pretty definitive answer."

Her brow rose. "You had to be in class."

He played a few chords running around his head, strumming gently. "So I'm not the villain anymore?"

"Oh, I'm still not happy with you, but I appreciate your reasons for pushing this class on me. And the results."

He nodded to the phone. "Go ahead and record."

"You're sure?"

"Positive."

She tapped the icon and they launched into the song one last time. When they finished, she pressed the stop button. A heavy silence blanketed the room.

Their eyes met. She leaned forward and when her sweet scent tugged him closer, he didn't fight the lure. His lips met hers and over the guitars, he kissed her. Softly, gently. Like the lyrics playing in his mind.

As the kiss grew deeper, Cassie abruptly pulled away. "You said we shouldn't."

He playfully bumped her shoulder with his. "You started it. Apparently you don't listen very well."

"I don't want—" She stopped speaking abruptly, rose and with stiff motions, placed her guitar in the case on the floor.

Clearly, something bothered her. "Don't want what, Cassie?"

She turned to face him, her brows angled in doubt. "This is all too much. Me volunteering here. You agreeing to help me, while battling all the unpleasant memories associated with music and your ex-wife." She ran a hand over her braid. "I guess what I'm saying is, I don't want to be a rebound for you."

"You think that's why I kissed you?"

"I don't know. You clearly haven't forgiven your ex."

Luke rose and carefully set his guitar on the seat beside him. Cupped his hands on Cassie's shoulders. "I would never treat you so cavalierly. I know how much it hurts."

She stepped back, putting distance between them. His hands fell to his sides.

"Then until you're sure how you feel about the past," she continued, "we should remain colleagues. I'll keep volunteering. You send me music students. Maybe we work on another song. But we stay professional. No more kissing."

"We already decided that and it's not working."

Cassie shut the case and flicked the chrome latches secure. "We work harder at keeping our word."

He shrugged off the letdown. "But kissing is a lot more fun."

She pointed a finger at him. "No charming me, Luke Hastings. Keep your word until you know what you want."

Letting out a heavy sigh, he lifted his guitar from the chair. "It won't be easy."

"If life were easy, we'd all be sitting on a beach drinking piña coladas. Unless you're lazy. Then you won't go anywhere."

"One of your mom's sayings?"

"Yes."

"Interesting view on life."

Cassie wrapped her hand around the handle and lifted the case. "I'll see you later."

He followed her as she left the room, his chest light even though she'd placed a moratorium on kissing. He'd have to get her to reconsider because the few kisses he'd experienced with her weren't enough.

Besides, in just the course of a conversation, she'd made him rethink his jaundiced view of his life. Made him face his ghosts and for the first time in two years, he was more than ready to exorcize them. There was no way he was letting her slip away, not when he wanted to learn so much more about her.

Once she'd crossed the gym and exited the building, he returned to his office. On his desk he found a store receipt.

Denny had asked for money to replenish the paints in the art room. Believing in the young man, Luke had given him cash and asked him to return the change. He read the sales total, then looked for the difference. No loose change on the desk. The good mood he'd enjoyed with Cassie evaporated.

CHAPTER NINE

EVERY TIME LUKE tried to grab a minute with Denny the next afternoon, either a group of kids surrounded him or Denny was busy with Klub projects. Luke was sort of relieved. He still had a hard time picturing Denny as a thief. While he'd rather be mulling over his time with Cassie, and where this attraction between them might land, he had a mystery to solve.

He'd called the police chief the night before, unsure on how to proceed given the circumstances. The chief urged him to file a report. He would, but first he wanted answers, starting with Denny. Maybe he'd just forgotten to leave the change.

When the young man finally emerged from the art room, Luke motioned Denny to come to the office. Denny trotted over, his long legs eating up the distance, securing his glasses as he went.

"You need me, Mr. H.?"

"I do."

When Luke closed the door behind them,

Denny's brow furrowed as he looked at Luke's face then the door.

"Is something up?"

Luke always knew Denny to be an intuitive kid. It didn't take much explaining to get him up to speed on a project or ways to draw attention to the programs at the Klub. He'd been all in from day one, which made Luke hate this situation all the more.

"I found the receipt on my desk last night for the art supplies you purchased."

"I got a great deal at the craft store." Denny's eyes danced with pride. "Probably saved us five bucks."

"I always appreciate a deal, but what about the change?"

"What about it?"

"There wasn't any."

"What are you talking about?" He pointed to the desktop. "I put it right there next to the receipt."

Luke shook his head.

"Mr. H., I swear it was on your desk when I left."

"Denny, sit down."

The teen's face went pale, but he did as Luke requested.

"Was anyone else with you?"

"Sure. Brandon and Kyle, but they were shooting hoops while I was in here."

"Anyone else see you guys?"

"Erin and her friends were hanging around outside, over by the picnic benches. It was late and most of the usual kids had gone home."

Luke personally knew the boys with Denny. He also knew Erin ran with a rough crowd, kids who stayed on the periphery of the Klub, never joining in.

"Mr. H., you're making me nervous."

The time had come to reveal the truth of the matter. "It seems we have a problem. Some money has gone missing from the Klub."

"What are you talking about?"

"Not only the change from last night, but the cash total didn't balance from the food we sold at the concert. Two hundred dollars is missing."

"Two… How would that much money go missing?" Denny asked.

"I'm asking you."

Denny blinked. "Why me?"

"You were in charge that night."

"I turned the money in. And you know I only run errands when you give me cash, like to the art store."

Luke nodded. "Normally I wouldn't need to check up, but this is serious."

Silence ticked for a beat.

"Wait. Are you accusing me?" Jumping up, Denny jabbed his glasses higher on his nose. "Mr. H., you know me. I'd never steal from the Klub."

"Then where is the missing change?"

"No idea." His voice rose. "I can't believe you think I'm guilty."

"I didn't say that."

"You didn't have to. I can read it on your face." He shot an accusatory glance at Luke. "After all I've done, you don't trust me?"

Luke leaned back in his chair.

Denny's reaction rang true. He was clueless about the missing money. Luke had dealt with enough teens to know when they told the truth or were obviously lying. The pain of Luke's accusation reflected in Denny's eyes. Luke had known the young man a long time and Denny's reaction was enough to back up Luke's next statement. "I do trust you. But you understand, I had to ask."

"Well, it stinks."

Luke hid a grudging smile. "It does. But I have a responsibility to the Klub, to the trustees and every kid who walks through those doors, to find out what's going on."

Denny sank down onto the chair. "Besides me, who else could be involved?"

Running a hand over the back of his neck, Luke frowned. "The missing money was only recently brought to my attention." He couldn't go into more details, but Denny's loyalty deserved the benefit of the doubt.

"So, now what? You watch everything I do?"

"For now I watch everyone's moves."

"Great." Denny rose, a scowl on his face. "I'm going home. See you later."

"Denny." Luke rose. "I'm sorry. You have to understand my position."

"I do. I know what the Klub means to you. I just never thought you'd throw me under the bus."

Before Luke could respond, Denny opened the door and bolted, nearly colliding with the mayor.

"Luke," she said, turning to watch Denny's escape. "Bad time?"

"No. C'mon in." He motioned her inside. "What can I do for you, Mayor?"

"I have a request."

This mayor skillfully rallied the troops before you realized you'd agreed to participate in her latest scheme. "Go ahead. Lay it on me."

Her good-natured laugh cut the tension of the last few minutes. "Since it helps the community, I'm hoping you'll agree."

Zoe Simmons had been mayor for less than

a year, but she'd put more energy into the job than anyone before her. Publicizing Cypress Pointe as a premier vacation destination was a key goal for her, along with the myriad of community projects she'd developed. An attractive woman with short dark hair, Luke appreciated her energy and knew if she came here personally, it had to be important.

"What do you have in mind?" he queried.

"I got a call from a local television news station, asking to do a special interest story about the different programs we support here in Cypress Pointe. The concert with Cassie Branford must have put us on their radar."

Luke hadn't thought much beyond the publicity the concert garnered beyond Kids' Klub. A by-product he should have considered.

"The Klub, especially the music program, has been such an integral part of the community I want to highlight both. Would you be interested in creating an original musical about Cypress Pointe? It'll be a different way to showcase all we do, rather than a stuffy old interview. This will be unique." She settled her purse on her lap before crossing her legs. "And I'd love you to pick out the kids to perform, if you agree, that is."

Had he heard her correctly? "Whoa. Wait a minute. Write the songs?"

"Hear me out." She slipped into her mayoral persona. "Luke, when you moved to town, you stepped away from the music business. Everyone respects your wishes not to revisit that time. But this is an opportunity we can't pass up. Who else do we know who can write original songs?"

Cassie came to mind, but she wasn't a resident any longer.

Zoe continued with her pitch like he hadn't just balked at her suggestion. "We can use this special interest opportunity to produce what I'm thinking of as a mini-commercial to spotlight the high school food bank, the clothing exchanges for new women in business and prom dresses for girls who can't afford one. And the Klub's success story gets billing along with the rest."

Success story? If only she knew. More like a memo to the individual stealing Klub money.

Luke's mind began to spin. "Slow down. You want to include all of it?"

"Why, yes." Zoe stared at him like she didn't get it. "We'll have a town picnic in the park and feature this musical for the local film crew. If all goes as planned, a larger network picks it up," she said, snapping her fingers, "and voilà, Cypress Pointe makes national news. In a good, come-spend-your-vacation-money-

to-support-our-programs kind of way. Not a
hey, we're-a-murder-capital, stay-away-from-
us, negative way."

Luke blinked. "You're serious."

She tilted her head. "Luke, you know I don't
fool around when it comes to our fair town."

Yeah, he knew. When Kids' Klub was early
in the planning phase, she'd wholeheartedly
been on board. Pushed it to her friends in local
government to make it happen, lobbied for a
seat as a trustee. As mayor, she took pride in
the time she'd invested in the Klub's success.
She'd loved the idea of Cassie's benefit concert and had helped to make it happen. How
could he tell her no? That he would never write
songs highlighting the programs she'd put her
heart and soul into.

"What's your time line?"

"Three weeks."

After closing his gaping mouth, he said,
"You're kidding me."

Zoe waved off his concern. "Look, you write
a few short ditties, the kids perform and we're
golden."

He picked up the pen on his desk and rap-
idly tapped it against the blotter. "Have you
ever written a song?"

"No, but I've written grant proposals and let
me tell you, those are time-consuming."

He nearly sputtered over her comparison between writing music and grants until he noticed the humor in her expression.

"Luke, I get that you don't snap your fingers and a song magically appears. Like I said, it doesn't have to be really long."

"I'm not sure what to say."

"Say you'll give it a whirl." She paused and by the twinkle in her eye, he knew he wasn't going to like what she said next. "Cassie Branford is in town. Recruit her to help."

"I can't bother her while she's home visiting her family."

"She's already volunteered her time for the Klub. Look at it as an extension of that."

Right. Ask an artist struggling with writer's block to team up with a man who has sworn never to write music again. Brilliant. Just brilliant.

"Can I think about it and get back to you?"

"Actually, no. I need an answer now."

He ran a hand through his hair. He hated creative deadlines. On the other hand, he could recruit help. Should he convince Cassie to join him? Add her talents to the mayor's request? Despite her star power, Cassie's gentle spirit drew him under her spell every time. So yeah, getting her on board would be a win-win all around.

"Some of the businesses in town already agreed to do whatever we need to make the best of this opportunity," the mayor continued, pulling him from his thoughts. "We really need you, Luke."

For a guy who'd originally come to town wanting to be left alone, he sure was in high demand.

"I'll see what I can come up with."

Zoe's wide smile took over her face. "I knew I could count on you."

He grudgingly shook his head. "You're good, you know that?"

Her grin turned cagy. "They don't pay me the big bucks for nothing."

"I didn't know you could do well financially in local politics."

"You can't, but I love this town so it evens out." She picked up her purse and stood. "I'll check in periodically. When I have a formal date and time for the filming, I'll let you know."

In high gear, Zoe left his office. Three weeks? Could he come up with something by then and teach the kids new music? Looked like he didn't have a choice. He grabbed his cell phone and hit his contacts, scrolling for Cassie's number. As the phone rang, he wondered how he'd go about asking her to help.

When her voice mail picked up, he blurted, "Cassie. It's Luke. Call me back. We have an emergency."

"How can you be so calm about this?" her mother asked, pointing a dirt-covered trowel at Cassie.

She'd arrived at her mom's house thirty minutes earlier, hoping for a little mothering and maybe an invitation to dinner. She'd found Dottie out back, wearing a wide-brimmed straw hat over her short blond hair. A long-sleeved shirt and capris protected her fair skin from the damaging rays of the sun as she tended to the colorful garden that encompassed the backyard.

"I didn't say I was calm. But I'm not as wigged out as I was."

"How do you lose the ability to write a song?" her mother asked.

"Nerves," Cassie answered from her seat on the suspended tree swing positioned nearby. She rocked back and forth, enjoying the lazy afternoon. Under the warm sun, her skin baked through the sleeveless, layered tank top and skinny jeans. Even her toes, exposed by her bejeweled platform sandals, tingled. She'd pulled her braid into a bun on top of her head, exposing her tender neck to the heat.

"Why didn't you say something sooner?"

"I was trying to deal with the block on my own. Then I got a crazy idea and didn't want to jinx it."

"Do I want to know?" her mother asked as she resumed her digging.

"When I saw Luke Hastings at Dad's wedding, I decided to ask him for advice."

Dottie's hand stilled, tool stuck in the soil. "Luke? I thought he was out of the music business?"

"He was. Is." Ever since he'd kissed her she'd been confused about the man. "But he agreed to give me pointers and last night we actually came up with something I could work with."

"So your talent is coming back?"

"Slowly. When I got back to Lauren's place I came up with another tune. Stayed up until early this morning working on it."

Her mother sat up straight, twisted to face Cassie. "Does Travis know?"

"I was hoping to get it under control so I didn't have to tell him."

"He won't be happy you kept him in the dark. He cares about you."

Cassie knew. But she also understood the demands of the industry. Travis might care about her, but he had a steady career on the upswing. "I still have time until I need to be in the studio."

"Time to create enough songs for a record?"

She tightly linked her hands together in her lap. "I guess I'll find out."

Her mother fell silent as she resumed her digging. Cassie closed her eyes, basking in the sunshine, savoring the sweet scent of her mother's blooming flowers. A bee buzzed by, busy seeking out nectar. Kind of like how she'd been searching for anything that would coax her muse back. Never in a million years had she expected her nectar to be Luke. As she swayed, her limbs grew heavy and after a long night expelling creative energy, her head lolled to the side as she started to doze off.

"So tell me, dear. Why are you really here?"

Cassie's eyes snapped open. Good grief. Was she really that transparent? Sure, she'd had another reason besides confiding in her mother about her writing problems. She just hadn't expected the woman to get to the next point so quickly.

"Can't I come by and visit my mom?"

"You're a busy, accomplished woman who usually calls if she wants to shoot the breeze. You only stop by when it's serious."

Pulling herself upright, she tried to decide

where to start and ended up blurting her real intentions. "Mom, have you forgiven Dad?"

Her mother had just picked up a small plastic pot containing a flower. At Cassie's question, the pot tumbled from her hands, soil scattering as it bounced on the ground. "You could have picked an easier question," she muttered as she scooped up the fragile blossom and started over.

"Sorry. You know how I get when I've been around him."

Dottie finished her task of planting the tender shoot before moving over toward Cassie. She removed her gloves and tossed them on the grass.

"You two have always been like oil and water."

"Seems to be worse as I've gotten older."

"I don't know about worse. Maybe you understand life a bit more now that you've matured."

"How do you mean?"

Dottie tipped her hat back. The beautiful face, with an ever-ready smile for her daughters, showed few wrinkles. She'd aged well, despite the tough years raising the girls alone. "As a child, you only remembered your father walking away. What I kept you from seeing were the times we argued. The ugly encounters between us." She shook her head. "We fought like cats and dogs.

"Your father and I were star-crossed from day one. I thought I loved him and, as I learned the hard way, he was merely in love with the idea of love. He never made a secret of the fact that his musical ambitions came first. I thought I could deal with it, and sadly, I couldn't. You picked up on my emotions. In the end, you and your sister suffered the most."

"Lauren is convinced he's changed."

"And you're not?"

"No."

Resting her hands on her knees, Dottie composed her features. "Does not believing he's changed keep you from forgiving him?"

"Yes. How could I ever trust him after what he did to us?"

"Trust and forgiveness are two different things. You can forgive, even if you don't ever trust him."

"What's the point? He has this unrealistic view of us as a family. I don't know if I can ever please him, or if I even want to."

"The point is, you forgive him so *you* can move on. Holding on to the bitterness of a situation that you have no control over is not healthy. Moving forward as the independent woman you've become will only make you stronger and show your father you're not easily swayed by what is important to him."

"He makes me…crazy."

"Family usually does." Dottie joined Cassie on the swing. "To answer your question, yes, I've forgiven your father. I'll admit, it took a long time, but when I finally realized we were both to blame, it took out some of the sting."

"But I'm not part of the problem. I was born into it. So why do I always feel like I'm lacking in his eyes?"

Her mother brushed a flyaway strand of Cassie's hair. Placed her soft hand against Cassie's cheek. "My dear, adults sometimes make the mistake of putting their issues above the needs of the children. You never did a thing to influence how your father and I felt about each other. I realize the disappointment from your youth colors the way you deal with your father, but you're an adult now. You can decide to keep him at arm's length or give him a chance."

"It's so hard," she whispered, blinking against hot, unbidden tears.

"The human heart has a great capacity to forgive and love. Can't you afford your father some grace?"

Cassie blinked away the moisture. She'd

been harboring her hurt and confusion for so long it had become a part of her.

"What if I forgive him and I still don't measure up?"

"Oh, Cassie. You're a wonderful woman. You decided to pursue your music all on your own. Look at the road you're on. I don't know how Robert could see otherwise."

Still, every time she was with her father she couldn't miss the cold air of disapproval. Could it be because of her attitude toward him? Could he be part of the reason she was blocked? The thought unsettled her but as she looked back, the timing fit. The album bombed. Dad wanted to insert himself into her life. The stress caused her to question herself, just like when she was a kid. It made sense.

"Thanks, Mom, for talking about this. I know the breakup was hard on you."

Her mother patted her hand. "In the beginning it was. But the three of us became stronger as a result. Lauren is good at her job. You've become a major success. And once I knew you girls were going to be just fine, I met the love of my life. So it all worked out."

Cassie's heart warmed at the mention of her stepfather. "Bud was after you for years, you know."

Dottie giggled. "He said the first time he delivered our mail he fell in love with me."

"How could he not? You are beautiful and kind."

"I'm happy to call him my husband." Oh, boy. Cassie recognized her mother's look. "I wish you girls would find good men to settle down with."

"Mom, women don't need men in their lives to be complete."

"Yes, but being with the man you love is fun. It's an adventure. A journey you never want to end."

An image of Luke flashed in her mind, one with him leaning against the doorframe, relaxed, a smile on his lips, his eyes hooded and mysterious as he looked at her. Is that what her mother was talking about? The chills and excitement she couldn't deny whenever she was with him?

"You should have written greeting cards for a living, Mom."

"I would have been good at it, too."

They both laughed.

As Dottie gathered her gloves and trowel and placed them in her basket, she said in an offhand way, "Lauren thinks you have a thing for Luke."

"Right to the point, Mom," Cassie sputtered.

"Both of my daughters are unmarried and in no hurry to walk down the aisle. I'm not getting any younger and I want to see you settled."

The swing shot out from under Cassie's legs as she got up. "What is it you used to say? You can't hurry love if your heart is unconscious?"

"Maybe not hurry, but I can push you two in the right direction, anyway."

Cassie laughed and kissed her mother's cheek. "Let's go inside for some tea. All this talking has made me thirsty."

"More like you want to change the subject."

Once indoors, Cassie picked up her phone from where she'd left it on the counter. Scrolling through her messages, she discovered a voice mail from Luke. Tapping his number, she listened. When she heard the word emergency, trepidation flooded her. Had something happened at the Klub? Was Luke okay?

"Mom, I'm going to take a rain check."

"Is everything all right?" Dottie asked as she washed her hands in the sink.

"I got a message from Luke. I need to go to the Klub."

The I-told-you-so expression Cassie hoped to avoid reflected in her mother's eyes. It didn't take a genius to figure out her mother's excitement over Cassie's concern for a man she didn't want to admit she was attracted to. And then Luke's words clicked. "We have an emergency." *We?* When had he begun to consider them a *we?* After the two kisses she'd lost sleep over? Him confiding in her about his past? Or was he strictly talking about the Klub?

Her mother broke into her rambling thoughts. "Hurry along, then."

Cassie waggled a finger at her mother. "Get that idea of me with Luke out of your head."

"A mother can dream," she declared with a theatric sigh.

So could Cassie, she silently admitted, struggling to imagine life without the hardheaded man in it. Independent woman or not.

CHAPTER TEN

OUT OF BREATH, Cassie raced into Luke's office. "What's the emergency?"

Luke looked up from his desk, tossing aside his pen as he advised, "Slow down."

She gulped in fresh air.

"Your message sounded urgent." She took a moment to glance around. "The building is still standing. No police cars with their lights flashing outside. So what's going on?"

Luke's face took on a sheepish look. "I'm sorry. It seemed like an emergency at the time, but since I called you, I've calmed down."

Cassie jammed her hands on her hips. "Enough suspense. Tell me!"

"The mayor stopped by. She's lined up a special interest TV news story featuring all the community projects in Cypress Pointe. She wants Kids' Klub involved."

She narrowed her eyes. "I rushed over in a panic all because of a TV piece?"

"She wants me to write original songs and

have the music students here play for the cameras."

Now she understood his initial panic. "I see. It's one thing to help me ease back into writing, but this? Makes it all too real."

"To me, it qualified as an emergency."

"I get it." She placed a palm over her racing heart. "Next time think before you scare the life out of me."

"Sorry."

She grinned. "Somehow I doubt you are."

He returned the grin, which turned her legs to jelly. "Then you won't be surprised if I ask you to join me in this writing endeavor."

"You want my help?" Surprise and pleasure flooded her.

"I asked, didn't I?"

Indeed he had. With that self-satisfied expression, she wondered if he wanted to work or maybe sneak more kisses. She wouldn't mind the latter, but she'd meant what she'd told him. He had to figure out where his head was concerning his ex-wife.

"Suppose I say no?"

"You'd do that to the kids?"

"No, Mr. Guilt Trip." She rolled her eyes. "I'll do it because I'm really connecting with them."

"Any plans later on?"

"I don't know. Suggestions?"

"How about coming by my place? I'll cook and we can discuss themes."

She ran the end of her braid through her fingers. "You just expect me to drop everything?" A lady had to play coy from time to time, didn't she?

"Oh, you're busy?" he played along.

"No, but you didn't know that."

"So you'll come over?"

She aimed for nonchalance, even as the prospect of spending time alone with Luke thrilled her. "I suppose I could eat."

"And share your brainpower. We've got three weeks."

She blinked. "Three weeks? Are you kidding?"

"Nope. You haven't met Zoe yet. If you had, you'd understand."

"Sure, I'll be by. Can I bring anything?"

"Your guitar."

"Got it."

"Oh, and one more thing. I invited some of the core group of kids over later on. Getting their input would be a good idea."

So much for any inkling of romance on the horizon.

"See you at my house in an hour?"

"I'll be there."

She turned, her mind already thinking about songs and kids and time alone with Luke, to find Mandy Rose hovering in the doorway. Her trouble radar immediately went off the charts.

"Oh, wow. I came by to talk to Luke but Cassie, you're here, too." Mandy's shark smile never quit. "Now I can interview you both."

Cassie recognized the urgent ambition in Mandy, the need for a current story, which she expected from the reporter. What she didn't like was the speculation as Mandy glanced between Cassie and Luke.

"Can I come in?"

Shouts echoed from the gym down the hall.

"I was just leaving," Cassie said, trying to brush away the guilt from Luke's imploring expression. If she left now, maybe they wouldn't end up a rumor in the paper. *Dear Readers, make up your own mind about Cassie and Luke. Are they a couple? Decide after I give you my theory on the tidbits they don't want to share.*

"Please, stay. I have questions about the television spot. Input from both of you would be amazing."

Mandy might be laying it on a bit thick, but she had a point. As much as she wanted to leave, Luke could probably use her assistance.

Without waiting for an answer, Mandy took

a seat, settling in comfortably. Luke scowled, a clear sign that Cassie needed to hang out so he didn't say something he'd regret. He'd been out of the tabloid's range for a few years now, which made him rusty and apt to say what was on his mind. She still dealt with the paparazzi on a regular basis and could deflect with the best of them.

Mandy pulled up her recorder app and set her phone on Luke's desk.

"The mayor filled me in on the upcoming special interest story. She mentioned you'd be coming up with new songs, Luke."

He sent her a bland smile. "The mayor has a way of recruiting the entire town in her special projects."

"So you'll be writing for the first time in years?"

"It looks that way."

"Any trepidations? After all, it's been a while since you had a hit."

Ouch. Even Cassie felt the sting of her remark.

"I'm hoping this will be a group project."

Mandy turned to Cassie. "You two are collaborating?"

"Like Luke said, it's a group project. Some of the Klub kids will be involved, too."

"Not really your style, Luke."

"The mayor wants the Klub represented, so…" He held up his hands as if to say, *ask all the questions you want, I'm sticking with minor details*. Cassie hid a small smile of respect.

"Do you have any ideas percolating in that musical mind of yours?" Mandy pressed.

He quirked a brow. "I just learned about this an hour ago."

Mandy cocked her head. "And?"

Cassie took the lead on this question. "Don't you usually take time to go over your notes and research before you file a story, Mandy? You know, to get your information straight?" She knew she shouldn't, but she enjoyed the slight frown the reporter couldn't hide over her question.

"Certainly."

"Songwriting is the same. We need time."

"We?"

"We, as in songwriters in general."

"So the two of you aren't working *together*?"

Cassie bit back a frustrated sigh. Did this woman want a story about the Klub or the possibility of her and Luke becoming an item?

A loud crash sounded in the gym, followed by a yell. Cassie scrambled aside when Luke jumped up and sprinted out the door.

"Goodness, what was that?" Mandy said as she stopped the recorder.

Cassie followed Luke and found the gym swarming with chaos. A boy sat on the floor, cradling his arm, with a metal basketball rack upended beside him. Balls bounced unhindered across the vast room. Luke squatted beside the boy, speaking quietly as loud conversation ricocheted around him. After a few moments, he assisted the boy to a door on the far side of the gym.

Mandy joined Cassie. "So much excitement."

"I suppose it's normal, given kids like to play hard."

Mandy arched a dark eyebrow. "I'm wondering if the same can be said of you and Luke."

Her gaze shot to the reporter. "I beg your pardon?"

"I find it hard to believe you're in Cypress Pointe, supposedly working on material for a new record, and you're spending time at Kids' Klub, which happens to be run by Luke. Are you sure there isn't any…after-hours collaborating going on?"

Her sly tone grated on Cassie's nerves.

"Mandy, I appreciate your need for a story, but I'm merely volunteering here. I talk to Luke to find out where he wants me plugged in. That's it. Nothing more."

"If you insist." She dropped her cell phone

into her oversized tote. "But whether you like it
or not, Cassie Branford in our town is a story."

"And despite your digging, there's nothing
to tell. I'm home, visiting family and helping
a worthy cause. End of story."

"We'll see."

At Mandy's parting words, a shiver of unease slithered down Cassie's spine.

AN HOUR LATER, Luke pulled into his driveway.
He'd already driven Todd to the emergency
room, where he met the boy's parents. Looked
like a broken arm, but X-rays would confirm
his suspicion. He'd left before the doctor diag-
nosed the patient, having discussed the situation with Todd's parents. Thankfully, the Klub
had insurance for incidents just like this. Even
so, he hated when any of the kids got hurt, especially since horsing around resulted in an
accident or two.

Hadn't he and his brother spent a few hours
in the ER when they were younger? Usually
after they were out causing trouble. It seemed
like eons ago, attesting to how far apart he and
Mark had drifted. Once, they'd stuck together
like glue, a dynamic duo joined together when
their parents couldn't be bothered. Now the
only time Luke saw his brother was when he
paid a visit to the jail, and then the strained

relationship left them at odds. At least Todd's parents were there for him. Luke and Mark could never say the same for their folks in any situation.

He'd just slammed his car door shut when a red convertible pulled into the driveway. Cassie, right on time. As she waved, the stress of the last hours washed away.

"How's Todd?" she asked as she exited the car, reaching into the backseat to remove her guitar case.

"Probably end up with a cast, but his folks were with him when I left."

Her sparkly sandals clacked against the brick pavers as she crossed the driveway. "I don't know how you do it. When I saw his pale face, my stomach turned over."

"Thankfully most accidents at the Klub aren't usually that severe. A cut or bruise on a good day."

"Are you sure you still want to do this? You must be exhausted after everything."

He'd been bone tired when he'd pulled up, but spending time with Cassie would definitely be the prescription the doctored ordered. He held up a to-go bag. "I've got dinner. Stay."

"I can't refuse after you went to the trouble to call in an order."

"This is the best I could pull off today. Hope you don't mind takeout."

"Not under the circumstances."

He nodded toward the house. "Let's go inside."

As they approached his custom-made home, he wondered what she thought. Just because he'd stepped away from the music industry didn't mean he hadn't been wise with his money. Growing up without much had made him watch every penny he'd ever earned. But did she think him pretentious? Showy? And why did it matter? He'd never considered another's opinion when he'd purchased the newly constructed house. He'd bought it for the semi-secluded location and proximity to the Gulf, never to impress.

After unlocking the glass-etched front door, they stepped into a sweeping foyer. The chill of the enclosed house greeted them. From here you could see into a great room and through the long bank of sliding doors overlooking the ocean vista.

"Impressive." Cassie closed the door behind them.

His exact thought the first time he'd walked through the doors. "It's home."

"You don't sound very happy about it."

"Don't get me wrong, it's nice, but it's also

just a place I rest my head. I'm hardly ever here."

They crossed the casual great room decorated in warm colors to complement the chocolate brown leather sofa and arm chair. Natural fiber baskets, light woven throw rugs and a sixty-inch television screen along one wall were the only added touches. He suddenly realized the great room could use a female touch.

Cassie beelined straight to the windows. "That's a shame. With that view, I'd be out on the deck all the time if I lived here."

Visions of her sunbathing during the day, camping out around the tabletop fire pit in the evening or whipping up a romantic dinner for just the two of them in his kitchen flitted through his mind, like her presence here would be a normal occurrence.

"Wow." Her voice shook him from his thoughts. "This has got to be the most spectacular view in Cypress Pointe. Beats my one-bedroom condo back in LA."

As he watched the rapt expression on her face, he silently agreed. When she turned to join him, he led her to the kitchen and set the takeout bag, with the escaping aroma of Italian herbs and spices, on the granite counter.

"Oh. My. Gosh." Cassie stopped at the entry

arch, eyes scrutinizing the room. "This kitchen is amazing."

When he'd moved in, he hadn't really considered the perks of a spacious and inviting kitchen. Stainless steel appliances contrasted with the dark wood floors. A roomy eating nook beside the windows complemented the cozy space. When he was home alone, the place only seemed to resonate emptiness. Not tonight.

Satisfaction welled as he watched Cassie carefully set her case on the floor before roaming the large, state-of-the-art kitchen. "Please tell me you moonlight as a professional chef."

"Unfortunately I eat at the Klub more than I do here."

"Now, that's a downright shame."

"You cook?" he asked as he removed two large containers from the bag, still warm after the trip home.

"Occasionally." She gravitated toward the floor-to-ceiling windows in the eating area. "I'm usually busy, but if I had a place like this, I'd learn real quick."

He pointed to a drawer at the end of the counter. "Mind getting us some silverware?"

"Sure."

"The plates are in the cabinet above."

While she went to work, he backtracked into

the great room, unlocked the doors and slid the entire bank to one side, leaving the view unhindered. The early evening air swept through the closed-up house, bringing with it an earthy scent, a testament of life outside the four walls. Two palms flanked the deck, long fronds rustling in the breeze. Tall oat plants hugged the structure, along with a splash of yellow beach buttercups scattered along the crushed shell and pebble path leading to the private beach. The Gulf waves lapped against the sugary-white sand not too far from the expansive wooden deck.

"How about we eat outside?" he suggested.

"You don't have to ask me twice."

After filling two goblets with ice and water, Luke carried the containers to a table easily able to seat eight located directly in the center of the deck. Cassie followed and before long they'd dished out a savory dinner of lasagna and chicken parmesan, with a side of crusty bread.

"I hope you like Italian. Fortuna's has the best in town."

"Smells awesome." She took a bite and sighed. "Tastes even better."

He paused as he lifted his fork, caught by her enamored expression. As he'd come to know her, he realized she lived every experience to the fullest. Unlike the rut he'd dug himself into.

"You're not eating," she observed.

He shook off his thoughts as the zesty pasta and tomato sauce slid over his tongue. He took a moment to enjoy the spicy sensation instead of eating just to get it done, like he normally would. Tonight was about taking things slow and appreciating every second.

"So, how long have you lived here?" Cassie asked between bites.

"A year now. I bought this place from a local builder."

She glanced around the tropical setting. "Teaching school must pay better than I imagined."

"No. Smart savings, despite signing over my biggest hit."

"Still kicking yourself?" she asked with a rueful expression.

"No, actually. I needed a clean break, so in the long run it worked out."

"I've only collaborated a time or two, so thankfully I never found myself needing to cash out of a song."

"It's kind of like cutting off your arm and willingly handing it to someone else."

"An arm? Really?" She chuckled. "It's crazy how protective we authors can be."

"Not the best analogy while we're eating."

"Not the best analogy anytime, but I get it."

They resumed their meal in silence. As the sun descended, the blue sky slowly transformed into a deeper purple, with streaks of orange and yellow dancing across the horizon. The muted hues cast a glimmering glow over Cassie as she looked out over the water, the subdued light highlighting her tanned skin, calling attention to the delicate bone structure of her cheeks, reflecting the sheer joy etched on her lovely face. Even the orange streak in her hair stood out. Unique, just like the woman taking his breath away.

A mighty kick of attraction seized him.

A hunger for the kind of life he'd always wished for growing up seemed possible as he stared at her. She had no idea the life she brought to an occasion, the contagious energy radiating from her, whether she commanded a crowd of fans or encouraged a group of teens to find their inner voice. Cassie was the real deal.

Did he dare pursue a relationship with her? Did he trust his instincts when it came to this woman? He'd been wrong before, not even thinking twice about getting involved with Tracy, and look where it had landed him. Sure, he was older. But wiser? The jury was still out on that decision.

When she faced him, he inhaled sharply. He wanted…so much more than he could put into words. Maybe with Cassie.

"Would it really be so bad?" she asked, pushing her plate away. "Writing again?"

"Other than the fact I swore I'd never go there?"

"Sometimes life has a way of changing your perspective."

"As I'm finding out." He took a sip of the cold water, his fingers coming away wet from the condensation on the glass. "Any more progress on the songwriting front?"

Her face lit up, excitement fueled by her passion. After his songwriting career ended, the Klub had become everything to him, but had he ever exuded that much enthusiasm? Yes, his mission for troubled kids went soul deep, but if he were honest, he'd admit a creative part of him was still buried deep inside. He'd thought he'd let it die when his marriage fell apart, but found that now he wanted to resurrect the spark, even against his own reservations.

"I started another song when I went home the other night," she went on to say. "The melody popped into my head on the drive home. I stopped on the side of the road to hum it into my phone recorder." She fell back against the seat cushion. "That hasn't happened in ages. When I started playing around with it, a story popped into my head, so I went with the vision."

It nipped at him that she hadn't included him in her newest burst of inspiration. Why, when he'd told everyone who would listen that he'd never write again?

"I'm still nervous about continuing on my own, even with the new burst of creativity."

"I remember those days. How a melody would grab hold and not let go until I'd played it out. Turned it into more than a flash of an idea clamoring inside."

"This songwriting opportunity. Think it'll wake up something inside you?"

His gaze traveled from the deck to the beach beyond. "I'm not really sure."

"Luke, you made a great impact with your lyrics and melodies. Your fans would love it if you treated us to your talent again."

Maybe that was the problem. He'd let it die too easily. He'd said he wouldn't try again, but maybe he was afraid it would be too *easy* to write again. Like he hadn't lost the artistic spark that fueled the original music artists wanted to record and listeners wanted to buy. Could that be the reason he was so willing to help Cassie shake up her abilities? To test his theory?

"I guess whatever we come up with for the mayor's special interest story will determine what the world gets from me in the future," he said.

"I admire you for agreeing. You didn't have to."

"No, but Zoe would have hounded me." He threw off his qualms. "Maybe it's time."

"To start again?"

He nodded.

"How about with me?" she asked, her voice small.

He froze. He'd thought about working with her. But the memory of their kisses stopped him. He'd been romantically involved with his last partner. He wasn't sure he wanted to travel that same path with Cassie. He wanted something different with her.

"Forget I mentioned it," she said, her actions jerky as she jumped up and began to clear the table. Dishes in hand, she scrambled past him until he stopped her by laying a hand on her arm. Their gazes met and he glimpsed the uncertainty there. He'd made her unsure of herself and hated it. He wanted the confident, joyous woman back.

He rose. With a slow motion, he lowered her

arm until the plates settled on the table. Easing closer, he slid both hands over her cheeks. His thumbs brushed her lips, catching the soft sigh escaping there. A gull cried out in the distance. The breeze stirred up the salty ocean air. Static moments stretched between them before he lowered his head, brushing his hungry lips over hers.

Home. Kissing her was like coming home. Something he hadn't allowed himself to dream about in a very long time. He'd shut that part of his yearnings away, thinking he'd never have another chance. That the Klub would be his only family. Until tonight. Until this woman.

The looming shadows surrounded them. He savored this stolen moment with Cassie, unsure if they'd share this special connection again.

As her arms circled his waist, his hands slipped into her hair. He slowly freed the neatly bound braid, silky strands running through his fingers. A hint of the berry scent he'd come to associate with Cassie escaped and mingled with the warm night. The kiss went deeper, turning his world upside down. His heart, so long still, beat in an erratic pace. All because Cassie walked into his life.

In the enormity of the situation, his hands trembled. Cassie, sensing a shift, broke the kiss and moved back, releasing him from her gentle embrace.

"What's happening?" she whispered, her eyes glittering in the last of the setting sun.

"I'm not entirely sure, but I like it."

She stepped back again, released an unsteady sigh. "I never intended this when I asked for your advice. I thought you'd kick-start my muse and we'd part ways. This thing between us is becoming rather...complicated."

"It doesn't have to be."

"Doesn't it? I have a career I hope to return to. You have a job and run the Klub. And you haven't told me if you've gotten over your ex yet, which is sort of a deal breaker between us."

He couldn't honestly admit he'd forgiven Tracy. But he didn't think about her nearly as much, nor did the driving anger that once claimed every aspect of his life continue its stranglehold on him. Now spending time with Cassie surpassed those old emotions, replacing them with an anticipation to see what he'd do with his life when the sun rose every morning.

She must have taken his silence as confirmation that he hadn't forgotten Tracy. Shaking her head, she crossed her arms over her chest. "Never mind. Let's just get to work and forget this conversation ever happened."

"No, I—"

His declaration died on his lips when the doorbell rang.

"That must be the kids." Cassie pulled her hair into a ponytail and secured it with the band he'd unconsciously tossed onto the table. "I'll clean up out here while you see them in."

He watched her gather up the plates and carry them to the kitchen. A sense of emptiness slammed him. When Cassie went back to LA, is this how he'd feel? Missing her each day? Wondering where she was and what she was doing? After Tracy decimated their marriage, he'd decided he'd never let a woman have that much power over him again. But in a short period of time, Cassie was proving to be an exception to that rule.

CHAPTER ELEVEN

THE NIGHT SKY sparkled with stars. Stars Erin loved to make wishes on, even when they didn't come true. Silly idea, really, but one she grasped with the hopes of a child.

"You're awfully quiet tonight," Erin said as she plopped down into a lawn chair next to Denny. After they'd worked for a while, he'd retreated to the far side of the deck, away from the rest of the group. "That's usually my thing."

"I've got some stuff on my mind."

She should have brought a jacket tonight, not because of the temperature, which was warm. More to hide behind. "I'm here if you want to talk about it."

"Right. Like you're always so chatty about stuff bothering you."

Score.

When Denny asked Erin to join the group going to Luke's house, she wasn't sure. Denny was always inviting her to come along to different activities. She usually held back, falling into the easy habit of hanging with Gary's crowd, even though she'd rather be with Denny. So tonight she'd given in, dressed up in a cute little dress and boots, let her long hair fall loosely around her shoulders, not that she wanted to impress him or anything, and tagged along. But boy, she missed the usually carefree Denny.

"I don't really care for Mr. Sad and Dark."

"Yeah, well, he's here tonight."

"You're kinda scaring me."

Denny blew out a breath. Pushed his glasses over his nose.

"Can't be that bad," she said, keeping her tone light.

"Mr. H. thinks I did something I didn't do."

"That narrows it down."

"I'm not kidding, Erin."

"Neither am I. What's going on?"

He went silent again. Gazed over at the other kids having fun with Mr. H. and Cassie. They should be with the group, drinking soda and chowing down on chips, but from the moment they'd arrived, Denny had been distant.

Here she'd been, all excited, spraying perfume before leaving the house, trying not to notice how good Denny looked tonight in a dark shirt and jeans. More and more she wanted to be with him, which was risky. Having one foot in Denny's world and the other with her semi-delinquent friends tugged at her lately, so when Denny called, she couldn't wait to get together. She hadn't expected this rotten mood, so unlike the guy who always tried to cheer her up.

Finally, Denny removed his glasses and rubbed his eyes. "Mr. H. thinks I stole money from the Klub."

For a second, she stopped breathing. Mr. H. suspected Denny? Oh, no, now what? How could she tell Denny it was her?

"You? No way."

"Some money went missing. I was in charge of it."

"What happened?"

He shifted in his chair to better face her. "Remember the food we sold at Cassie's concert?"

"Yeah."

"It didn't add up."

She tried to keep her tone even. "Oh, but why would Mr. H. blame you?"

"Looks like I lost some other change, too."

"How do you lose change?"

"No clue. I swear I put it on his desk but when he checked, it was gone."

"This is bad." And she knew bad from experience. Thinking of the stolen money, she wanted to throw up. She made excuses in her head, like her parents wouldn't give her an allowance or she had to prove herself to Gary. It was stupid and now came back to bite her.

"I've been trying to figure out who might have taken it," Denny said, his voice low so the others wouldn't hear. "But it's hard to believe it even happened." Defeat smothered the hope in his eyes.

"I, um, kinda know how it feels to disappoint an adult. I mean, you know, people you love." She pulled at a snag in her tights. "My parents don't really like me."

"That's crazy. How could anyone not like you?"

She tossed out a bitter laugh. "It's the truth."

He returned his glasses, tilted his head. "Why don't they like you?"

"I turned out like my sister."

"What did...? Wait, I remember. She got pregnant."

Embarrassment made her jaw tense.

"But you're not pregnant." His eyes went wide. "Are you?"

"No! It's just, she left and my parents take it out on me."

"Sometimes adults stink."

A surprised laugh escaped her. She glanced over at Mr. H. He and Cassie were strumming away at their guitars. Alan joined them while Kyle and Taylor came up with silly song ideas.

"Someone should tell Kyle he sounds like a cat who just got run over." Erin grimaced after Kyle broke out in a song.

When Denny didn't have a comeback, Erin knew things were bad.

"I bet Mr. H. really doesn't think you took the money," she told him quietly.

"How can you be sure?"

Battling her shyness with him, because really, why would he want her for a girlfriend? Her parents barely tolerated her. She spent time with kids who were not the best role models. Far from the kind of kids Denny was usually with. Face it, she was too much trouble.

Going for it, Erin reached over and linked Denny's fingers in hers. "Just like me, deep down he knows you could never steal."

Denny glanced down at their entwined hands and back again. Tightened the grip between them.

"So what do I do?"

"Prove him wrong."

"I can try." His forehead wrinkled as he thought. After a few moments, he glanced at her. "If you take your own advice."

What? How had he turned the topic around? "We aren't talking about me."

"Maybe we should."

She yanked her hand from his, embarrassed all over again. "Maybe you should just worry about yourself."

"Erin, I like you. I just… I want you to be okay."

She shook her hair. Let it fall over her face. "Leave it alone, Denny."

"I don't think I can."

Just what she was afraid of. Denny always meant what he said, always did the right thing. As much as she wanted him in her life, she didn't know whether to be happy or scared.

"TIME TO HEAD HOME," Cassie announced after they'd been working for over an hour.

"Everyone have a ride?" Luke asked.

They all responded, except Erin. She stood aside, her face closed off. Cassie shut her case and walked toward the girl.

"Need a ride home?"

"I don't want to bother you."

"I don't mind. It'll give us a chance to talk."

"Why would you want to talk to me?"

Because you're hurting, she wanted to say, but knew better. Teen Angst 101. "It'll be fun," she said instead.

"Um, okay."

Cassie didn't miss the longing glance Erin

sent Denny's way. What was up with those two? Normally Denny was right in the action, but tonight he'd been quiet. She'd noticed them in conversation, away from the other teens. Obviously upset about something. Possibly the missing money. Denny was too conscientious to let it go.

Belongings gathered, Cassie followed the group to the front of the house. As the kids walked to the cars, she stopped on the front step. Faced Luke. Her stomach dipped at his shuttered gaze. He'd initiated the kiss, but was he regretting it now?

She cleared her throat. "Thanks for dinner."

"I'm glad you came over. It put the kids at ease knowing you're involved."

An awkwardness stretched between them. There were so many things that needed to be said, but as Luke gazed at her, his dark eyes glittering in the porch light, her mind went blank. What was wrong with her? Why did this man always reduce her to bumbling? Spending more time with him hadn't made her more comfortable. Just the opposite. Ever since that first kiss she found herself waiting for the next one, even though he clearly hadn't gotten over his ex. She shook her head. *Get it together, Cassie.*

"So, um, call me when you set up the next meeting," she said, stepping away.

"I will. Cassie…"

She stopped. Looked up at him. "Yes?"

"This thing isn't over between us."

A shiver of anticipation swept over her. A glorious shift of emotion and excitement. He could reduce her to tangled knots in seconds flat. And because of that power, he could never know his effect on her until they came to terms with where this relationship was headed.

For tonight, she'd leave him hanging. Give him a taste of the turmoil sizzling in her. Wanting more, which, despite his words to the contrary, he wasn't ready to give. Right now she needed distance.

She nodded and strode away. Took in jerky breaths of air before joining Erin.

"Sweet ride," Erin said, admiring the convertible.

Cassie pulled her head into the present. "Thanks. I decided to splurge when I came to town. Rented the coolest car on the lot."

A look of disgust crossed the teen's face. "My mom drives a minivan."

"We can't all pull off this look," Cassie said, hiding her smile as she placed her case on the backseat.

"Yeah. My mother would have a stroke if she had to drive a convertible."

After the two buckled up, Cassie took off, following Erin's directions to her street address.

"So, what do you think about this whole musical idea?" Cassie asked as the wind blew through her hair. Tonight the humidity was minimal, cooling her flushed face as she tried not to dwell on Luke's parting words.

"It's okay," Erin called over the sound of the engine. "Usually I'm not in with the music crowd, but Denny asked me to come tonight."

"He must have thought you'd have something to share."

The teen shrugged. "I like choir, but mostly I sing in my bedroom."

Cassie turned on the radio, scanned the stations until she came across a popular song. "It's just the two of us. What do you say we belt this one out?"

Erin shot her a disbelieving look. "Are you serious?"

To verify her intentions, she started singing. Erin laughed, then joined in. By the time the last note faded, they'd harmonized like old friends.

"Erin, you have a beautiful voice."

Erin slid down in her seat. Twined her hair around a finger. "It's okay."

"Better than okay. Trust me, I know." As she issued the compliment, a thought hit her. "Why don't I ask Luke to let you sing at the filming?"

"Me?" She dropped her hand into her lap. "I don't know."

"It'll be fun."

"Aren't you going to lead?"

"No. This is about Cypress Pointe. I want Kids' Klub in the spotlight."

"I… I'll… Maybe."

Recognizing the girl's reluctance, Cassie reined in her excitement. "No pressure, okay? Let me know at the next meeting."

Cassie pulled up in front of Erin's house. No lights shone through the windows. No porch light greeted her. In the looming shadows of the tall oak trees, the house seemed deserted.

"Are your folks out?"

"No." Erin opened the door to quickly exit. Concern swamped Cassie when she noticed Erin wouldn't look her in the eyes.

"I bet they fell asleep and forgot to leave a light on. No biggy. There's a key around back."

Something was off here. As much as she wanted to pry, Erin effectively put up a barrier. "If you're sure."

"Yep. I gotta go. They're expecting me by now."

"Okay. If you need anything—"

"Nope. I don't." Erin jogged backward, sending an offhanded wave. "Thanks for the ride." She turned and took off across the grass, disappearing around to the back of the house. Cassie waited, motor idling, until a dim light appeared through one of the windows. She still couldn't shake the uneasiness, but finally put the car in gear and set course to Lauren's place.

Once she arrived, she noticed a strange car in the driveway. Lauren hadn't mentioned company. Of course, the two had only passed each other occasionally the past few days. Cassie hadn't been privy to her sister's calendar.

Grabbing her guitar case, she went inside, containing a groan when she found her sister entertaining her father and his new wife.

"Dad. Angelica." She set the case down and walked into the living room. Her father rose, giving her a quick peck on the cheek while Angelica wrapped her in a floral perfume embrace. "I didn't know you were going to be here."

"It was a last-minute thing," Lauren rushed to say. "I tried calling but your voice mail picked up."

"Sorry I missed your call."

"You've been a stranger since we got back

from our honeymoon," Angelica scolded as she resumed her seat on the sofa, smoothing the flowing skirt of her bright dress over her legs. Cassie nearly swooned over the designer shoes. Between her hair and makeup, the woman knew how to pull an outfit together.

"You know how it goes. Songs to write. Kids to mentor."

"How is the writing going?" her father asked. As usual he sported a button-down dress shirt and slacks with a crisp crease. She half expected a tie, even for a family visit.

"It's going." She noticed the teacups on the coffee table. "You know, a cup of tea would be great right now."

Lauren jumped up. "I'll get it."

Unsure how to proceed, she took a seat on the other side of the room from her father. His intense scrutiny made her uncomfortable. Was she in trouble for not visiting them? Or was he just in a mood?

"Where were you off to tonight?" Angelica asked conversationally. Bless her stepmother, she always missed the tension in the air.

"I was at Luke Hastings's house. Some of the kids from the Klub stopped by so we were hanging out."

Her father nodded in the direction of her guitar case. "I heard about the mayor's upcoming news story. Any chance you were working on original material?"

Great. Not a discussion she wanted, but knowing her father, it was inevitable. "Yes. The mayor gave Luke a brief idea of what she wanted covered so we sat down to try a few sounds."

"You should invite me to your next session. I'd be more than happy to lend my name to the process."

And there it was. Cassie glanced at her watch. Less than ten minutes for his pitch.

"I'm not in charge, Dad. I can't really say who gets invited."

"Then put a word in for me with Luke."

Talk about awkward. "I'll mention it but I can't promise anything."

Angelica took a sip from her cup and placed it back on the saucer. "I don't know why the mayor didn't ask you first, Robert. Teaming up with Cassandra would draw more attention to Cypress Pointe."

"I agree." His face grew animated. "I should make an appointment with her. Mention the possibility."

No. No. No. There would be no teaming up. "It's about the town, Dad. Not us. It's better if we stay on the sidelines."

Her father looked at her like she'd lost her

mind. "Cassandra, the mayor wants to draw attention to Cypress Pointe. We *are* the draw."

Good grief. Did he even listen to himself?

"You really have no—"

Lauren bustled into the room. "Here you go." She handed Cassie a cup and saucer.

"Thanks, sis." Cassie took a bracing sip, actually glad for her sister's interruption. The less said, the better, because the determined look on her father's face told her he wasn't going to stop until he secured a place in the mayor's news story.

"Dad, how would you have time, anyway?" she asked. "Don't you have a busy schedule?"

He shot his wife a quick glance before answering. "I have a concert scheduled next month. Since my time here is limited, I want to get involved with the project now."

"Do you still want us to come out to visit?" Lauren asked. "I would love to spend a few days in LA."

Their father stared at her for a second.

"You mentioned us all getting together in LA," she prompted.

"Yes. Of course. We should set up a date."

Had he forgotten the invitation already? Cassie hated the uncertainty in her sister's eyes, brought on by their father's carelessness.

"I can't make any promises. I'll be in the studio soon."

"And we'll be back at our place by then," he rushed to say. "I could stop by the studio. Lend a hand."

Okay, why was he pushing so hard? He'd been on a campaign since the wedding. "Dad, what's up? You seem awfully interested in what I'm doing. Don't you have enough appearances to preoccupy you?"

His shoulders tensed. "My schedule has some holes in it."

Finally. Truth time.

"So being with me helps you...what? Get attention? A foot in with the studio?"

"You make it sound like I'm only interested in the industry, not you girls."

"Suppose I can't help you? Are Lauren and I still welcome to visit?"

"Of course," Angelica interjected.

Cassie noticed her father remained silent. Deciding to forgive the man when she couldn't get a handle on his intentions was extremely difficult. His air of desperation made her suspicious, but for the sake of the family, she really needed to coexist with him until she could deal with his insistence on being part of her life.

She glanced at her sister. "Then I guess

you'd better book a flight. Looks like you're coming to California."

Lauren beamed. "We could plan some day trips. Go to the beach."

"And shop," Angelica added. "We must shop. I know the most darling boutique you girls will love."

"If I'm not working, I'll certainly make time." She glanced across the room. "How about you, Dad?"

"Hmm. Yes. We'll figure something out."

The distracted air returned, like the wheels in his mind were turning. She'd love to know what he was up to.

Angelica stood. "Since our future visit is decided, Robert, we should be heading home. Lauren has to work tomorrow and Cassandra has been busy since she came to town."

Lauren and Angelica gathered up the empty cups to carry into the kitchen, leaving Cassie alone with her father.

"Cassandra, I have a request."

She winced. "What is it?"

"Could you put me in touch with your manager?"

Surprised, she asked, "Why? You know Travis."

"I would like it done in a professional capacity."

Interesting. "Are you saying you want him to represent you?"

"Yes."

"I can put a word in, but I have no idea if Travis is taking on new artists."

"That's all I ask."

Cassie glanced to the kitchen. The women were still chatting about shopping, so she decided to wade in deeper in the conversation. "Dad, what's going on with you? Really."

His brows rose. "What makes you think anything is going on?"

"First, you've been after me to include you in whatever I'm doing since I got to town, and second, you want to talk to Travis. I thought you had a full schedule of concerts?"

"I don't like to admit this, but I have fewer and fewer dates booked. Ever since I took time off to write the movie score, the orchestras I work with have found other conductors."

Now she got it. "So what's your plan?"

"Find more movie opportunities. I enjoyed the creative energy of cinematic music."

"So why push to perform with me?"

His grin, when it crept across his lips, turned sheepish. "Exposure. I want to make sure the movie people know I'm around."

"And if that avenue doesn't pan out?"

"Then maybe you can give your father a job playing piano when you go on tour."

Yeah, that wasn't gonna happen. "Hopefully, it won't come to that."

"Because you don't want me around?"

Truthfully, yes, because Dad being around meant she'd have to face her feelings for the man. Instead, she answered, "I know how much you want to do movies so I'd like it to happen for you."

He smiled, genuine for once. "Thank you. We've been at odds for a long time. Maybe this gap in my schedule will give us time to reconnect."

Which implied they'd been connected to begin with, but she got the point. "You still have a name in music, Dad. I'm sure the right opportunity will open up for you."

"In the meantime, I meant what I said. I'd like to help you and the Klub."

"I'll talk to Luke."

"So we're okay?"

She nodded. "For now." She couldn't promise the future.

Angelica walked into the room, putting an arm around Cassie's shoulder. "I'm so happy to see you and your father getting along. He does miss you."

Cassie bit her tongue. She'd always remember how he'd left them, the hurt, anger and uncertainty, but maybe they could move into a new phase as a family.

Once their parents left, Lauren flitted off to the kitchen. Cassie followed, leaned against the wall and crossed her arms over her chest.

"So, you and Dad?" Lauren said as she placed the cups in the dishwasher.

"I'm trying, but I'm not making any promises."

"Why do you always doubt him?"

"Experience."

"He's changed."

"So you've said." She held up a hand when Lauren opened her mouth, ready to argue. "But we're talking."

"It's a start." She looked over her shoulder. "Are you really going to take them up on the offer to visit when you get back to LA?"

"Sure, but I'm staying at my own place." She raised a brow. "I'll leave my door open for you just in case."

"Why do you do this?" Lauren slammed her hands on her hips. "He said we're welcome."

Cassie shrugged. "I hope he means it, I do, Lauren. For your sake."

"I don't need your pity."

"That's not what I'm giving. I'm being cautious. For both of us."

"Dad loves us. He's making an effort. Can't you cut him some slack?"

"Actually, I have." She pushed from the wall. "I had a long talk with Mom. She urged me to forgive Dad, so I'm going to give it a shot."

Lauren ran over and threw her arms around Cassie. "Thank you."

"Whatever happens between us will take time."

Lauren pulled back, her hands still gripping Cassie's shoulders. "But it's a start. You've been so adamant about not wanting Dad in your life. Just you wait and see, things will be better."

Cassie hoped so.

"So, the special interest story?" Lauren asked as she returned to her task. "You and Luke?"

"Yes, we've teamed up. To write. Nothing more." Maybe if she kept saying those words she'd believe them.

"And your other problem?"

"He helped me break the block by asking me to teach a songwriting workshop at the Klub. I got some ideas from the kids and then Luke pushed me creatively, so we'll see."

"You can do it, Cassie. I know you can."

"Thanks."

Her sister's confidence in her ability meant

a lot to her, but it didn't write songs. She still needed to put in the hours.

Picking up her guitar case, she went to her room and closed the door. Lifted the guitar from the case. "Well, Ginger. It's just you and me."

Settling on the bed, she plucked a few chords. Closed her eyes. Recalled Luke's kiss. She picked up her pencil and scribbled into the open songbook.

Moonlit night, his arms around me,
Dreaming again, afraid it will end.
He's captured my heart,
there's no running away,
When I wake up in the morning,
I hope he says he'll stay.

Yep, that kiss was tattooed on her memory. And since she couldn't shake it, went with the flow. She'd learned a long time ago to trust her instincts and this was one of those instances. She may have more questions than answers about her future with Luke, but it certainly made for a good song.

Three down. A dozen more to go.

CHAPTER TWELVE

THE NEXT MORNING Cassie sat in Cuppa Joe, sipping the most awesome coffee she'd had in weeks. Chatter abounded as locals caught up on daily events. The air was pungent with both the scent of Columbian beans and sugary-sweet treats.

How long had it been since she'd stopped and listened to people around her? Been curious about town happenings? Been involved? Probably not since she'd left Cypress Pointe. Her rise in the music world had been her main focus for years and once she reached the goal of signing with a label, recording and touring became the be all and end-all of her life. Sitting here among neighbors and friends who knew and obviously liked each other, she discovered she was... lonely.

Most of the time she was surrounded by all sorts of people, except the ones who mattered most. She lived on the far side of the country, away from her family. How she missed spending time with her sister, even if they playfully bickered over some nonsense. Or dropping in on her mother just like the other day to glean her wisdom and love. Was it possible to be homesick but too busy to realize it?

Wow. The revelation shook her. While her career was important, she'd sacrificed much to attain her goal. And if she didn't come up with new material soon, all she'd worked for could be gone with the snap of a finger. Then what would she do?

Suddenly her pleasant outing turned somber.

She'd been awake until the wee hours of the morning, putting the final touches on the new song. Only once before had she written a song she knew was destined to be a hit, and the Kiss song, as she'd come to think of it thanks to Luke, gave her the same vibe. Excitement finally started to well in her, but she wasn't ready for the studio.

After another bracing swallow, she picked up her phone. Time to check in with Travis. He'd left her a few messages, but she'd been putting off returning his calls. Between the slow success of actually creating a number of songs, and her father's request to talk to her manager on his behalf, she needed to bite the bullet and touch base.

After dialing the number, Travis picked up. "Hey. How's my favorite gal?"

"I'm fairly certain you say that to all your female artists."

"I'm an equal-opportunity manager. I love you all."

She chuckled. "Yes, you do. So that's why I'm checking in."

"Listen, Cassie, you've got me worried. Why haven't you been in touch?"

She bit her lower lip. "I haven't been completely up front with you."

A pause. "I don't like the sound of that."

"It's nothing earth-shattering. At least not now."

"Just tell me."

Here goes. "When I came to Cypress Pointe, I told you I was going to work on new material. Problem is, I've been suffering from a bout of writer's block."

"How bad?"

Cassie smiled. How like Travis to get right to the bottom line.

"Bad enough that I only have three songs so far."

She heard his breath exhaled over the airwaves. "Why didn't you say something?"

"Because I was worried enough as it is. Talking about it makes it real, which in turn makes me more nervous."

"We have to get you some help."

"Already taken care of."

"How?"

"I ran into a songwriter at my father's wedding. We've been working together on my problem."

"Would this songwriter be Luke Hastings?"

"How do you know?" she sputtered.

"Honey, I have my finger on the pulse of the music industry. When a major talent like Hastings disappears, I still keep tabs."

"Now I just feel silly."

"No, you made a good call. Enlisting Luke will get hits on this new record. So, you've made strides?"

"Some."

"You know, writing a song with him will really boost your creds. He's an icon and collaborating will make the label very happy."

"I'm not certain he wants any credit."

"Cassie, I don't have to stress the importance of this next record being a hit."

No, he didn't. She thought about it every second of every day.

The bell above the door tinkled as new customers walked in. A tall, dark-haired man walked by with his arm around a snappily dressed woman with reddish hair. She was just about to look away when she noticed the third person in the trio. Luke. She shifted away.

"Cassie, what's wrong? You blanked out there."

"Sorry. I'm in a busy coffee shop."

"Back to business. What's your plan?"

"To keep coming up with songs."

"You only have a few weeks."

"Please, don't remind me."

"Then I'm gonna say it again—get Hastings on board. The label will be thrilled."

She glanced at Luke who stood in the order line, chatting up the couple. What would he say to her manager's idea of collaborating? Did she dare ask?

Lowering her voice, she said, "Travis, you can't say anything about Luke. No one is to know we're working together."

"You gotta be kidding. This is big news."

"I'm not going to blow this chance by spooking Luke. If you say anything, how long will it be before the tabloids get wind? I can guarantee he won't talk to me afterward. Then my plan goes up in smoke."

"I understand. Just promise you'll keep me in the loop. If you're still having trouble, call me. We'll figure something out. Together."

"You know, for a guy who plays favorites, you're okay."

"Buttering me up, are you?"

"Of course."

His chuckle assured her he was on board, even if grudgingly. Now she had to launch into the next part of the conversation.

"While I still have you on the line, I have a request."

"Hit me."

"Since my father's wedding, he's been making overtures to connect himself professionally with me. I wondered what the big hurry was and finally got to the truth last night. He wants to do another movie score and asked if I would talk to you about maybe representing him."

The long silence made Cassie nervous.

"I'm gonna be up front with you, Cassie. No one wants to work with Robert."

Despite her strained relationship with her father, Travis's words shocked her.

"Why not?"

"He has a reputation for being difficult. Likes to run people over to get what he wants."

"I had no idea. I mean, I know what he's like when he wants something, but others in the industry are aware of it? Sounds pretty serious."

"I'm afraid so. As much as I'd do anything to help you, in this case, I'll have to pass."

She tugged at her side braid. Her father was not going to be happy with this news. And he'd likely blame her. "Thanks for hearing me out, Travis."

"Cassie, there's more."

Oh, no.

"He's been casually dropping hints that the two of you are a package deal. I've had a few calls on the subject. Assured certain people that's not the case."

"Why didn't you tell me?"

"I know how…difficult your relationship is with Robert. I just handled it for you."

How like Travis. To look out for her welfare, unlike her very own father.

"I'm… I don't know what to say."

"Say you'll keep writing. Keep your father away from your career. Make me and the label proud. You need a hit, Cassie."

No pressure, right?

The daunting task of making so many people happy made her stomach revolt. The coffee she'd enjoyed moments earlier now burned, leaving a sour taste in her mouth. She said a hasty goodbye to Travis and gathered her things. Before escaping, she chanced one last look at Luke. To her surprise he was already watching her, his brows angled over his eyes. Their gazes met, held, and a jittery warmth crept over her. Time to go.

Once on the sidewalk, she panicked, unsure of which direction to run. Desperate, she caught sight of the town gazebo in the distance.

She stumbled in that direction, gulping fresh air as she went.

At the park, she ran up the steps of the gazebo, dropped her belongings and plopped down on the bench. Lowered her head between her knees. *Breathe. You can do this.*

But could she?

Travis's words weren't meant as a threat, but his intent was clear. Perform or the label drops you. Maybe even Travis, too, if things went sideways. If she didn't get inspiration soon, she might be back to booking gigs in local clubs. While she'd loved it on her way up, she didn't have the enthusiasm for that life. She wanted stability, which was not a cohesive concept in the creative world. One day you were on top, another no one remembered your name. That was why she needed the next record to be a hit, or her short-lived success might crumble.

And what about her father? He lived for his career. This news would be devastating to him, but worse was his underhanded way of grasping her coattails. So he'd developed a negative reputation in the business. How was it her problem?

"Cassie. Are you okay?"

Her head jerked up. Silhouetted by the bright sun behind him, Luke stood in the entryway, his broad shoulders filling the space.

"You took off from Cuppa Joe's like you'd gotten bad news."

She tried to speak, but found her throat blocked. Tears swamped her. How she hated this loss of control, especially in front of Luke.

When she didn't answer, his shoes thumped over the wooden floor as he crossed to sit beside her.

"Cassie?"

She held up a hand. Mentally got her act together. Luke didn't need to be privy to her problems. She hated being so needy and vulnerable around the man she'd only wanted to impress. The man she was so easily falling for. The man who couldn't let go of his past.

"It's nothing." She strove for a wobbly smile. "I was talking to my manager. Going over career logistics. You know the drill."

His steady gaze revealed he wasn't convinced by her answer. "You seem pretty rattled."

"I'm counting the days until I go back to the studio, Luke. So yeah, I'm a bit off."

"Nothing new has come to you?"

Yeah, lyrics about his kisses. Like she was going to admit the truth. "I came up with another song last night."

"You still need more."

Yes. She did. Staring over the pristine beach

adjacent to the park, with the sugary sand glistening and the clear blue water meeting the horizon, she breathed a silent prayer. "Yeah. You'd think with this beautiful view, how could I not come up with a winner?"

In reality, she needed to sit here. Soak in her surroundings. Children scampering about and laughing, parents watching their children with eagle eyes as they played in the surf. Bodies lined up to bathe in the sun, spreading coconut-scented lotion on pale skin. Boys throwing a Frisbee in the ankle-deep water while girls walked by, whispering about those same boys.

It may have been years since she was a teen, but she recognized it all. Running with every bit of inspiration the beach scene offered her, she dug her songbook from her bag. Scribbled her observations.

"Let me guess. You got an idea?"

"I don't know why I didn't come here sooner. I love the beach. I always loved lying back, dozing off after a late night by the town bonfire, my sunglasses on so no one knew I was asleep."

They looked at each other. Said simultaneously, "Sleeping in Sunglasses."

Cassie held up her hand for a high five. "Cool name for a song."

Chuckling, Luke slapped her hand with his.

He lingered, the rough calluses on his fingers from playing the guitar brushing over her tender skin. Their gazes met. Held. To her dismay, the heavy longing weighing her heart for this man overwhelmed her and soon, they both dropped their hands.

Luke settled back against the bench. When he spoke, his voice was thick. "Just let it flow, Cassie. Naturally. You know you can't force it."

She peeked at him, then grinned.

"My inspiration could be you, you know. You show up and…" she said and snapped her fingers in the air. "I get an idea."

"That's a nice compliment, but it's all you."

"Tell that to my manager."

"He's breathing down your back?"

"No. Concerned, naturally, but always supportive." When he wasn't piling on the pressure of her commitments.

"Write down your impressions. If you want, we could go over them later."

"I don't want to bother you."

"Actually, it would kind of be a trade-off."

"How?"

"The band is playing a wedding Saturday night. Ryan's baby is sick and his wife is stressed, so he cancelled. I was going to ask if you'd fill in for him."

"I'd love to."

"Great. There's no pressure, but you should also know it's an audition, too. The couple I was with in Cuppa Joe? They're getting married in a few months and will be at this reception. They haven't booked music for their event yet, so we have to make a good impression or they're going with a DJ." He shivered in mock disgust.

"Are you going with the standards?"

"We usually do."

"Then I shouldn't have any problem following you."

He placed his hands on his knees, pushing off as he stood. "The reception starts at seven."

"Wait." She looked up. "Before you go, I have a question."

He nodded.

"Have you heard Erin sing?"

"Not solo. But I have heard her harmonize with a group."

"I was thinking, what if we get her to lead the song for the news story? It'll include her in something important, maybe give her some confidence."

Luke lowered himself back to the bench. "I like the idea, but Cassie, I have to warn you, getting close to Erin might not bring the outcome you expect."

"She's obviously struggling. It probably has to do with her home life."

"No doubt. But until she's willing to sit down and talk to one of the counselors the Klub keeps on staff, I wouldn't delve too deeply into her problems."

"All I want to do is show her I care."

"Which you should. Anything beyond that, you're treading on thin ice."

"Then why have volunteers at the Klub?"

"To steer the kids to professional advice."

Made sense. But Erin had touched a kindred spirit inside her. Cassie only wanted the best for the teen. "I get it, Luke. I won't play counselor, but I will continue to involve her."

"Then ask her to sing. The others will be on board and maybe it'll be the tipping point to get her to open up." He stood again. "Do you want me to pick you up Saturday?"

"Sure. It's a date." Which it wasn't, but she liked the sound of it.

"It's a date." His eyes grew smoky for a moment, then he pivoted on his heel and walked back to Main Street.

Cassie watched him go, admiring the sway of his shoulders, his confident stride. Oh, she might as well admit it. She had it bad for Luke Hastings.

With a sigh, she turned to the beach scene.

A sort of peace came over her and she spent the next couple hours playing around with lyrics and melodies. Maybe she'd have a complete song list before she boarded the jet back to LA.

"So, HOW DID you feel about the first set?" Luke asked Cassie as she stepped from behind the keyboard. Tonight she'd dressed in sleek black leather pants and a black tunic that screamed pop star. A spunky smile curved her lips, a welcome sight after the uptight expression he'd witnessed a few days earlier.

"The bride and groom look happy, so there's your answer," she said as she adjusted her chunky necklace.

The young couple, Bart and Jewel, danced to the entire set. The crowd, rowdy and upbeat, lifted the energy level on the outside patio of the Grand Cypress Hotel. The night, just now turning an inky black, tinged with sparkling stars, was still young, with plenty of dancing in store for the guests.

He shouldn't have been surprised when Cassie harmonized with him like they'd been singing together forever. He'd noticed their ease initially at the Klub concert, when they'd naturally combined their voices. She exuded talent, no doubt about it, but when they sang together, his admiration for her went deeper.

A time or two he'd looked over and their gazes met and held, banding his chest tight. He'd had to look away to concentrate on the words of the song he was singing. Yeah, Cassie had that much of an effect on him.

Sonny and Brian had jumped off the make-shift stage as soon as the last song ended, leaving him alone with Cassie. Well, alone as anyone could be at a reception full of people. If he were smart he'd join his buddies, but the lure of Cassie kept him in place. Her playful expression tied him up in knots because, let's face it, he couldn't deny his feelings any longer. He could make excuses all he wanted, but the truth stood before him, her hair in her usual braid, a mean green streak threaded through the twist, a smile on her lips and a twinkle in her eye. All he wanted was to run off with her. Write songs together. Sit on the back deck at his house and spend time getting to know every detail about her.

The truth had slowly snuck up on him. He'd spent too much time over the past two years trying to justify his anger at Tracy. Cassie's presence in his life had actually been the cata-lyst to let it all go. Life was changing and he'd yet to catch up, but tonight was different. To-night he needed to let Cassie know how he felt.

Yes, he'd intentionally kept her hanging

when she'd asked about where he stood with his ex-wife. At the time, he hadn't wanted to discuss Tracy or the past. But the bleak expression in Cassie's eyes told him he had to make a choice. And fast. Otherwise she'd leave town and he might lose her.

Asking her to play with the band hadn't only been about filling Ryan's place. He hoped to have a conversation later that might change both their lives.

A shout of laughter yanked him from his thoughts. He wasn't sure how the night would end, but right now he should focus on the job at hand. "I was wondering if you wanted to add one of your songs to the next set."

"Uh, I'm flattered, but Luke, this is your band. I'm just the help tonight."

"Hardly. Look, everyone here knows who you are. Might as well throw in an extra number. Who else can say Cassie Branford played at their wedding reception?"

"I'd be honored… If you don't mind."

"I wouldn't have asked if I did."

"True." She bit her lower lip before saying, "How about throwing in one of your songs?"

That old familiar panic tightened his throat. "We don't usually do my music."

"So tonight we mix things up. Give the newlyweds a treat."

His one rule, no music from his past, seemed foolish. Tonight was about new beginnings. Why not give it a go? "Any suggestions?"

"'Won't You Love Me Always.'"

"Wow. That was fast."

She grinned, very unrepentantly. "I've always loved that song. Singing it with you would be a dream come true."

Or a disaster. That had been the first song he and Tracy had written together. Their first hit, launching their career. But if he wanted to let the past go, that meant moving beyond the memories. The songs he'd written with Tracy would never go away, but the heaviness accompanying each one had lessened. Maybe singing this particular song with Cassie was just what he needed to completely wipe away regrets. After all, the beginning of his career hadn't been all bad.

"We'll trade off. One of your songs and one of mine," she said with that cocky smile that always took his breath away.

"Deal."

"I'll let the guys know." She turned to walk to the steps at the end of the platform when Luke called out to her.

"Wait."

She turned back. "Something wrong?"

"No. I wanted to thank you."

When she tilted her head, he looked away. "No need. Playing tonight has been lots of fun."

"Not for filling in. For the past few weeks. Getting to know you. Seeing you with the kids."

An attractive blush swept over her fair skin.

"And I owe you."

Her questioning brow rose.

"I never answered your question about my ex. I'll admit, I hadn't meant to forgive her any time soon, but being with you has made me rethink many things in my life."

Her expression softened. "Are you saying there's a chance we can build on this attraction?"

"I'd like to."

Her grin started slowly, blossoming into a full-fledged smile as her eyes lit up. "I'd like to, as well."

Nerves hit him like when he was a teenager, asking a girl out on a first date. "Okay, then."

"So, where do we start?"

He leaned down and spoke into her ear, his breath sending a cascade of shivers over her skin. "I'd like to start by kissing you, but I noticed Mandy Rose lurking around. I don't want this new relationship becoming fodder for the tabloids, especially before we figure it out. Been featured in those rags enough."

She smiled at their secret. "I understand. And as much as I second kissing you, there are some things that should stay private for now."

"And we need to get ready for the next set."

As the band members returned, Sonny brandishing a napkin with a woman's phone number on it, Luke told them about the change in the lineup.

"Dude, are you sure?" Brian asked, shock in his voice.

"We never do your songs," Sonny chimed on the tail of Brian's question.

He sent Cassie a covert look. "Maybe it's time for a change."

The band mates exchanged confused glances. Brian shrugged it off. "Whatever you want, man."

Sonny settled behind the drums, a happy grin on his face. "You do know that song is a real chick magnet. Thanks, buddy."

Luke chuckled. Leave it to his friends to make light of this major decision.

Before long they launched into the music. The dance floor filled. When Cassie played her song, the guests hooped and hollered. *This is good*, he thought. Maybe the reaction of the guests would help her to loosen up. Inspire new songs.

When they started "Won't You Love Me Always," surprised gasps flitted across the patio. But soon, the outdoor lights faded and couples took to the floor, embracing as the romantic lyrics promising a lasting love drew them together.

He met Cassie's gaze. Her eyes shone with tears, but she smiled reassuringly. And his stomach took a nose dive. He couldn't fight it any longer. Their connection was strong and after tonight, he owed it to both of them to truly see what might come of their future.

To counter the mood after his hit, they played a rowdy song before taking a break. The noise level continued as the guests mingled and the bride and groom made a spectacle of cutting the cake.

"I need more water," Cassie said as she held up an empty bottle.

"Let's go to the bar."

He took her elbow and escorted her from the stage. The natural way they moved together, like a long established couple, didn't skip his attention. Weaving through the crowd, they spoke to guests before reaching their destination.

While Cassie asked for water, someone from behind slapped him on his shoulder. He turned to find his cousin Dane beside him, his girlfriend, Nealy, on his arm.

"Great set. You guys sound good up there."

"Cassie joined, so that explains it all."

"I don't believe so," Dane said, his expression serious. He knew the history behind Luke's song.

"Excuse me," Nealy said as she placed a kiss on Dane's cheek and went to chat with Cassie.

Luke recognized the pensiveness on his cousin's face. "Okay. Let me have it."

"You look happier than I've seen you in a long time." Dane stated the fact Luke had finally come to terms with.

"It's Cassie."

"Is she behind you finally acknowledging one of your hits?"

"Yes."

"And how do you feel about that?"

"Like you're a shrink making me examine my inner emotions."

Dane chuckled. "And if I were, what would you tell me?"

Luke unscrewed the top of the water bottle Cassie had passed to him. "Do you remember a few weeks ago when I told you I'd try dating again? Thought maybe Cassie might be a good distraction from the past? Somehow it's turned into more."

"I'm not surprised. You just hadn't found the

right woman to make you see there is more to life than wallowing in what you can't change."

"I initially thought Cassie might be the catalyst to get me out of the rut I'd dug myself into, but..." He paused, lifted his shoulders in a shrug. "This sorta crept up on me."

"Embrace it."

"Am I rushing this? What if things get turned around and I end up hurting her?"

"And what if Cassie turns out to be the love of your life? She's not anything like Tracy and it's pretty clear she's interested in you."

He glanced over at Cassie engaged in animated conversation with Nealy. "It appears that way."

"Then stop worrying. What will be will be."

"When did you become so enlightened?"

"When my soul mate came back into my life."

"I'm happy for you, Dane. I know you'd never gotten over Nealy."

"The years apart were probably good. We needed time to mature and now we're solid." Dane elbowed Luke. When he looked down, Dane partially pulled a blue velvet box from his jacket pocket. Luke's gaze flew back to his cousin.

"You're going to pop the question?"

"Tonight."

Luke slapped him on the back. "It's about time."

"I expect those will be Nealy's exact words."

Dane dropped the box into his pocket just as the women joined them.

"I was telling Cassie how excited Jewel was when she found out Cassie was singing with the band," Nealy said.

A happy glow surrounded Cassie. "It's only temporary, but it's been fun."

Another couple approached the group.

"Way to go, Hastings." Max Sanders, and his fiancée, Lilli, grinned at him. "Convincing Cassie to play with you tonight sealed the deal. We pick you for our wedding band."

"You know you were always gonna choose Sandy Palms."

"Yeah, but making you sweat was fun to watch."

Lilli playfully slapped Max's arm. "You guys, always getting the better of each other."

The males in the group exchanged satisfied glances.

"I'm happy this is our final decision," Lilli sighed. "I feel like we've been planning this wedding forever."

"Couldn't convince her to run off to the courthouse?" Dane asked his friend.

"Tried." Max beamed at Lilli. "But she

wants the whole shebang." His loving expression said she was worth the wait.

"So, you'll all be there to witness our special day," Lilli said. "And Cassie, you're more than welcome to come."

Cassie's brows rose over surprised green eyes. "Thank you. I'll have to check my schedule, but I'd love to."

"Then it's settled," Lilli announced.

"We need to get back onstage," Luke interjected. Standing here, talking to his friends and the women they loved made him hopeful that he and Cassie might join the happy group as a couple one day.

Once again he led Cassie across the room, this time reveling in his decision to move things forward with her, instead of coming up with every problem he could think of to discourage their budding relationship.

"It was nice of Lilli to invite me to the wedding, especially since we just met."

"That's what I love about Cypress Pointe. The people here treat you like long, lost friends."

They passed the bottleneck crowd hovering near the stage. Cassie spoke over the loud cacophony surrounding them.

"I may be in the studio," she said, moving closer to speak into his ear.

"And if you aren't, would you agree to be my date?"

Cassie stopped. Her smile beamed. "Yes."

Soon the band was back in place. As Luke pulled the guitar strap over his head to settle the instrument on his chest, he scanned the crowd. His friends, people who had accepted the broken man who first came to town, smiled at him. The same folks who rallied around Kids' Klub when he took steps to turn his dream into reality. His joy dropped momentarily when he glimpsed Mandy Rose off to the side, an enigmatic smile on her face, but he turned away and stamped out the four-beat intro to the next song. For now, he was going to stay in the moment.

Two hours later, the band packed up. The bride and groom left on a sea of well-wishes as they hurried off to their honeymoon destination. After that, guests slowly headed home for the night. Luke and Cassie stepped from the hotel into the fragrant spring night, strolling toward the parking lot. The sense of contentment that had escaped Luke for far too long wrapped them in a soft blanket. When they stopped by his car, he snapped a fuchsia hibiscus blossom from a nearby bush and slipped it into Cassie's hair.

"Quite the romantic, aren't you?"

"I'll admit, I'm a bit rusty."

"I'd never have noticed."

"And we both know you're sweet to say so."

Cassie laid her hand on his chest. "Thank you for singing 'Won't You Love Me Always.' You have no idea how much it means to me."

"If it makes you happy." Luke tilted her chin with his knuckle. Feasted on her lovely face for long seconds before leaning in for a much-needed kiss.

Cassie wrapped her arms around his waist as his lips brushed hers. The decision to tell Cassie how he felt, to trust her, almost overwhelmed him. When he pulled back and saw what he hoped was love shining in her eyes, words escaped him.

Unable to keep from kissing her again, he bent his head. In the quiet night, his cell phone blared from his pocket. He groaned and rested his forehead against hers.

"Welcome to my life. Always one emergency or another."

Cassie gently pushed him away. "You should answer. What if it's one of the kids?"

Yanking the offending device from his pocket, he quickly sobered when he read the incoming number. "It's the police station."

CHAPTER THIRTEEN

WHEN THEY RUSHED into the brightly lit, over-crowded station, the first face Cassie recognized was Kyle's. He and the police chief were battling in a heated conversation, until the teen noticed Luke.

"Mr. H., you came."

"What's going on?"

"Seems Mr. Snyder here forgot our last conversation," the chief growled.

Chaos reigned as parents and youngsters she didn't recognize spoke over each other to get to the root of the problem. Cassie gathered there had been a shoplifting incident. Did Luke deal with this sort of thing often?

As she listened closely in order to collect more information, a few of the people directly in front of her shifted and she caught sight of Erin sitting alone on a bench on the other side of the lobby. The teenager stared at her boot-shod feet, arms tightly crossed over a green-and-white-striped dress, while the other kids explained their sides of the story. Where were her folks?

Easing away from the confusion, Cassie crossed the room and sank down next to Erin. The girl glanced up momentarily. Her eyes conveyed humiliation and she pulled her hair over the side of her face.

"Quite a mess," Cassie said softly.

Erin shrugged.

"With all the accusations being tossed about, do you want to tell me what's going on?"

"Mr. Thomas caught us lifting some soda and chips from his convenience store."

"Us? You included?"

Erin pressed her lips together.

"I know Kyle, but don't recognize anyone else. Who are the others?"

Shrugging, Erin said, "Just some kids from school."

Cassie searched the crowd. "Denny's not here."

"Why would he be?"

"I thought you two…"

"He doesn't hang with this crowd."

"I see." She brushed her shoulder with Erin's, her mouth close to the teen's ear. "So why do you?"

Erin went still.

"It seemed like you and Denny were rather…"

close the other night. I thought you might want to spend time with him."

"He'd never hang around with these kids."

"So let me guess. You can't decide which group of friends to be with?"

"What makes you an expert on kids?"

"I was one once."

Erin rolled her eyes. Oh, the attitude. Cassie hid a grin.

"You aren't the first girl to hang out with people she shouldn't," Cassie told her.

"Like you ever did?"

"For a while." Erin tried to pretend disinterest, but Cassie sensed otherwise. "My parents were fighting and had just gotten a divorce. I was mad at my dad, so I started sneaking out at night. Until I came home late and found my mother scared to death. I'll never forget the look on her face. We talked and I decided on a different path."

"Lucky you. My parents don't care."

Luke's warning resonated in her head, but instead of taking heed, she decided to be a friend to a girl who desperately needed one. "And why is that?"

"I'm a disappointment." She chewed on her thumb nail. "Their words."

"Because you've gotten in trouble?"

"Um, I haven't before tonight."

Interesting. "Then why would they be disappointed?"

Erin went stonily silent again. Okay, new tactic.

"So are you going to call them?"

"Are you crazy?"

"You'd rather sit here all night?"

A phone shrilled in the background, barely audible over the noise level. Cassie almost missed Erin's next words.

"They wouldn't come even if I called, so why bother?"

"Because they might surprise you."

Cassie read the doubt on Erin's face, which barely covered the equally strong longing beneath the surface. "What if I called them for you?"

The opening Cassie had hoped for slammed shut. "Why don't you leave me alone? I didn't ask for your help."

"No. You didn't. But I'm betting you want it."

Suddenly, Erin's eyes misted. Her body seemed to sink into itself and her breathing became ragged. Concerned, Cassie placed a hand on Erin's shaking shoulder.

"I can't… I don't deserve any help."

Cassie scanned the group. Was Erin talking about her friends? Didn't want them to see her weakness? The tough girl who deep down wasn't so very tough? She stood, taking Erin's arm to pull her up and lead her toward the ladies' room.

"Hold on," the police chief called out. "I need to talk to that young lady."

"A minute?" Cassie asked.

The chief must have noticed Erin's shaking shoulders and relented. "Ten minutes."

Cassie nodded and shuffled Erin away from the others. Once inside the empty bathroom, Cassie wet some paper towels and held them out. "Wipe your face," she commanded.

Erin obeyed, taking the towels with trembling fingers. When she finally composed herself, she said, "You must think I'm an idiot."

"No. A little off the path, perhaps."

"I don't want to spend the night in jail," she whispered.

"Then let's straighten this out."

"Without calling my parents?"

Cassie sighed. "We'll try. On one condition."

Erin's brow rose.

"You meet with a counselor at Kids' Klub."

The moody expression returned. "Those lame adults?"

"It's either yes, or you can spend the night in lockup."

Erin tried for an expression of suppressed

disgust, but the shiver still shaking her shoulders belied the sting. "Fine."

"I'm going to ask you a question and I want the truth."

Erin's eyes narrowed.

"Did you steal anything from that store?"

She opened her mouth, seemed to think better of it and sagged against the wall. "No. Not the store."

"I didn't think so."

Something close to relief flared in Erin's eyes. "Why would you believe me? Especially considering who I was with?"

"First, because you're not a bad kid, Erin, no matter how much you believe otherwise. It's obvious you have some issues at home, but deep down you're a good person."

"You don't know me."

True, but she had to finesse this for Erin's sake. "I saw you running back and forth at the concert when you were giving Denny a hand. You showed up the next morning and chipped right in serving breakfast. I know you enough to be right, Erin. Secondly, I don't know those other kids, but considering the phone call Luke received, and the fact that the chief didn't call you by name, shows you aren't a regular here."

"I'm not."

"Then I'll make sure the chief knows, okay?"

The room went silent. Cassie held her breath, waiting for Erin's answer.

"I... Okay."

Cassie took her hand and they walked outside. The crowd had thinned with only a few adults and their children. She scoped out the chief and headed in his direction.

"Chief. A word?"

The bear of a man lumbered to them.

"Erin is ready to talk to you when you're free."

Fear shadowed the girl's face. The chief pulled himself to his full height and waited. It was a great intimidation tactic because even Cassie was spooked.

Erin visibly swallowed before speaking. "I... um...didn't steal anything from the store."

"And you expect me to believe you with just your say-so?"

All the color rushed from Erin's face. "I swear."

The chief rocked back on his heels. "The store owner didn't ID you and no one gave you up so..." He turned to Cassie. "You'll vouch for her?"

"Yes."

"Then you're free to go." He pointed a thick finger at Erin. "I don't want to see you again because next time you won't be so lucky."

Cassie sensed her hand holding Erin's kept

the girl from buckling in relief. When the chief winked at Cassie, she realized their good fortune. Until Luke joined them, a handsome scowl on his face.

"You need a ride home, Erin?"

"Yes," came the quiet reply.

"Let's go."

They piled into Luke's car for a silent journey to Erin's house. Once again the house was dark when they pulled up, shrouded in shadows. Uninviting. Cassie exited the car to let Erin out of the backseat. She brushed the hair away from Erin's eyes.

"Are you going to be okay?"

Erin shrugged.

"I'll be checking to make sure you make an appointment with the counselor."

Erin took two steps away, twirled around and rushed back to wrap Cassie in a tight hug. "Thank you," she whispered fiercely, then ran off to the back of the house. As she did the other night, Cassie waited for a flicker of light inside. Only then did she slide back into the front seat.

"I'm exhausted." She rubbed her neck, trying to ease the tension. "How often do you do this?"

"More often than I'd like." He put the car in gear and drove off. "I called Erin's folks.

Assured them she was okay and told them I'd drive her home. I could tell by her father's clipped tone he wasn't happy."

"I don't think any parent wants to receive that phone call."

"No. But it bothers me that they didn't come get her themselves."

"The family issues I'm worried about?"

"Probably." He blew out a breath. Sent her a glance. "This wasn't how I planned on ending the night."

"While far from romantic, I'm glad you were there for the kids." She turned toward him. "I think I got through to Erin."

"In what way?"

"I told her I'd stick up for her to the chief if she made an appointment with one of the Klub counselors."

"No kidding? She went for it?"

"She's not as tough as she wants everyone to believe. Plus, she was legitimately scared."

"Yeah. Tonight was a first for her."

"As opposed to the others?"

He nodded. Cassie found the concern etched on his face as attractive as a full-blown smile. Anyone could rock the styled hair and those soulful brown eyes, but his support for the kids touched her heart.

"Take Kyle, for instance. Third strike."

"Which means?"

"I have to pull him from the musical."

"Ouch."

"It's tough, but I have to follow through." He paused. "My brother and I had a tough childhood. Got into plenty of trouble. I learned a long time ago I can't give in or the kids will walk all over me. I warned Kyle. Gave him plenty of chances. He made his choice."

She reached over and took his hand. "I'm sorry, Luke."

"It's part of the job."

From his own experience, Luke understood the consequences at stake for each and every child under his watch. Cassie may have gotten a crash course tonight in dealing with Erin, but she didn't know how he stayed so strong, how he didn't fold every time a kid needed help. Her respect for his stand grew leaps and bounds. He cared, more deeply than he would ever let anyone know.

"There is one thing that concerns me," he said, breaking into her thoughts.

"What?"

"The stolen money from the Klub. I don't believe Denny took it, but he wasn't the only one with access. I figured out that Kyle and Erin were with him both times money went missing."

She really hoped Erin had nothing to do with the theft. She'd sworn she hadn't stolen from the convenience store, so Cassie could only have faith that Erin steered clear of any other shady business. "Who do you think took the cash?"

"I don't know, but it's time to find out."

Cassie roused at the conviction in his voice. "Do I want to know how you're going to prove it?"

"Probably not."

THE NEXT WEEK flew by. Cassie held another songwriting workshop and the kids found time to work together on the television music. Denny seemed back to normal. Kyle hadn't taken the news of his third strike well.

Two things, however, remained in the forefront of Luke's mind. How to move forward with Cassie in this relationship and finding out which one of the kids had stolen Klub money.

He mentally reviewed the money situation first. The commonalities were Denny, Erin and Kyle. He'd already dismissed Denny as a guilty party, but remembered the boy's crush on Erin. Young men had done worse than keeping a few bucks to impress a girl, but it didn't feel right. He didn't know Erin well enough to decide how much influence she wielded over Denny or if she'd pocketed the cash. Cleary she was troubled. And Kyle? He couldn't stay on the straight and narrow.

He'd already put them to the test, albeit secretly. He'd asked Denny to run to the store, a task the teen had accomplished without incident many times before. When Luke gave him petty cash to cover the purchase, he'd balked, but Luke told him to handle it. He'd watched as the pack of kids went off together. Then he'd waited. But upon their return, Denny left the exact change. Really, Luke shouldn't have been surprised now that Denny, or the real culprit, was on high alert. He should have realized solving this mystery wouldn't be that easy.

Which brought him to his next quandary. How to move forward with Cassie? His instinct to trust Cassie in the romance department was hard earned because of his past mistakes with Tracy. Yeah, he could admit now that he'd made blunders, too, maybe put his career first. Now that he'd made the decision to dive into this new relationship, he wanted to treat Cassie right. Rusty after a lengthy period of not competing in the dating game, he'd suggested a picnic lunch at the park, hoping for time alone to get to know her on a deeper level, as well as work on her music.

On the following Saturday, just before noon,

he walked out of Pointe Cafe with a large to-go bag in hand, nearly colliding with his cousin Dane.

"Whoa. Where's the fire?" Dane asked as he veered out of harm's way.

"Sorry, man. Got lots on my mind."

"Yeah? Better be a pretty brunette with a braid."

A vision of Cassie brought out a smile. "Bingo."

"So, what, you planned lunch?"

Luke grimaced at his cousin's amused face. "You already knew, didn't you?"

"When you call Nealy for advice, it's pretty much like talking to me."

On a chuckle, Luke held out his hand. "I hear congratulations are in order. Nealy told me you proposed."

Dane shook his hand. "And you acted suitably surprised, right?"

"Hey, I wouldn't blow her big moment by admitting I knew beforehand."

"Thanks." Dane cocked his head. "So, what's going on with you and Cassie?"

"Lunch. Some time alone. You know the drill."

"Been a while, but yeah, I get it." Dane stuffed his hands in his pockets. "So, you're finally putting the past behind you?"

"I was afraid I might blow it with Cassie when she asked me if I'd forgiven Tracy. But keeping Cassie in my life is more important than holding a grudge."

"Wise choice. It's time you enjoy life."

Luke restlessly shifted the bag in his hand, more than ready to get started on this new life. "I'm not arguing."

Dane nodded. "Go on, then. Sweep Cassie off her feet."

He grinned. "And I know the perfect way."

Luke stopped by his car to retrieve his guitar and a blanket, then headed to the prearranged meeting spot. He spread out the blanket under the shade of a wide-limbed oak. Pink and purple flowers circled the base of the trunk, adding a burst of color, mingling with the sea breeze to create a natural perfume. Glancing at his watch, he realized he was ten minutes early.

The noonday sun sifted through the canopy of leaves, warming his shoulders under a short-sleeved polo shirt stitched with the Kids' Klub logo. Was he underdressed in this casual shirt and slacks? Should he have made more of an effort? Cassie really had him twisted in knots for him to be worrying about his clothes.

"That frown better be because you've missed me," Cassie said as she set her case on the grass.

Her sunny smile matched the bright yellow sleeveless top she wore. Her braid flew over her shoulder as she plopped down beside him. Her fragrance, more potent than the nearby flowers, enveloped him.

"I have missed you but you never make me frown."

Cassie snorted.

"Okay, maybe once in a while."

"You sweet-talker, you." She leaned over to gift him with a quick kiss to the cheek. "I'll take it."

As much as he wanted to haul her into his arms and kiss her senseless, he'd decided to put the brakes on. More talk, less kissing for now. Especially in a public park, where rumors could start.

"I hope you're hungry."

"Starved. I met Erin at the Klub earlier. She made an appointment with one of the counselors."

"I heard."

"Since I kinda pushed her, I wanted to offer moral support."

"So how'd it go?"

"Not sure. She wasn't very chatty afterward. Said she needed to get home."

"It's a start, Cassie. A good start."

"I hope." She bit her lower lip. "I want her

to figure her life out now before she gets into any deeper trouble."

He leaned back on his elbows. "Let me ask you something."

Cassie crossed her legs into a lotus position. "Shoot."

"Do you think Erin had anything to do with the missing cash?"

She grimaced. "I wish I could give you an honest answer, but really, who knows what goes on inside a person's head?"

"That's my problem, too. I'm not sure who to believe." He told her about his failed experiment.

"You didn't expect it to be so easy, did you?" she asked with an amused expression.

"I did. Only because I want to get to the bottom of this."

"That makes sense." She tugged at a blade of grass. Ran it through her fingers. "A lot of Luke Hastings is at stake at Kids' Klub."

"Probably more than I even realize."

"Because you care so much?"

"I told you my brother and I didn't have an easy upbringing. Our parents weren't around and when they were, we couldn't rely on them, so we were troublemakers." He paused. Decided to lay it all on the line. "When I came to Cypress Pointe and started teaching, I realized looking at certain kids in class was like looking in a mirror. I was so messed up over Tracy, I needed an outlet for the hurt, just like they did. Kids' Klub became that for me."

"You've probably saved many kids from traveling down the same road."

"I hope so. When you invest in something so personal, it takes your heart and soul."

"So your ex didn't totally wipe you out emotionally?"

"No. But it was a long time before I figured it out." He sat up, pulled up one leg and rested a forearm over his knee. A bee buzzed by and he absently brushed it away. "Given how I grew up, I wasn't sure I wanted a family," he said in a quiet voice as he stared over the vast green expanse of the park. "Tracy and I talked about it. Put it off. There were always excuses. I guess I look at the teens in the programs as the only children I'll ever have."

Cassie placed a hand over his. "But deep down you wanted one of your own?"

"Yeah. I did." He drew in a breath. "My ex is pregnant."

"Oh, Luke."

"It's funny. I think even from the beginning I was waiting for Tracy to somehow let me down, just like everyone else in my life had before her. Makes me wonder if I'd pushed her to be unhappy. To act on my worst fears." He shook his head. "Even she saw that we shouldn't have a family together. She was right."

Cassie remained silent as he let the truth sink in. He'd never given them a chance. He'd been waiting for Tracy to disappoint him and in time, she'd achieved his self-fulfilling prophecy.

"I was angry, but now…I'm reconciled. She has her life." He met her gaze. "Now I hope I have mine."

Cassie's features softened and he thought, yeah, maybe I want a life with this woman. He cleared his throat, "So, lunch?"

Blinking away the sheen in her eyes, Cassie reached over for the bag. "I'm ready."

It didn't take long to dive into the gourmet turkey and cheese sandwiches on focaccia bread. As they munched on chips, Cassie filled him in on a new idea for a song that had woken her in the early hours. He sipped iced tea from a tall cup, watching her animated face. Her muse was returning. Gone was the insecure songwriter he'd met mere weeks ago. Instead, a confident woman sat beside him. The woman who had made a name for herself, and would continue to be a success in the music world.

Once they polished off the last of the food,

Cassie bagged up the waste and carried it to the nearby trash can, resuming her seat as Luke grabbed his guitar and nodded to her case. "Let's write a song."

She stilled. "Sure you want to do this?"

He got out a notebook. "Actually, I've come up with some thoughts."

"Really?" She scooted closer. "Let's see."

He chuckled and opened the notebook. "It's pretty rough."

"I'm sure it's great."

"Maybe. The idea came to me this morning. It was still dark. I'd poured my first cup of coffee and wandered out to the deck. The sky grew lighter and then this spectacular sunrise, with all sorts of mellow colors streaking across the horizon, caught my attention. Insects started buzzing and I heard a dog bark in the distance. A fishing boat chugged through the water, leaving behind a foamy wake. It was like the world waking up around me so I came up with this theme. Life and love and finding your place in the world."

Cassie took the notebook from his hands. Read over the page before digging a pencil from her bag. "There's another layer here, Luke." An intensity seemed to overtake her as she added her own words. Before long she glanced at him. "Now we have something."

For the next hour they rearranged the words, came up with a stirring melody. He hadn't been this creative in a long time. Writing songs for the news story was one thing, but this, writing with Cassie, was entirely another. He'd gone with his instincts and she'd taken it to another level. The old adrenaline kicked in. He knew as soon as they'd completed the song that she had another song for her album.

The last note Cassie strummed floated in the breeze, touching his soul. Once he'd thought no one could beat him and Tracy as songwriters. They'd been after commercial success, cranking out hit after hit. It had been a blast, been all he'd thought he wanted out of life. But he'd discovered otherwise. The Klub, with all the messy emotions of working with teens, spending hours worrying about finances and whether they could afford to buy the current property, filled the void songwriting left behind. He should be happy exactly where he found himself, so why did he feel like he was at a crossroads?

He watched Cassie scribble a few final flourishes to the page in her cherished songbook filled with music that would once again make her a star.

All she wanted was to be true to herself. And she'd succeeded. While he was honored to work with her, he had to question if he re-

ally wanted any part of the old life. The acco-
lades. The invasion of his privacy. He didn't
miss that aspect one iota. What he valued was
making a difference in troubled teens' lives.
Could he somehow have both?

Today showed him he could still write a
lyric, tap out a melody. But music wasn't his
sole purpose any longer. His life was here, in
Cypress Pointe, not clear across the country
where Cassie made her music.

The sound of a car horn, followed by yell-
ing, yanked Luke back to reality. Kids on bikes
zipped by on a path, folks rushed about Main
Street. People living their daily lives in this
sleepy Florida town. A life he'd signed on to.
A life that would never keep Cassie here.

"This is so great," Cassie said as she returned her guitar to its case. "My manager is
already going nuts over us writing together."

"You told him?"

"Why wouldn't I?" She turned quickly toward him, her braid whipping over her shoulder. "He's relieved and knows the label will
be thrilled."

Which meant he'd become a public figure
again. A place he didn't miss and would rather
not return to. "I'd really rather you took all the
credit."

"I can't, Luke." Her brow wrinkled. "Wait.

Why don't you want anyone to know we collaborated?"

"I'm not part of the life any longer, Cassie."

"Still, it doesn't mean you shouldn't receive any recognition. Yes, we worked on this together but your observations gave it life."

"Think of it as a gift."

Cassie stared down at the page where they'd made notes. He couldn't decipher her closed expression. Silently, she tore the paper from the notebook, slowly folded it in half. Stored it away in her guitar case. Leaving him to wonder just what she was going to do with their song.

CHAPTER FOURTEEN

"PRACTICE WENT PRETTY GOOD, don't you think?"

Erin absently nodded at Denny's question, her mind a whirlwind following the late afternoon practice session. All week they'd been working on the music for the news story. Tomorrow after school she would be singing in front of her friends, reporters, cameras and, worst of all, her parents. Why had she mentioned the concert to them? Deep down did she want them to see her in a different light? Maybe finally have something nice to say to her?

They walked down Main Street, in the direction of the park. The burger she'd eaten for dinner soured in her stomach, like an elephant sat on her belly and pushed the food into her clogged throat.

"Erin?"

She glanced over at Denny, his eyes questioning behind his glasses. He was always so positive. Why couldn't she be more like him, even though it irritated her at the same time?

"Yeah, I guess."

"Thought you'd be more fired up about the solo. No one else but you was asked to sing alone."

"Don't remind me." She placed her hand on her lurching stomach, sure she'd be sick. She never should have gone with Denny to the restaurant after practice, but he'd been so excited when she said yes. And after being accused of stealing money from the Klub, it was the first time in days he'd seemed like his old self. And when they walked to the restaurant, he'd taken her hand. A funny sensation had washed over her. She'd never felt it with another guy. Every time she was with Denny, she was all jittery and happy. While she liked it, she didn't examine it too closely, afraid of what she might discover about herself. Or admit Denny was the guy for her. If she told him the truth about the missing money, would he hate her for keeping it from him? Help her instead of turning on her?

"Are you and Mr. H. doing better?" she asked to get her mind off the nerves.

Denny shrugged. "He says he believes I didn't take the money. It hurts that he even questioned me in the first place."

"Welcome to my world," she grumbled.

"Still having trouble with your parents?"

"I guess." She hesitated, then blurted, "I told them about the concert. They're coming."

"That's great." There it was. The optimistic grin that assured her everything would be okay.

"I don't know. I'm sure they'll find something wrong with my voice. Or my clothes. Or even why I volunteered in the first place."

"Stop worrying so much."

"You sound like the counselor at the Klub."

She'd followed Cassie's ultimatum and made an appointment. The lady behind the desk hadn't been so bad. Nicer than the high school counselor she'd reported to when she'd skipped classes. This lady seemed to care about Erin. So she'd spilled about her family; her parents hating her because of her sister's actions. Why she acted out. She'd come close to confessing about the money. The truth ate away at her every day, but still, she kept quiet.

The counselor suggested she try to find a common ground with her parents to rebuild the relationship. Erin hadn't been convinced, but decided to test the suggestion by mentioning the musical to her parents. To her surprise, they'd asked questions. Seemed interested instead of discouraging. Said they'd be there to hear her solo.

But what if they were lying? What if they didn't show? They couldn't be that cruel, could they?

The more she thought about it, the more her stomach twisted. "I don't feel good."

"You look kinda green." Denny took hold of her arm and hurried her to the public restroom at the edge of the park. She dropped her backpack and ran inside, making it to the stall just in time to lose her dinner. Resting against the stall she blinked back hot tears. Could she be any more pathetic? Denny must think she was the weakest human on earth and after this, she wouldn't blame him.

After getting her bearings, she cleaned up, tried to fix her hair and stepped back outside into the evening shadows. Her heart sank when she saw Gary and his gang circling Denny like he was their prey. Kyle and Brandon were hovering, too. Weren't they Denny's friends?

She walked over, ready to jump into the fray when Gary stopped her.

"You with this guy, Erin?"

"I'm—"

"Since when did you start hanging out with losers?"

The boys laughed at his remark.

"It's not what it looks like," she said, then cringed when she glimpsed Denny's hurt expression. "I mean, we were talking about the Klub."

"Nerd stuff, I bet," Gary said, reaching out to knock off Denny's glasses.

Denny slapped his hand away. "Cut it out."

"Make me."

Denny moved closer to Erin. "Let's go."

He reached out for her hand but she hesitated. If she left with him, she'd never hear the end of it. But if she didn't, Denny would probably never speak to her again.

"I…um…"

"Can't talk to the loser?" Gary taunted and the group laughed again.

She tried working this dilemma out in her mind, but before she could control the bile rising up in her throat again, Denny dropped his hand. His face pale, he inched away from her. She couldn't miss the disappointment in his eyes. Just like her parents. Just like Cassie when she found Erin at the police station. When would everyone cut her some slack? Give her time to figure things out?

"Are you coming?" Denny asked in a quiet, controlled voice.

She swallowed hard. Glanced from the group back to Denny. "I…"

"I guess that's your answer."

Face composed, Denny turned on his heel and walked away.

She almost hollered at Denny to stop. What had she done? She frantically searched for her backpack. Gary sauntered over and casually wrapped his arm around her shoulder.

"You made the right choice."

She ducked under his arm. "Get away from me."

Gary dropped his arm. "What's up with you?"

"You're a jerk, you know that?"

Gary's face turned incredulous. "You actually like that guy?"

"He's a nice guy. A lot better than you'll ever be." She faced Kyle and Brandon. "Hypocrites."

"What?" Gary sputtered, then started laughing hilariously. When he caught his breath, he pointed to her and told his friends, "What a loser."

Is that all he could name anyone? Loser? Denny didn't deserve what she'd done to him. He'd been looking out for her and this was how she repaid him? She didn't merit him as a friend. Or ex-friend. Yeah, her hesitance had defiantly blown things with Denny.

"You need to add to your vocabulary, Gary," she snapped and walked away, leaving her backpack and so-called friends behind. All she knew for certain was that she had to get far away before she let anyone else down. Right now, where to hide or what would happen in her future loomed before her, even without answers. Breaking out into a run, she headed for the beach and didn't look back.

AN ODD QUIET hovered over the Klub. He'd worked late into the night, grading papers for his English class. A task overdue. Since the request to write songs and get the music together for the special interest story, he'd been lax about his school load. In reality, he'd wanted to take Cassie to dinner, but she begged off. Something about a family thing. So he'd taken advantage of the rare peace to get his grading done.

The music session earlier that afternoon went well. The kids were pumped, ready to put into practice what they'd been learning. Cassie had assisted him, encouraging the kids and making the overall tone of the upcoming event fun. Her ready smile never ceased to amaze him. He savored every minute spent with her. Coming to Cypress Pointe after the divorce, teaching and starting Kids' Klub, hadn't given him the sense of completeness he now experienced with Cassie. Witnessing her passion to overcome writer's block had compelled him to confront the ghosts of his past and he'd always be grateful for her place in that change. They hadn't made plans or spoken about the future, but he hoped for one with her just the same.

While he was happy with Cassie, the mystery of the money thief continued to bug him. After much thought, he put another plan in place. At practice, he'd mentioned to Denny, in front of all the kids present, that he'd left cash in his top drawer so they could buy matching T-shirts for the news story. He hoped the culprit would take the bait, since he'd gotten a teacher friend from school to help him rig a hidden security camera. If anyone entered his office, an alarm would sound on his phone. Yeah, he was that desperate to smoke out the guilty party.

In addition to the camera, he'd marked the money with invisible ink, showing only when held under a black light, revealing lines across the bills.

Now he could only wait and see if anyone took the bait. Tomorrow was going to be hectic. The camera might be his only chance to capture the truth. Denny and Erin had never returned from dinner and the other kids were long gone, so he wondered if, or when, the thief would strike again.

Finished grading, he gathered his papers and locked the office. He turned, startled to find Cassie's father standing a few feet away.

"Mr. Branford. I didn't hear you come in."

"Call me Robert." He held out his hand. Luke took it, wary of the man's presence.

"Robert. How can I help you?"

The man smiled, but it didn't reach his eyes.

Luke had been around enough troubled kids to be leery of a smile with no substance.

"First, I stopped by to congratulate you on creating music for the special interest news piece. The mayor must have forgotten I was in town when she approached you."

"I didn't know you'd be interested in working on our small musical."

"When you love music, nothing is small."

Somehow Luke doubted that. "Sorry not to include you."

Robert brushed off Luke's apology. "Neither here nor there. Actually, I have a proposition for you."

"I don't know, Mr.…ah, Robert."

"Please, hear me out. As you might know, I wrote the score for a movie a few years back."

"No, I hadn't heard."

A shadow passed over Robert's eyes. "It was a major action film." He visibly collected himself. "Anyway, I have been looking for opportunities to write again. I may have a handle on a project and I want to know if you would be interesting in penning a new score with me."

"That's not really my area of expertise."

"You know music."

"I do. And while I appreciate the offer, I'm pretty busy here with the Klub."

He started to walk away, but Robert blocked his path.

"My offer will also benefit your kids program."

"In what way?"

"I could volunteer some time here. Teach students how to score music. Maybe give those interested a look at how an orchestra works."

Luke had to admit, a renowned conductor offering his time here was a coup for the kids serious about pursuing music.

"The mini-concert your kids are performing is an example of where my expertise can come in handy," Robert continued. "There are certain goals serious musicians must reach. Taking part in this news story is one of them, but I can offer more exposure."

"So you're saying that in order for my kids to learn from your expertise, I need to work with you?"

"Oh, no," Robert rushed to say. "You misunderstood. I merely think an exchange can be accomplished that will benefit everyone. Cassie included."

His interest spiked at her name.

"And how is that?"

"I get the impression you and my daughter are coming up with some songs. Or maybe there's more between you two?"

Luke kept silent on the subject. If Cassie hadn't filled in her father, he wouldn't.

"If the three of us put our considerable talents together, we could corner the film market."

Luke wasn't interested in cornering any market except one that helped his kids. He thought his exit from the music industry would be a big clue, but Robert had missed it.

"Cassie's okay with this?"

"Cassie and I are sorting out our difficulties. She said herself she wants us to get closer. Working together will fit the bill."

His answer wasn't a yes, but Luke hadn't been privy to their family conversations. He knew Cassie and her dad were at odds, but had she had a change of heart?

"And here's another incentive," Robert went on to say. "My daughter Lauren mentioned you still don't have all the funds needed to buy this property. If we work together, I'll donate the rest of what is needed."

Whoa. The final piece to giving the Klub a permanent home. The goal he'd been striving toward for a long time now. "It's a very generous offer."

"I can be a very generous man." Robert shrugged. "With our names linked, you can be a success again."

"I'm not looking for the spotlight."

"Really? Then why else would my daughter have sought you out if not to give her career a boost?"

He didn't want to question the idea, but could this be the reason Cassie approached him initially? To connect her name to his? She'd mentioned that her manager wanted the label to know they were collaborating. For publicity on her part? He couldn't imagine her using him, but the reality niggled at him. She'd needed to come up with music, fast, and requested his help. So she volunteered for a few hours when the payoff was getting songs for her new record. She'd never said she would stick around Cypress Pointe. So maybe courting him for his help had been her game all along?

No. Their kisses told him otherwise, right? But still, she hadn't said she'd stay in town, even though he never asked. Why hadn't he asked? Because he was afraid she'd leave him for her career? For the fame? Just like his ex?

He'd made a conscious decision to move out of the spotlight. Liked his life this way, stress-free from reporters and gossip and innuendo. But Cassie would still have plenty of publicity and touring to do once her next record was released. Could that be why he hesitated bringing up a future with her?

He had to believe she'd been truthful with him. That she wouldn't involve his name for publicity, no matter how much she wanted a hit.

"You'll understand if I need to think about it."

Robert nodded. "Of course. But just know, this is a limited-time offer. My daughter and I will be returning to LA soon, so we'll need an answer."

A string attached. Why wasn't he surprised? Because of the air of desperation about the man?

And they were leaving together? After the way he'd seen Cassie wrestle with feelings for her father after their run-ins, he highly doubted it. But what he didn't have any doubts about was Cassie leaving. The clock had nearly ticked down to the end of her stay here. He was still processing the idea of her a full country away from him.

The older man's footsteps echoed in the empty gym. Luke waited until he left to switch off the lights, his heart heavy as he plunged the building into darkness. He didn't bother engaging the security alarm, wanting instead to have the silent alarm notify him from his phone. No point in scaring off the thief if he could catch the person in the act.

He returned home, but sleep eluded him. Thoughts of Cassie leaving, songs in hand, bothered him. He'd picked up the phone half a dozen times to call her, each time putting it down. But all his silent reassurances about their relationship didn't help. Not until he spoke to Cassie himself. He dialed her number.

"Hello," came her sleepy voice.

"Did I wake you?"

"Luke? No, well, yes, I just dozed off for a minute. Is something wrong?"

"I wanted to give you a heads-up."

"That sounds ominous."

He loved how she could take any situation and insert humor in it.

"It's about your father."

"Great." He heard wrestling on the other end, like she was moving about. "I'm sorry in advance."

This time he chuckled. "He stopped by the Klub with a proposition."

"Of course he did."

"He wants us to collaborate on a movie score with him."

Silence, then, "Come again?"

"According to him, our names linked together will give us an edge in the movie industry. Implied you were with him on this."

"All I did was encourage him to go after his dream."

"He wants to. With us."

"Never going to happen."

"There's more."

She sighed. "There's always more."

"He suggested that if I help him, he'll volunteer his orchestra expertise at the Klub."

"Really? How big of him. You know he's all about the show, right?"

"Yes."

"Good, because if you take him up on his offer, he'll never follow through."

"I already figured that out."

"He sure covered all the angles."

He heard a heavy exhale on the other end of the phone.

"Luke, I don't know what to tell you. If you want to accept his help, you should."

A beep cut into the conversation.

"Hold on," Luke told her. He checked the phone screen. Someone had set off the hidden camera alarm in his office. "I have to run. The trap I set up at the Klub worked."

"Trap? What trap?"

"I'll talk to you later."

"No, wait. What did you do?"

"I'll explain it all tomorrow, I promise," he said, then ended the call.

With lightning speed, he threw on a T-shirt and shorts. Stepping into boat shoes, he grabbed his keys from the counter and ran out to his car, speeding all the way to the Klub. The building was dark, exactly as he'd left it. He jumped out of the car, stopping long enough to observe his surroundings.

A bird cried out overhead as it took flight from a tree branch. The sound of bass thumping in a car sound system carried from the main road. A paper wrapper flitted by in the gulf breeze. The lights over the door and at the corners of the buildings shone, revealing nothing.

Dialing his phone, he put in a call to the chief.

"Gardener."

"Sorry to bother you, Chief. A silent alarm went off at the Klub. I'm going inside."

"Don't. Wait until I get there."

"And miss catching the thief? No way." He thumbed the off button and slipped the phone into his pocket. He started to move when car lights flashed across the building. Looking back, he saw Cassie jump out of her convertible and rush toward him.

"What are you doing here?"

She brushed the hair that escaped her ponytail from her eyes. "You tell me about a trap and I'm supposed to sit at home and wait to find out what happens?"

"I don't suppose I can convince you to stay here?"

She rolled her eyes at him like he was dense.

"Didn't think so. Follow me."

Cassie stayed at his side as they moved in a crouched run up the sidewalk. Luke scoured the surroundings, but everything remained calm. He unlocked the door and stealthily moved inside, keeping Cassie behind him. After listening for any sounds, he jogged across the gym and motioned for Cassie to do the same. His office door was closed. Reaching out, he turned the knob. The door banged against the wall to reveal an empty room.

"Shoot," he muttered under his breath.

"Should we check the other rooms?"

"Let's split up."

Taking a quick inventory of the building, they found nothing out of the ordinary. He switched on the overhead gym lights as the chief walked in, weapon in hand.

"There's no one here," Luke informed him.

The chief holstered his firearm. "You know you aren't very good at taking direction."

"Not when the Klub is at stake."

Then the chief noticed Cassie. "What'd you do, call in the troops?"

"Trust me, I didn't expect reinforcements."

The chief nodded, looked like he was going to argue about both of them being there, then changed his mind. "Anything missing?"

"Let's check."

The three went back to his office. The first thing he did was search the desk drawer. "The cash I left here is missing."

"What about the other rooms?"

"Nothing's disturbed. Whoever took the money knew it was in here."

The chief's brow rose. "Care to explain?"

Luke did. About his plan, the camera and the marked money.

"I'm impressed."

"Don't be. These are talents I picked up from being a troublemaker."

A deep chuckle rumbled in the chief's chest. He looked around and bent to pick up a pink paisley backpack. "Yours?"

Cassie looked over. Her stomach dropped. "Erin's."

"Could she have stolen the money?" the chief asked.

"No way," Cassie came to her defense.

"Cassie, Erin knew about the money." Luke turned to the chief. "So did a bunch of other kids, but I don't see her breaking in. Not her skill set."

"She was at the station the other night with kids who do fit that set."

"You released her," Cassie reminded the chief.

"Doesn't mean she wasn't involved," he replied. "I'll go by her house tomorrow. No point waking the family until we have more proof."

"More proof than her backpack?" Luke asked.

"I'd like to find the marked money in her possession."

Luke nodded. Made sense.

"There should be more proof." He rounded the desk and stood on his chair. With the small screwdriver attached to his key chain, he loosened the screws on the air vent. Inside, he retrieved the security camera. "We can check the memory card and see who was here."

He ejected the small card and booted up his computer. In minutes, he fast-forwarded through the grainy images on the screen until dark figures appeared. Two people slinked inside, one moving directly to the desk while the other stood by the door. From the angle, Luke couldn't see much, but he did have a perfect view of the desk. The problem was, the figure wore dark clothes and a cap pulled low, obscuring his or her face.

"I can't make out any features."

"Me, neither," the chief seconded.

They watched as the figure opened the desk drawer, pocketed the money, closed the drawer. Then the two figures disappeared from the camera frame.

"So much for my inspired idea," Luke muttered.

"Run it again," the chief commanded.

He did as asked.

"Stop."

As he studied the frozen frame, Luke noticed something new. "Does that look like blond bangs under the cap?"

"Sure does."

Luke looked at the chief. "Erin has blond hair."

"Long, if I remember correctly."

"That doesn't mean it's her," Cassie added.

"She could have stuffed it up under the hat," Luke reasoned.

The chief peered at the screen with an objective eye. "Coulda, but it seems more like the build of a boy."

"It could be anyone," Luke said, reaching out to shut off the device.

"Wait," Cassie placed a hand on his arm. "What's that logo on the cap?"

Luke studied it, but the image was too dark

and grainy to read. "It looks familiar, but I just can't place it."

"Let me have the footage," the chief said. "My guys can enhance the picture. We might get a lead yet."

Luke ejected the card and handed it over. "Sorry to wake you for nothing."

"Oh, this ain't nothing. We'll figure it out Luke."

Yeah, but would he like the results?

The chief pocketed the card and took the backpack. "I'll send my guys around in the morning." He nodded to Cassie. "Good night."

A heavy silence settled in his office.

"So what happens now?" Cassie asked in a weary voice.

"We let the chief investigate. Go on with the musical tomorrow."

Cassie dropped into a chair. It was then Luke noticed the rumpled T-shirt and shorts. She must have run right out of the house. The fact that she'd rushed over in her casual clothes warmed his heart.

"You shouldn't have come."

"Like I could stay home." She bit her lower lip, the worried expression she'd lost returning. "You don't really believe Erin could be involved, do you?"

"I can't say for sure."

Her shoulders slumped. "I thought I'd made some headway with her."

Luke crouched down beside her. Laid a hand on her bare knee. "It takes more than a few hours spent with these kids to make any inroads."

"I get it now. I'd just hoped…"

"Hope is good. I have to wake up with it every day, or the disappointments would pull me under."

She looked up. Met his gaze. The compassion in her eyes made him realize he loved her. More than he thought possible. The revelation shocked him to his core.

Stifling a yawn, she stood. "I should get home."

Luke stepped back. "We have a busy day tomorrow."

He walked her to the front door. She started to leave, then turned. "Would it be okay if I dropped by Erin's house tomorrow?"

"I'd let the chief handle this, Cassie. He knows what he's doing."

"Right. I'll see you at the park."

Luke leaned against the doorjamb, making sure Cassie made it safely to her car. When her taillights disappeared in the distance, he stayed, thinking about her.

Now that he'd admitted the truth of his feelings, what would he do with them? Cassie was going back to LA, back to the industry he'd walked away from. How could he reconcile her fame-driven choices with the quiet, private life he needed?

CHAPTER FIFTEEN

TWO HOURS BEFORE the filming on Friday afternoon, Cassie, along with Luke and the kids involved, met at the makeshift platform set up for the performance. The news outlet had already arrived, setting up cameras and equipment. A lively crowd gathered in the park, spreading out blankets to get a good view as they came out to support the mayor and her newest publicity event.

Everyone involved in the news story dressed in a Kids' Klub T-shirt and white jeans, with only Cassie in high-heeled boots. Most wore reasonable footwear, like sneakers or ballet flats. She could only blame her choice on her slavery to fine shoes.

While the kids loitered, laughing and horsing around, Cassie paced, frequently checking the time on her phone. So far Erin was a no-show. No one had seen or heard from her. Her parents were worried, proving to Cassie they did care about their daughter. If Erin would let them know she was all right, then Cassie could calm down. Only Denny seemed as distracted as she, his gaze moving from the crowd to the main street, as if he, too, were waiting for Erin to arrive.

"Pacing isn't going to solve anything," Luke told her for the fifth time.

"It makes me feel better." She recognized nervous energy and the only way to dispel it was to move. Constantly.

When her cell rang, she nearly dropped it in her haste to answer. Frustration swept over her when she realized it wasn't Erin. "Travis."

"There's my favorite gal. Got a minute?"

She glanced at Luke, held up a finger and walked a few yards away to stop under the shade of an oak tree. "What's up?"

"Good news. There was an opening so I booked the studio. You start recording next week."

"What?" Panic swept over her. "I still have a few weeks left." She should have been more annoyed with her manager's move, but her concern for Erin took precedence right now.

"We take what we can get. This is a positive move to show the record label we're all in."

She'd be in once she knew Erin was okay.

"Is your song list ready?"

She peered around the thickening crowd,

searching for a familiar blond head. "Not enough for an entire album."

"We'll go with what you've got so far and hope for the best."

She would have cried if she weren't so side-tracked.

"Making any headway with Luke?"

With songs or the attraction neither could deny? She didn't want to say too much. They'd worked on songs, but he didn't want credit. And when she went back to LA, where would that leave them?

A steady tapping, like a pen on a desk, sounded from the phone. "Are you listening to me?"

"Yes." She moved to the other side of the tree for a different view. "Studio. Songs."

"If I didn't know better, I'd say you aren't all there right now. We've been working toward this day, Cassie."

Actually, before she'd come up with the new songs she'd been dreading stepping foot in the studio again, but with Luke's help and a bit of Cypress Pointe inspiration, she was finally ready to return to work. As long as they found Erin safe and sound. "I'm sorry, Travis. I'm worried about one of the kids from the youth program."

"Cassie, get your head in the game. Come

next week, you'll be in LA. You should be more worried about the studio execs than a kid in a small town."

Yet here she was, anxious over the welfare of a girl she'd only met not long ago. Her frustration grew, reflected in her tone. "Travis, now isn't a good time."

His voice went hard. "Get focused, Cassie. Your career depends on it."

He hung up, his words ringing in her ears. Okay, she might be anxious to return to the studio, but right now all she cared about was finding Erin in one piece. The record executives would have to wait. Her career would be fine, she assured herself. She could only deal with one crisis at a time.

Luke strode over, lines around his eyes, his blond hair darker under the canopy of the leaves. "Erin?"

"My manager."

His brow rose in question.

"He called about the studio date. Things are moving forward."

He stuffed his hands in the front pockets of his jeans. "Good for you."

"Can we talk about it later?" She ran a hand over her braid, a new black streak threaded through her brown hair, scanning the crowd again. She didn't care about the record, her manager, the label, or anything else just then. She'd always made sure to jump when they snapped their fingers, even when it seemed they required more and more of her time and loyalty. They'd moved up the studio date for Pete's sake.

"Sure," came Luke's terse reply.

"Sorry. I didn't mean to sound so short."

"You're worried."

"Aren't you? How can you be so calm?"

"Look, the chief is looking for Erin. Her folks have been notified."

"What if she doesn't make it? Who will sing her solo?"

"Taylor can fill in if necessary. We'll have to hope for the best."

Which wasn't enough for Cassie. She wanted to take action, but didn't know what action to take. If Erin didn't show up here at the park, Cassie wouldn't have the first clue where to search for her.

"Let's run through the songs again," he suggested.

"You're trying to distract me."

"Is it working?"

"No."

He ran a hand over his jaw. "Me, neither."

They'd returned to the stage when Denny hurried over to Cassie. "I haven't been able to find Erin. Where is she?"

Hiding, Cassie assumed. No one said it, but she was sure they were all thinking it. "You know Luke's office was broken into last night. Her backpack was found there."

"Yeah." He rocked back on his heels. "It might have been my fault."

"What makes you say that?"

"We were together at the park last night. We kinda had a fight, well, not a fight exactly. Anyway, I left her with Gary and his gang."

"Doesn't mean she broke into the office."

"I don't think she would, but her not being here looks bad."

The television reporter arrived with the mayor. Everyone performing gathered around for instructions on filming.

"I need to talk to the tech guys before we start." Luke placed his hand on her arm. Even in the tense setting she couldn't ignore the shiver of pleasure from the merest touch of his fingers. "You sure you're okay?"

"Yes." She waved him off with a reassuring smile. "Go. Do your job."

When her cell rang again, Cassie stepped away from the group. Her blood raced when she read the unknown number. "Hello?"

"Cassie," came a quivering voice.

"Erin. Thank goodness. I've been so worried about you."

"I'm at the hospital."

Cassie's heart sank.

"I'm not hurt," Erin rushed to say.

A strangled breath escaped Cassie. She could barely say a word as relief flooded her.

"I'm here with a friend."

Cassie finally found her voice. "Erin, people are looking for you."

"I'm sorry I didn't call my parents. It's just…"

"I'm coming to get you."

"Please," Erin pleaded with a sob.

Cassie ended the call. She searched the crowd for Luke, but couldn't locate him. Where had he gone? Without taking time to search, she ran to her rental car, nearly turning her ankle in her high heels. "What were you thinking?" she muttered before making it to the vehicle. Once on the road, her speed getting to the hospital would have made a race car driver green with envy. She rushed into the building, heart pounding as she searched the faces coming and going. Erin hovered just inside the lobby.

"Erin." She rushed over just as the young girl burst into tears. Cassie wrapped her in an embrace and pulled her away from the busy entrance. Finding the waiting room, she pulled Erin aside and took her by the shoulders. Pierced her with what she hoped was her best you'd-better-tell-me-everything look. "What happened?"

Sniffling, Erin ran a finger under her nose. "Denny and I had a disagreement last night. I really hurt him. It's what I do, disappoint and hurt people." She hiccupped. "So I took off. Ended up at a friend's house. She was driving me home after lunch when a tire blew. She swerved off the road and hit a tree."

Cassie looked her over. "Are you injured?"

"No. But Kelsey banged her head on the steering wheel. Another car stopped and called 911, so I came to the hospital with her."

Cassie placed a shaky hand over her chest. "I was so worried when we hadn't heard from you."

"I'm sorry. I know I'm supposed to be at the park, but...I can't face Denny. I blew it. Mr. H. will never let me sing today."

Denny and singing were the least of Erin's worries. "So you were with your friend all night?"

"Yes."

"And she can vouch for you?"

"I slept at her house." Erin's brows angled downward. "What's with all the questions? You're freaking me out."

"Luke's office at the Klub was broken into

last night. The police found your backpack there."

The color leached from Erin's face. "But I couldn't... Wait. I got into a fight with Gary and walked off. I left my pack with them."

"Them?"

"Gary, Kyle, Brandon. A few others." She stopped talking as the gravity of the situation sank in. "Do you think I broke into the office?"

Cassie gently pushed her down into a nearby chair. "I didn't think so. But the evidence..."

Erin's mouth hung open. "I... This can't..." she sputtered.

"You have an alibi. That's good."

"For last night." Her eyes filled with tears. "Not for the night of the concert."

"What are you talking about?"

"I took the missing money."

Cassie's stomach flipped. "Erin, why?"

Tears poured down her cheeks now. "I don't know. It was there. I kept thinking, if I get caught, my parents will have to pay attention to me. But then I realized how bad it was and Mr. H. blamed Denny. I didn't know what to do."

"Oh, honey." Cassie pulled her into her arms.

Erin's sobs broke Cassie's heart. When the tempest passed, Cassie wiped the moisture from Erin's face. "I'm not gonna sugarcoat this. This is bad. Do you still have the money?"

Erin nodded.

"Then you can return it. Maybe Luke won't come down so hard on you."

"He should." Erin sniffed. "But I didn't have anything to do with the other money."

"We can prove you weren't at the Klub last night."

"My parents are going to kill me." Erin placed her palms on her forehead and bent over. Long blond hair hung over her face and her shoulders began to shake.

Cassie rubbed her back. "It'll be fine."

Erin's head shot up. A wild look flared in her eyes. "Are you crazy? My parents think I'm a mess. I chose those kids over Denny and everyone will know I'm a thief. I'm a loser, just like Gary said."

"Gary doesn't know a thing. Look, Erin, just because you've made some mistakes, that doesn't define who you are."

"Why are you even bothering with me?"

"Because I see the hard time you're going through. But I promise, it gets better. You want to change, right? Be the girl you used to be?"

Tears rolled down Erin's face. "I want my parents to love me again," she whispered.

Emotion clogged Cassie's throat. She took a few breaths. "Then don't let anyone else decide who you are. Choose your own path. Make your parents proud. It's not too late to tell the truth."

Erin brushed away the tears. "You make it sound so easy."

"It won't be. But you do have friends who will stand by you. I will. And I'm sure after you straighten things out with Denny, he will, too."

Fresh tears formed again. "Do you really think so?"

"Yes. But first, we have to let the chief know where you've been and get to the park. We only have an hour."

Pulling the phone from her pocket, Cassie called the police station. She explained Erin's alibi to the chief, who said he'd be right over. Erin would come clean to Luke about the rest after the concert. Once the chief arrived, spoke to Erin and corroborated her story with Kelsey, he announced she was free to go.

With thirty minutes to spare, they made it back to the park.

As they began to cross the neatly cut grass, Erin looked down at her outfit in horror. "I can't go onstage like this. Not in the same clothes from yesterday."

"Not a problem." Cassie nodded to a woman approaching them. Erin gasped when she glimpsed her mother.

"I called her while you were busy with the chief," Cassie said.

"But why?"

"Those steps I was talking about? Better now than later."

Erin's mother, a small woman with honey-blond hair, whom Erin greatly resembled, tentatively moved forward, folded clothes in her outstretched hands.

"Mom?"

The woman placed the clothes in Erin's hands. Tucked a strand of hair behind her daughter's ear. "Kelsey's mother called last night. I knew where you were." The woman swallowed. "She also told me how upset you were over your sister leaving. Your father's and my reaction. Then she called to tell me about the accident. That you were okay." Tears shone in the woman's eyes. "I realized how close we came to losing you. I...we...haven't been fair to you, Erin. You aren't your sister and we never should have compared you both."

"I don't know what to say," the teen said, wonder and hope in her eyes.

Cassie tapped her shoulder. "Say you'll talk to your folks later. You need to change, pronto."

Erin's mother nodded. "We'll talk later."

"Come on." Erin grabbed Cassie's hand and

pulled her to the restroom. "What am I going to say to them?"

"First, you tell the truth. Then how about everything you've been holding in?"

"That will take a while."

Cassie laughed. "You have all the time in the world."

While Erin disappeared inside, Cassie lingered outside. In the distance she saw Luke directing the kids. She'd texted him with a heads-up on Erin's arrival. He'd demanded to know what was going on. Yes, even in a text she could hear the authority in his tone. She'd miss that about him when she left. Truthfully, she'd miss everything about Luke, but he hadn't asked her to stay.

Bottom line, she'd fallen in love with him. Probably since she'd first heard "Won't You Love Me Always." From the beginning, the lyrics moved something deep inside her. A love for music. For words. A poet's soul. And when she finally met him in person, her heart came alive, like she was stirring from a long sleep. So yes, she would always love Luke. He held her heart and didn't even know it.

"I'm ready," Erin said as she exited the building, dressed like the rest of the team.

"Then we'd better get going."

Cassie followed Erin to the staging area,

holding back. She couldn't face Luke yet, not with all these unsettled emotions bombarding her. Luke's strong voice, his command of the situation, only made her heart ache. He loved Kids' Klub. If she told him how she felt, could he love her as much in return?

FILLED WITH EXCITED kids and parents, the Klub gym echoed more loudly than usual. Luke scanned the scene, trying to catch a glimpse of Cassie. She'd promised to explain later, but just said that Erin was off the hook for the office robbery when they'd arrived just in time for the musical to take place.

The news story went off without a hitch. Well, he'd waited long enough. He wanted answers.

Along one wall, long tables were set up for drinks and donated food for the celebration. Once again, the generosity of the families in this community blew him away. All everybody wanted was the best for Cypress Pointe, himself included. And while he wanted Kids' Klub to be a permanent part of the town, he admitted he'd been thinking a lot about his future. A future that included Cassie? He had to find out before she headed back to the studio.

He felt a tap on his shoulder. He turned to find Cassie and Erin.

"We need to talk. Your office?"

The serious expression on Cassie's face made him nervous. "Sure."

They wove through the noisy crowd. Once in the office, he closed the door to face the women.

Cassie nodded to Erin. "Go ahead."

Erin's face turned ashen. She dug into her jeans pocket and extracted a roll of bills. "This is the missing money from the concert. I took it."

Erin was the thief? She'd been on the list, but he'd never seriously considered her. Big mistake.

"I don't have an excuse, other than it was stupid. I wanted my parents to notice me. I thought taking the money would somehow make them see me, but then you blamed Denny and it got out of control." She held out her hand. "I went home after the news taping to get the cash. I told my parents what I did."

Luke took the bills from her outstretched hand.

"I'm ready to tell the police what I did, but I had nothing to do with the other money. I swear."

He stared down at the cash. Then at Erin. Saw the misery and despair in her eyes.

"You realize if I go to the police," Luke said, "you'll have a juvenile record."

"I understand," she croaked.

Luke saw the repentance in her expression. The acknowledgment that she'd accept her punishment.

"But under the circumstances, I'll keep this between us."

Erin sank against Cassie, who wrapped a supporting arm around her.

He met Cassie's eyes and she mouthed a silent thank-you.

"You'll have to make it up to the Klub by volunteering here, agreed?"

Erin straightened. "Anything. And just so you know, my parents are punishing me."

He almost laughed at the joy on her face when she admitted to being punished, but he got where she was coming from.

"Can I go now? I need to tell Denny the truth."

"Yes. Make an appointment with me next week. With your parents."

"I will," Erin said then slipped out the door.

"Cassie, you know?" he asked as he tucked the money in his pocket.

"I only found out a few hours ago."

He blew out a breath. "I know I put Erin on the suspect list, but I gotta admit, I never really suspected her."

"She's a confused, lonely girl."

"Who has a great advocate."

Cassie shrugged, but his words put a smile on her face.

"Once we figure this all out, maybe things can go back to normal."

"Normal is overrated."

He grinned. "Listen, Cassie, I wanted to talk to you about—"

A knock at the door cut him off. The chief entered."

"Got a lead on the suspects from last night."

"Great. How?" he asked.

"My guys were able to enhance the camera footage and make out the logo on the ball cap. Same logo Dan Snyder uses for his fencing company."

"Kyle."

"Yes. With the picture enlarged, I was able to recognize his features and ID him. Also got a better angle on the second figure. Gary. They must have left Erin's backpack behind to make her look guilty."

Luke tried to fight the frustration of this setback. He'd hoped Kyle would make positive strides, but this was strike four. "So now what?"

"Already sent one of my officers to pick up Gary. Now I insist Kyle and his father follow me to the police station." Scowl lines creased the chief's forehead. "Sorry to ruin the party."

They left the office. Luke watched the chief approach Mr. Snyder, whose face went slack in disbelief, then red with fury. He marched over, the chief on his tails, to drag Kyle away from his friends. Before long the teen was coming up with loud excuses as he left the building.

Cassie hooked her arm through his. "Luke, I'm sorry."

"He'll have no option now but to own up to the consequences of his choices."

They stood together for a moment before Cassie said, "All this excitement is a bit...much."

Something about her subdued expression made him nervous. "How about we escape outside for a few minutes, grab a little fresh air by the picnic benches? I wanted to talk to you anyway."

She nodded. With his hand on the small of her back, they left the crowd. As he did, several people congratulated him. Yeah, the news spot was a success, but he didn't deserve this much praise. It was all the mayor's idea.

They'd just reached the door when Mandy Rose sauntered in. Her delighted smile sent a warning through him. "Just the couple I wanted to see."

"We were leaving," Luke said.

"Hang on a minute. I need to thank you."

"For what?"

"My newest scoop. The story has only been out a few hours and it's already trending."

He didn't remember seeing her at the mayor's event. "Thanks for covering the kids. It'll be a good news story for the town."

Mandy tapped her foot, a frown marring her forehead. "You haven't seen my exclusive?"

Cassie glanced up at him, confusion in her lovely green eyes.

Mandy produced a tablet from her tote bag, ran her fingers over the screen and handed it over for Luke and Cassie to see. The headline read Cassie Branford and Luke Hastings, Collaborators in Music and Love? Below the headline, a picture of Luke whispering in Cassie's ear, a secretive smile on her lips, caught his attention.

"What is this?" he demanded.

"Breaking news."

He skimmed the article, filled with innuendo about his relationship with Cassie, her time at the Klub and an insider scoop that they were writing music together.

Shocked at the accuracy of the article, he asked, "Where did you get this information?"

Mandy cast a sideways glance at Cassie before returning Luke's gaze. "I have impeccable sources."

Mandy took the tablet from his hands and tapped the screen. Held it up. "My story is going national. Look."

He focused on the screen again. Another headline, Is Luke Hastings Back?, ran in dark bold letters under the news section of a popular music magazine.

Suddenly a buzzing filled his ears. Cassie was saying something to him, but he couldn't make it out. He signaled for her to follow him outside, away from the noise and confusion.

They reached the picnic area, well away from the building and prying eyes. The low-hanging limbs with full foliage would give them a degree of much-needed privacy.

"You knew about this?"

She cringed at his sharp tone. "No. It's just as much of a surprise to me."

He began to pace as his anger mounted. "I thought we agreed. No publicity."

"Luke, I didn't tell her a thing."

"What about her sources?"

"How would I know?"

"Because she looked right at you when she said it."

"And if she looked at me when she accused

someone of robbing your office, would you automatically suspect me?"

He ran a hand over the back of his neck.

"Right. Because I'm still in the business so I leaked our relationship."

"You're heading back to LA. soon. Managers always want their clients in the spotlight."

"I asked Travis to keep quiet."

"Looks like he failed." He stared pacing again. "And where did she find that picture of us?"

"You don't remember?" she asked in a trembling voice.

He stopped. Stared at her.

"At the wedding. When I filled in for Ryan. During a break you were telling me about how much you wanted to kiss me."

The memory flashed in his mind. He'd spoken into her ear so no one could overhear. And Mandy had captured the image of their special moment together and used it against them.

Their gazes met. He read the hurt, the indecision in the green depths.

"Cassie, I—"

She held up her hand. "You've made it very clear that you don't want to be part of the music scene. I respect that, Luke, I do. So I would never go behind your back and suggest otherwise."

"I've been clear."

"Yes, you have." She paused, her throat moving. "Kids' Klub will always be number one with you. I get it. I guess I'd hoped you might want more with me."

He didn't respond. Couldn't. The moment of truth was upon him and he froze.

Cassie walked to him, laying her hand on his chest. Her eyes glittered with tears. "I love you, Luke."

His hand covered hers, yet the words wouldn't come. He'd thought he was ready to tell her how he felt, but the shock of his name aligned with hers made him second-guess all the progress he'd gained. His worst nightmare, happening again.

When he didn't move, she slipped her hand from his and stepped back.

"Someday you'll have to face up to the past, Luke. You won't be able to hide behind Kids' Klub, using the kids as an excuse not to move on with your life. I thought you would have learned that by now."

His chest ached and he could barely breathe, and still the words wouldn't come.

"But at least now I know where I stand." She took a shaky breath. "I can see how much this article is affecting you, so you don't have to worry, I won't record the song we wrote together. I'll make sure the tabloids know this was just a short-term volunteer gig for me and that we have only a friendly relationship. Once they see me back in LA, recording and going on with my business without you, your name will fade away again, just like you want."

When she walked off he called out her name. "Cassie, wait."

She turned. "For what? I may have hoped, but I see now this would never have worked between us. So I'm leaving Cypress Pointe." She bit her lower lip. "Goodbye, Luke."

She turned on her heel and hurried to the parking lot. Her convertible roared to life and soon a cloud of dust was all that was left.

He stood there, staring into the distance, wondering how he'd let this situation get so out of hand. Why hadn't he stopped her? Were her words true? Was he using the Klub as an excuse not to live his life? Was he so afraid of repeating his old life that he'd let the possibility of a new and better life get away?

"Hey, Mr. H, we need you inside."

Denny's words shook him from his thoughts. He moved up the sidewalk, numb. Had he really been that dense to let Cassie leave without telling her he loved her?

He met the teen at the door.

"You okay Mr. H.?"

"I think I just let the best thing to ever happen to me get away."

Denny blinked behind his glasses. "Cassie? She's gone?"

Luke tried to shake off the stupor hanging over him and failed.

"Because she's famous? I gotta say, Mr. H., I don't see the problem."

Luke's head jerked up. "What did you say?"

"Who cares? None of us here. We like Cassie and she sure makes you smile, that's what's important. You don't have to be part of her world to love her."

"Why are you telling me this?"

"Because you're always here for us, Mr. H. Now it's our turn to help you." He looked over his shoulder and waved. Erin came running over. Denny slipped his arm around her shoulders and she snuggled close. "Erin and I almost blew it because we have different friends, but you know what? Nothing in those two worlds is more important than we are together."

Nothing in those two worlds is more important than we are together.

Nothing was more important to him than Cassie. Not the past. Not the spotlight. Not her career. They could make this work.

Luke slapped Denny on his shoulder. "Thanks, Denny. You're pretty smart for a kid."

"That's what I've been telling everyone."

With his heart pounding, Luke set off for his car. He had to convince Cassie he was wrong to let her go. That he'd used his fear as a shield, but she'd worked her way through his defenses with her light and love. And just like that, a freedom he'd never thought to experience made his hopes soar. He could do this.

Darned if Denny was right. Who would have thought a sixteen-year-old would have wise words he needed to hear? He only hoped Cassie would listen.

CHAPTER SIXTEEN

CASSIE MANAGED TO contain the tears as she drove home. Once in Lauren's driveway, she ignored the moisture on her cheeks, refusing to give in to the pain. As she exited the car, she nearly tripped on her high heels. Hurt, anger and frustration had her yanking them off and hurling them into the front yard. Barefoot, she stomped to the house, then fumbled with the keys and the lock. She'd jammed the key for the second time when the door flew open.

"What's your hurry?" her sister asked, her amused smile fading at the sight of Cassie's face.

Just over her sister's shoulder, Cassie glimpsed her father standing under the arched opening to the living room. Great. Could this day get any worse?

"Cassandra, you look terrible," he stated the obvious.

"Dad!" Lauren gasped.

"Well, she does. It's not fitting for her image, either."

Cassie scrubbed her face. At this point, her mascara was probably streaked down to her chin.

"We have business to discuss," he announced, apparently unmoved by his daughter's distress. With a broad sweep of his hand, he motioned for Lauren to leave the room.

Her sister hesitated, looked at Cassie for guidance. Cassie nodded. Might as well get this over with before she suffered a complete meltdown.

"I heard the news about Mandy Rose and her headlines."

Swallowing a sudden lump of emotion, she said, "I'm fine." She couldn't remember a time her father had been concerned for her welfare.

"Do you realize what this means?"

She stepped into the living room, hoping for a comforting hug as her father kept talking.

"The word is out. The music industry will see that Luke is back in the picture. Now we can move ahead as planned."

Cassie stilled. "What plan?"

"To work on my music score. The three of us." He rubbed his hands together as he paced the length of the room. "I've already put together some ideas for a new concept. You'll contact Travis. Luke will work on his end. It'll be perfect."

"Perfect for whom?"

Her father stopped. Stared at her in surprise. "For all of us."

"Dad, we aren't helping you."

"What are you talking about? Of course you are. I offered Luke a large donation so he'll be motivated to do this."

"Wow. You bribed him?" This was news to her. Luke never mentioned the money—only that her father had promised his time to the center. Yet from the conversation they'd had the other day, she knew he wasn't throwing in with her father. Did that mean while Kids' Klub was important to Luke, he wouldn't sell his soul to keep it alive? That he really wasn't hiding behind the Klub like she'd accused him?

Her father grimaced. "*Bribe* is such an ugly word. I like *incentive* better. I merely suggested that a donation was on the table if he did his part."

"I can't believe you. Do you even care about what Kids' Klub does? How it helps troubled teens?"

"That's all fine and good but my career is in serious need of revamping."

A niggling thought bothering her suddenly became clear. "You're the source Mandy was talking about?"

"She mentioned my name?" His face lit up

and a satisfied grin crossed his lips. "I haven't read the article yet."

Cassie gaped at him. "You're unbelievable. Pretending to be a family? Getting Luke on board? All of this was about you."

"Stop acting like you're the only one with a reputation to maintain here," he snapped. "I need this."

"Well, I don't. I'm not working with you and it's pretty safe to say Luke isn't, either. Go try to coerce someone else to get what you want."

Her father's face turned a dangerous red. "You've always been ungrateful."

"And you've never been a father."

Her words hung in the air.

"You'll regret this."

"I doubt it."

He stormed from the house. When she heard the front door slam, she let out the breath she'd been holding.

Strung out from the encounter, she eased the elastic band from the end of her braid and began to loosen the plait. She heard a muffled sound and looked up to find Lauren in the doorway, her face pale, lips trembling.

"You heard all that?"

Lauren nodded.

"I'm sorry."

"No," came her shaky reply. "Deep down I wanted to believe he'd changed."

Cassie didn't know what to say. Her sister had to work through this disappointment on her own. Find her own way to deal with their father just as she had.

"Is this when you say 'I told you so'?" Lauren asked with a bitter laugh.

"Never." Cassie moved close and wound her arms around her sister. Hugged her tight.

"I should have listened."

"Now you know."

Both of their lives had been upended in the span of a few short hours. Cassie always suspected who their father was deep down. Hoped she was wrong, but with startling clarity realized now that his renewed interest in her life had diminished her confidence, contributing to the writer's block. She'd never reach his ridiculous standards, but now, after showing his true colors, his degrading words to *keep at it* would never ring in her head again. She didn't need to prove her worth to anyone but herself.

Lauren pulled away. "What an awful day."

"Preaching to the choir, sister." She brushed her loose hair over her shoulder. "I need to get far away from here." She moved past Lauren to get to her bedroom. Pulling her suitcase from the closet, she yanked open the dresser drawer.

"Cassie, you're scaring me," Lauren said from the doorway.

"I'm tired of trying to please everyone and failing," she said as she balled up the dress from her father's wedding to stash in the case.

"Hold on." Lauren grabbed her arm. "What happened? You looked devastated when you got home."

Suddenly all her energy dissipated. She sank onto the edge of the bed then slid to the floor, landing in a leap. Tears flowed freely now, heaving sobs strangling her. Lauren grabbed the tissue box and sat beside her, silently taking her hand.

When she finally got over the worst of the onslaught, she swiped at her face. Choked out the source of her meltdown. "Luke."

"Ah." Lauren yanked a tissue from the box. "Isn't it always a guy who brings out the best in us?"

Cassie sputtered at her sister's attempt at levity as she pressed the tissue to her face. Unfortunately, it was too little too late.

"Mandy Rose released a story about us, thanks to Dad. Luke didn't take it well."

"Luke is a stickler about his privacy."

Cassie's chest grew tight. "But he thought I leaked it for publicity."

"You'd never stoop so low."

"He thought otherwise."

Sniffles sounded in the quiet room.

"So you're leaving?" Lauren asked.

"What else can I do? I put the final touches on the song I came up with this morning, so I'm ready to start recording."

"How many songs do you have now?"

"Eight. I usually go into the studio with more, but I'm thankful I came up with that many." She glanced across the room to the closed guitar case containing the songbook full of her newest lyrics and melodies. "Nothing like cutting it short."

"Do you really have to go back?" her sister asked. Cassie recognized the sadness in her voice. Felt it to the depth of her soul. "I've loved having you around."

"I've been gone too long already. I have to be in the studio next week and still have to meet up with the band to go over the new material."

When she'd arrived in Cypress Pointe, she'd been sure her career was history. Coming up with fresh songs had been the hardest thing she'd ever done, but she'd confronted the block and overcome her fears. No, she needed to go back and remind the world who she was.

"Besides, I can't hang around here and risk

seeing Luke." She blinked back tears that wouldn't stop falling. "What a mess."

"I'm going to miss you."

Cassie rested her head on Lauren's shoulder. "At least someone will."

The sisters sat in quiet until the doorbell started ringing like crazy. Someone held their finger over the button, impatiently pressing.

"I suppose I should see who that is," Lauren said, standing.

"And I need to finish packing." Cassie hauled herself up as Lauren left the room. In reality, she really couldn't just escape like she wished. She had to say goodbye to her mother and Bud, stop in to make sure Erin was okay, say goodbye to the kids at the Klub. Plus, she'd promised Nealy she'd sing one of her songs at her engagement party tomorrow. So much for fleeing.

Loud voices carried her way. Heavy footsteps thundered down the hallway. Luke appeared at her doorway, Lauren right behind him.

"Sorry, sis. He shoved right in without being invited."

Of course he did. "It's okay."

Lauren looked at her. "Are you sure?"

Cassie nodded.

"I'll be out back on the patio if you need me."

Flustered now, Cassie grabbed a bunch of tops from the open drawer to dump on the bed.

"Running away?"

"No. Leaving a place where I'm not wanted."

He frowned. "That's not true. Everyone in Cypress Pointe loves you."

She shot him a sideways glare. "Not everyone."

He placed one foot in the room. Stopped. "May I come in?"

"Like I could stop you?"

"Yes, with one word you could."

With a sigh, she waved him forward.

"I owe you an apology."

Lifting her head, she said, "That's right, you do."

"Mandy's story caught me off guard. I don't take surprise well."

Cassie picked up another shirt, only this time she folded it in slow motion.

"I shouldn't have assumed you had anything to do with the story."

"I agree, but that's not the real problem, is it?"

Luke rocked on his heels. "No. You told me you loved me and I pretty much threw it back in your face."

Cassie looked over at him. Wanted answers. "Why?"

"A lot of people told me they loved me throughout my life. Most of the time they ended up hurting me." He met and held her gaze with an intensity that took her breath away. "You were right. I do hide behind the Klub. But you showed me that I should take a chance on love. Real love this time."

"And you'd recognize real love how?"

"By you telling me you wouldn't record our song."

Cassie placed the folded top in the case and grabbed another. "So, what, we just go back to…" she held out her hand to point between them "…whatever was happening between us?"

"We can try. It may be long-distance, with you recording and traveling, but we can work at it." He ran a hand through his hair. "I should have said it earlier, but I love you, Cassie."

She snorted at his declaration.

"Okay. Not the response I was envisioning."

"What else did you expect? With my busy schedule and all?" Surely he wouldn't miss the sarcasm in her voice.

"Right now, I'm not sure."

"Well, when you figure it out, let me know. If you'll excuse me, I'm busy."

"Tough room." He took a step back. "You can't leave town yet. You agreed to sing at Dane and Nealy's party."

"It's one of the reasons I'm not headed to the airport this second."

"I know I don't deserve to ask you this, but will you promise me you'll keep an open mind to the possibilities between us?"

Like she was ever going to stop loving Luke. But still, her heart couldn't cope with getting stomped on again.

"I'll show you how much I love you, Cassie."

Oh, how she wanted to believe him. Throw all caution to the wind and run into his arms.

If he'd told her he had faith in their relationship, that the music angle didn't bother him or that they'd meet halfway when it came to their schedules, maybe then she would have reacted differently. But she had no assurances. No proof he'd ever accept her career tied to the music industry. So she restrained herself in fear of taking another blow she'd never recover from.

"I'll be the judge of whatever you think is strong enough to change my mind."

A somber expression crossed his face before he left the room.

Once she was alone again, Cassie lowered her trembling body to the bed. Was she the biggest doormat on earth? First Luke was upset with her, then he said he loved her. And how did she respond? By wanting to forgive him, no questions asked.

But she couldn't. Not and still retain her pride.

Suddenly a huge weight settled on her shoulders. Travis and the label had been constantly after her to show her loyalty, to the point she'd almost lost her love and passion to write songs. Her father, always after something, never truly loving his children. And Luke, how did he expect them to have any kind of relationship if he wouldn't let go of the past?

She had to make changes or keep making the same mistakes. But how?

The words she'd shared with Erin echoed in her head. *Choose your own path.* Could she follow through with her own advice? She wanted to make her kind of music, but if the label disagreed, would she back down? Or Travis. Sure, he had her best interests in mind, but he still had his own rep to think about. Could she stand up for herself and finally be her own person? Recover if she walked away from the LA music scene because she wanted to control her destiny? Share the kinds of songs that touched her soul? Find a new way to share her craft and love of music?

She could, as long as she stuck to her own principles.

The revelation scared her, but made her lighter. She'd deal with whatever came at her.

It couldn't be worse than telling Luke she loved him, hoping for the same declaration and have him not answer her at all.

She still had a few days to come up with a plan, but she was finally going to live her life on her own terms. She'd make her stand with the label and take whatever consequences came as a result. With Luke, things were a little more murky because her heart was involved, but she wasn't going to sell her love short. Either they were in this together, 100 percent, or they weren't in it at all.

Squaring her shoulders, she went to the bathroom to throw water on her face. Grimaced at the reflection in the mirror. Blotchy cheeks and chipmunk eyes. Still, when she'd looked at herself in the mirror at her father's wedding, there'd been nothing but fear in her face. Now there was a spark of life. Taking command of one's own life had power.

Even if it masked a broken heart.

THE FOLLOWING EVENING, Cassie entered the exclusive restaurant fashionably late. Not to make a statement, but because of cold feet. She had no idea what Luke would do or say. How on earth could she sing a love song to the happy couple with her heart so bruised and battered?

Out of habit, she reached for her braid, only to come up empty handed. In a pique of independence, she'd decided to have her hair cut in a completely different style. Gone was the long, streaked braid that defined Cassie before this visit to Cypress Pointe. Now she sported a sophisticated, layered bob that brushed her shoulders. She'd added subtle highlights to her sandy-brown hair color. Now, dressed in a silver sleeveless sheath dress with black strappy heels, she felt like a confident, in-control-of-her-destiny woman, ready to take on the world.

Moving farther into the throng of guests, she searched for a familiar face. Nealy noticed her and hurried over.

"I wasn't sure you would come tonight."

"I told you I would and I always keep my word."

Someone called Nealy's name. "Get a drink. Mingle. It is a party, after all."

It may be a party, but all Cassie wanted to do was sing and leave. By the looks of the rowdy crowd, it couldn't happen soon enough.

Making her way to the bar, she asked for bottled water. Her throat, already tight with emotion, had her lowering her expectations of getting through a song without cracking. She swallowed the cold liquid anyway, making do with what she had.

"You made it," Dane said as he approached her. "Congratulations."

He grinned. "I'm a lucky man."

Wonderful. Great. What time was it?

"Do you mind if I put my two cents in where it isn't needed?"

"Why not?" Everyone else had. Her sister, mother and friends. They meant well, but she had to make her own decisions.

"Luke messed up. He knows it. Would you cut the guy some slack and give him a second chance?"

"And why would I consider doing that?"

"Because he's a good guy. Being with you makes him a better man."

At Dane's words, tears prickled the backs of her eyes.

"Like I said, it's just a suggestion."

He walked away leaving her to ponder his words. Suddenly the lights went down. From across the room, the sound of a microphone being turned on screeched in the speakers. Luke stood under a single light, his guitar strapped over his chest.

"Hello, everyone. Tonight we're here to celebrate Dane and Nealy."

Applause broke out.

"My cousin, who's had my back my entire life, is giving me the floor for a few minutes tonight." He cleared his throat. "You might have heard that Cassie Branford and I came up with a new song together. It's true. While I'm not back in the music business, I am hoping we'll be a team. So in honor of her, I want to debut our song, 'This is True.'"

Shocked, Cassie weaved her way through party guests to stop a few feet away from Luke. He started to strum the tune they'd come up with. When he sang, the lyrics resonated in her heart.

"This is true, the beating in my chest.
It felt like ages for true love to arrive.
I tried to deny the love shining in your eyes,
but I knew from the very first hello,
you held my lonely heart."

Cassie quietly sang along, word for word, each syllable etched on her heart. When he finished, the room erupted with loud applause. Luke put his guitar down and strode to her, pulling her to a dark corner of the room, away from the gaping crowd.

"I meant every word I sang, Cassie. Before you came into my life I was resigned to an empty existence. But you turned everything around for me and I'll be forever grateful. I love you, Cassie Branford."

Shimmery tears blurred her surroundings. Sound faded. It was as though she and Luke were the only two people in the room. "I guess you got the memo that grand gestures work."

"If it means convincing you that we're better together than apart, I'll keep coming up with gestures to knock your socks off."

"So this means we continue to collaborate? Maybe divide time between here and LA?"

"I'm ready to agree to anything that keeps you in my life. We can always decide on the logistics later."

She wrapped her arms around his neck. Emotion thickened her voice. "You didn't have to sing our song."

"Yes, I did. To tell the world I don't care who knows we wrote it together. Just as long as we *are* together."

"I think that can be arranged."

His eyes caressed her. "What happened to your hair?"

She ran a nervous hand over the styled tresses. "New Cassie."

"I miss the streak."

"For you, I can put it back."

He tilted his head. "Or maybe just stay as you are. After all, you are the music of my heart."

When he grinned at her, all her reservations,

about their love, life and future, drifted away. She'd never been so sure about anything in her life. "You and I are destined to make beautiful music together, Luke Hastings."

His hold on her tightened. "A Cassieism?"

"The best one yet."

* * * * *

If you loved this book, don't miss the other books in Tara's miniseries
THE BUSINESS OF WEDDINGS:

ORANGE BLOSSOM BRIDES
MAGNOLIA BRIDE
HONEYSUCKLE BRIDE
THE BRIDAL BOUQUET

Available now from Harlequin.com!

And watch for Tara's next romance, coming in December 2017 from Harlequin Heartwarming!

Get 2 Free Books,
Plus 2 Free Gifts—
just for trying the Reader Service!

Love Inspired®

Get 2 Free Books,
Plus 2 Free Gifts—
just for trying the Reader Service!

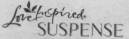

HOMETOWN HEARTS ♥

YES! Please send me **The Hometown Hearts Collection** in Larger Print. This collection begins with 3 FREE books and 2 FREE gifts in the first shipment. Along with my 3 free books, I'll also get the next 4 books from the Hometown Hearts Collection, in LARGER PRINT, which I may either return and owe nothing, or keep for the low price of $4.99 U.S./ $5.89 CDN each plus $2.99 for shipping and handling per shipment*. If I decide to continue, about once a month for 8 months I will get 6 or 7 more books, but will only need to pay for 4. That means 2 or 3 books in every shipment will be FREE! If I decide to keep the entire collection, I'll have paid for only 32 books because 19 books are FREE! I understand that accepting the 3 free books and gifts places me under no obligation to buy anything. I can always return a shipment and cancel at any time. My free books and gifts are mine to keep no matter what I decide.

262 HCN 3432 462 HCN 3432

Name	(PLEASE PRINT)	
Address		Apt. #
City	State/Prov.	Zip/Postal Code

Signature (if under 18, a parent or guardian must sign)

Mail to the **Reader Service**:
IN U.S.A.: P.O. Box 1867, Buffalo, NY. 14240-1867
IN CANADA: P.O. Box 009, Fort Erie, Ontario L2A 5X3

HHBPA17

Get 2 Free Books,
Plus 2 Free Gifts—
just for trying the Reader Service!

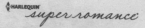

Get 2 Free Books,
Plus 2 Free Gifts—
just for trying the Reader Service!

Love Inspired HISTORICAL

LIHI7R

Get 2 Free Books,

Plus 2 Free Gifts—

just for trying the Reader Service!

HARLEQUIN®

HEARTWARMING™